Foreign Born

Foreign Born

John Herrmann

Introduction by Sara Kosiba

Edited by Ross K. Tangedal

Hastings College Press | Hastings, Nebraska

Production Staff

Sam Crossett
Alexandru Dan
Sydney Dexter
Erika Diaz

Sarah Knight
James Lapka
Hannah Meeske

Proofreader

Bruce Batterson

ISBN-10: 1942885644
ISBN-13: 978-1-942885-64-1

Manufactured in the United States of America.

Text is printed on acid-free, chlorine-free paper with 30% postconsumer recycled content. Cover is printed on 100% recycled paper.

Contents

Introduction

Sara Kosiba

> Americanization means, of course,
> assimilation. But that is an empty
> concept, a mere cry of rage or tyranny,
> until the question is answered which
> would never be asked were the answer
> ripe: Assimilation to what? To what
> homogeneous culture, to what folkways
> of festival and song, to what common
> instincts concerning love and beauty, to
> what imaginative passions, to what
> roads of thought?
> —Ludwig Lewisohn[1]

In the vast archival collections of the Harry Ransom Center at
the University of Texas at Austin lies a 207-page typescript of an
unpublished John Herrmann novel, *Foreign Born*.[2] The fact that
it survives at all is a testament to the fantastic efforts of research
centers like the Ransom Center to obtain and preserve even the
obscure bits of American cultural history. John Herrmann has
long been relegated to footnotes in American literary history, often
described more as a "friend of" more famous figures than an author

---

[1] From *Lewisohn's Up Stream: An American Chronicle* (Boni & Liveright, 1922): 235.

[2] My 2014–2015 research fellowship at the Harry Ransom Center was funded by the Andrew W. Mellon Foundation Research Fellowship Endowment. My ongoing research on John Herrmann has also been funded by two Faculty Development Committee Research Grants from Troy University.

in his own right. While Herrmann's life history and literary works have languished in relative obscurity for the past several decades, the rediscovery of *Foreign Born* at this juncture in American history provides a particularly timely opportunity to learn about our past and to reflect on our present. Herrmann's novel, written in the 1920s, examines the U.S. home front before and during World War I, particularly the impact of the war on the German American community. As we commemorate the 100th anniversary of United States' involvement in that war, events in the novel inspire reflection on the past and on how much humanity has learned from those events.

In October 1924, John Herrmann returned from a two-year sojourn studying and traveling in Europe with two promising new prospects. The first was an exciting new romance with an American woman he met in Paris, fellow writer Josephine Herbst. The two had spent several months together in France, and they returned as passengers on the *Rochambeau* listed as husband and wife on the manifest, despite the fact that they would not become legally married for almost two more years. The other promising development was that he carried on that voyage the manuscript of his first novel, *What Happens*, which Herrmann hoped to place with a U.S. publisher. However, the optimism of their return would be short lived. After a few weeks together in New York City, Herbst travelled back to Iowa to visit family, leaving Herrmann still shopping his novel and trying to find a job. Unsuccessful, he returned home to Lansing, Michigan, and his letters from the time show his frustrations with the publishing world and in trying to navigate his own ambitions and his parents' expectations. In January 1925, while still in Lansing and about to leave for a job in Detroit, Herrmann passed the time by starting a second novel, *Foreign Born*, describing it in a letter to Herbst as a

> book about a German American during the war
> which I hope to work on there and possibly finish
> off. He started out one hundred percent with son
> and wife of English descent. He is respected in the
> community and a [R]otarian. The war makes him
> pro-[G]erman, his wife and son against him. Family
> breaks up almost. Business goes bum, he must resign

> from the [R]otarians, son goes to war, open break
> between father and son. Father must buy Liberty
> bonds[,] refused[,] has trouble with Security League,
> starts buying bonds and using them in his business,
> people think he has become patriotic, he still talks
> pro[-]German stuff though. End of the war, son
> back, business fine making much money, Rotarian[s]
> take him back, and the book ends with a speech
> he is making before the Rotarian[s] on hundred
> percent Americanism. How does that sound roughly?
> (Herrmann to Herbst, 21 Jan. 1925)[3]

Herrmann continued his efforts on the new novel while working as an assistant manager at Sheehan's Book Store in Detroit. *What Happens* was still circulating among publishers but was finding little encouragement, as they found the novel problematic for the time due to its references to masturbation and pre-marital sex.[4]

By the end of July 1925, eager to reunite with Herbst in New Preston, Connecticut, where she had set up house for them, Herrmann left Detroit with a completed manuscript for his second book. Herrmann wasted little time getting the new novel circulating among publishers. A letter dated 16 September 1925 from Horace Liveright to Genevieve Taggard, a fellow writer and friend of Herrmann's, notes that the firm of Boni & Liveright was reviewing the manuscript. Clearly, that early effort did not work out, as later reader reports and letters regarding *Foreign Born* continue into 1926 and 1927. While all of the reports reject the novel, all of them also note some potential in either the ideas or in the writing. A reader's report still attached to the manuscript at the Harry Ransom Center—dated 25 September 1926 and simply identifying the reviewer as "a well-known newspaper man, editorial writer and dramatic critic"—begins by stating "I like this for its simplicity and its straightforward honesty" and notes that "The half

---

[3] The original letter has a number of typos in this section that I have corrected for ease of reading. No substantive changes have been made.

[4] See Sara Kosiba's introduction to *What Happens* (Hastings College Press, 2015) for more on the novel's publishing history.

cynical and wholly artistic restraint" is "perhaps equally ahead of its time—certainly above and beyond current popular taste." For that reason and some of the novel's other flaws, the reader concludes, "Publication of such a study could be financially warranted only by literary quality of a higher order, a broader perspective on the era depicted and more salient skill in narrative and character drawing" (qtd. in Herrmann, "Foreign Born [Part 3 of 3]"). The firm of J.H. Sears & Company actually wrote favorably to Herrmann about the book in October 1926, commenting that they felt they might be able to publish the book with a few changes. Their reviewer characterized the novel as a "satire of high order" (H.M.W.). The requested changes are not specified in the correspondence, and the firm never ultimately published the book. Simon & Schuster and Charles Scribner's Sons also turned the novel down, with famed editor Maxwell Perkins writing Herrmann, "It is extremely interesting in respect to literary method and in respect to the insight into human character. It does not[,] however, seem to us that we could publish it successfully enough to justify us in undertaking it" (Perkins).

Many of the criticisms of Herrmann's novel in the 1920s are still true today. The writing style of the novel is not very eloquent. It is indeed underdeveloped. The dialogue is often simplistic. As a literary and historical artifact, however, the novel has a great deal of value today for its fictional portrayal of real-life events and for its insightful examination of the irony so often found in human experience. The story unfolds much as Herrmann's 1925 letter to Josephine Herbst describes. The Weiman family immigrates from Germany in the late nineteenth century and sets up a shoe store in the small city of Fairbanks. Eventually, the son, Ernst, takes over the family business. He is a prosperous member of the community and well-liked by the townspeople. While the Rotary Club mentioned in Herrmann's letter to Herbst never makes a specific appearance, Ernst is a member of the "business men's club." He also socializes with the local Liederkranz Society, a German singing club. As conflict in Europe develops and events lead to World War I, the Weiman family's German heritage leads to more scrutiny and judgment from the community. Ernst does not like war, but he supports Germany's right to defend itself and refuses to demonize or condemn the German people. He wants peace between two countries he loves so well. This attitude leads to a drop in business, ostracism from the general community, and a greater affiliation with the local German Americans. Ernst's American-born wife, Helen, rather lukewarm about her husband to begin with, turns even colder toward him, as she is also facing criticism from the community, and his son, Charley, disagrees with his pro-German views. One by one, many of Ernst's other pro-German friends cave to social pressure, particularly after the United States enters the conflict; they all begin flying American flags in an effort to prove their Americanism. The Liederkranz Society disbands. Those who do not align themselves with public expectations of patriotism are hassled or face vigilante justice. Ernst is repeatedly pressured to buy liberty bonds to avoid this fate. Charley eventually runs away to enlist as a soldier, and only after that point does Ernst begin to cave a bit to patriotic social pressure, mainly in support of his son, but he still maintains his concern for the German people.[5] The novel's original ending shows Ernst having regained his status in the community and scornful of how easily he has fooled his local community into thinking he agrees with their perception of 100% Americanism.

The city of Fairbanks is clearly modeled on Herrmann's hometown of Lansing, Michigan, and many of the surrounding details in the text are also either autobiographically based or drawn from local news and events. Herrmann's grandfather and namesake, John Theodore Herrmann, immigrated from Darmstadt, Germany, in 1872 and established a prosperous Lansing tailoring business in 1878, one that was eventually taken over by his sons upon his death ("Merchant Tailor Firm" 51). Therefore, the Herrmann family's German roots were similar to those of the Weiman family. Herrmann's grandfather, according to his obituary, was a member of the local Liederkranz Society ("John T. Herrmann Dead"), and Herrmann himself noted attending a Lansing Liederkranz concert in a 9 December 1924 letter to Herbst. Early in the novel, the city of Fairbanks is described as the home of a prosperous wagon works.

---

[5] Charley is seventeen when the United States enters the war and enlists when he turns eighteen; Herrmann would have been close to the same age at that time. There is no evidence that he tried to enlist in the war.

The Lansing Wagon Works was a prosperous business, founded in 1881, and would transition into the automobile age by becoming the Lansing Body Company (MacLean and Whitford 34, 58). Later in the novel, Herrmann contrasts the wagon works in the fictional Fairbanks with the Olds Motor Works in Lansing (86). A pioneering automobile manufacturer, Ransom E. Olds assumed control of his father's Lansing-based engine company in the late 1800s and began designing motor cars. As the company expanded, Lansing remained a base of operations, although Olds would resign from the company in 1904 and eventually found a new Lansing automobile company, the REO Motor Car Company, later that same year. Olds' reputation was well established in the city, and the reference in the novel solidifies the fictional contrast to Herrmann's hometown.

The anti-German backlash depicted in the novel also has significant real-world ties to wartime Lansing, incorporating events and references that were similar to what was happening throughout Michigan and the United States as a whole during this period. As the United States entered the war, in Michigan "efforts were energized to repress opposition and to Americanize foreign-born nationalities. Rumors abounded about sabotage and disloyalty among the 80,000 Michiganians of German birth" (Kilar 38). These activities and this social climate clearly inspired *Foreign Born*. Herrmann's attendance at a Liederkranz Society function in December 1924 was notable, as the concert he attended was the first to be held after a three-year gap ("Three Years Silent" 12). Local news stories obliquely refer to the struggles the club had during the World War I years, with rumor of the sale of the Liederkranz Society hall as early as 1917 and finalized news of the sale in 1919. In 1919, the sale is described as being timely due to "the lack of interest in these societies by the younger set" ("Theater Added" 2), and yet, a mention in the 19 June 1922 *Lansing State Journal* notes a 200-person reunion of Liederkranz Society members ("City in Brief" 2). For such a supposed "lack of interest," the organization managed remarkable revival in only a three-year span, suggesting quite strongly that there was another motivation for the organization's demise. While there is no reference to the war years in the reunion mention, it is likely that the increasing anti-German sentiment in Lansing during World War I contributed to many German American families avoiding or hiding their heritage, thereby advancing the attrition that led to the sale of the Liederkranz Society hall and similar real estate owned by other German American organizations in Lansing. In *Foreign Born*, Ernst attends a meeting at the Liederkranz Hall shortly after the United States joins the war effort where the diminished membership votes to disband the organization in light of the social climate.

Attending the Liederkranz Society concert may have jogged Herrmann's memory to other anti-German circumstances in Lansing, inspiring the start of *Foreign Born* in the weeks that followed. Shortly after the United States enters the war, Ernst's father-in-law stops by the shoe store to caution Ernst about speaking out in public with his pro-German views. Cautioning him to be "a real good American," Charles Ross tells him to hang an American flag out front or else the Vigilance Committee might cause trouble for Ernst (152–154). The Vigilance Committee was a group of local businessmen and citizens dedicated to monitoring suspicious or unpatriotic activity. A little later, Ernst is visited by one of his friends, Harry Johnson, a member of the Vigilance Committee, who encourages him to buy liberty bonds, particularly if Ernst wants to keep from being labelled as unpatriotic in the newspaper. Ernst protests that the threat to publicly shame him is blackmail and a violation of his own freedoms, particularly freedom of speech, but his friend is unswayed and warns him that the committee will be making an example of noncompliant citizens in the community. Herrmann describes a Vigilance Committee that is far from just an innocent monitoring organization. In their desire to carry out their duties, they are not above coercing more extreme unpatriotic behavior that will allow them to take action. As Harry Johnson converses with Henry Miles outside of the shoe store about Ernst's lack of patriotic participation, Harry tells Henry, "All we got to do is get him to say something in front of somebody against the government the way we got Meisel and we can fix him all right" (168). Far from simply monitoring pro-German activity, the local committee is not above entrapment to punish those they deem un-American. However, despite such a strong outward appearance, the committee holds arbitrary standards, as Ernst's friend Roger Bartlett also refuses to buy liberty bonds, but members of the local committee are happy to simply write him off as a local eccentric, determining that he "couldn't possibly be a spy or really in his heart proGerman because he was almost pure English in his blood" (170).

While the United States was involved in World War I, Lansing had a very robust and active Vigilance Committee that was likely the model for the Fairbanks Vigilance Committee of Herrmann's novel. A large front-page headline in the *Lansing State Journal* on 3 November 1917 claimed "Final Report of Vigilantes Is Issued." The article details the actions of "The Committee of Twenty Five," who were tasked to "deal with persons in the city who were not doing their duty as citizens in supporting the [Liberty] loan and other measures" ("Final Report" 1). Describing their methodology and emphasizing that the committee gave every man confronted an opportunity to amend his wayward views, the article also explained that those who did not comply with the war effort were treated more harshly: "War is the most awful and exacting trial a people can be called on to undergo. In time of war no man may stand apart and plead selfish or trifling excuses in extenuation of his failure to give active and whole-hearted aid to his country. A sentence frequently used in the committee's conference was, 'You are either for the country or against it—you can't be on the fence.'" ("Final Report" 1). The paper published the names of individuals who "convicted themselves of being slackers," including Daniel Edwards, who simply had not bought a liberty bond, and Martin J. Stahler, who was "Solicited three times. Refused to 'put a dollar in the Loan'" ("Final Report" 2). The article then closed with the signatures of the twenty-five members and seven additional names. The Lansing Vigilance Committee's efforts were clearly popular, as other newspapers in Michigan praised their efforts, and a front-page article in the 24 January 1918 *Lansing State Journal* about a committee meeting proudly declared, "It was brought out that Lansing's plan is attracting attention from widely separated parts of the country. From Buffalo to Los Angeles have come requests for information as to how the committee was organized, how its work was carried on and requests for advice on inaugurating bodies elsewhere to deal with the slackers, disloyalists, and traitors" ("Vigilantes to Renew Activity" 1).

The most notable parallel between the Lansing Vigilance Committee and the enforcement efforts of the Fairbanks Vigilance Committee is in the particular actions described toward one

Fairbanks citizen, Wilhelm Meisel. In the novel, Ernst becomes passing friends with Meisel as the two talk about the German war effort and how misguided American perceptions of Germans are. Herrmann describes Meisel's effusive support of Germany despite the war:

> His butcher shop had German flags hung up in it and had a little box for taking contributions for the Germans' relief organizations and he was always talking of the glory and the good of Germany and he was always damning France and England and reviling them with ugly words and doing things like fingering his nose when he saw an Allied flag or a picture of some Allied general or anything almost that was Allied and of a nature he could finger his nose at. (134)

As the United States enters World War I, Meisel is judged very harshly by the local community. Locals pressure him to take down the German flag. Rotten eggs are thrown at his butcher shop. Eventually, Ernst hears news of a German spy being tarred and feathered, and it turns out that the "spy" is Wilhelm Meisel. The newspaper account that Ernst reads explains that Meisel was "tarred and feathered because he had desecrated the American flag in front of some men calling on him to sell him liberty bonds. He had poured excrement on the flag" (175). In pursuit of justice, "a group of people who were unknown had called him from his store and rushed him into a high powered automobile and rushed him out of the town to the golf links, and just as dusk was falling they tarred and feathered him" (175). Earlier in the novel, members of the Vigilance Committee imply that they have goaded Meisel into such outrageous behavior, but it is clear they are quite happy to make an example of him whether the charges against him are sincere.

Meisel's circumstances have parallels to a prominent incident in Lansing during World War I. On Friday, 2 November 1917, William Saier, owner of an established Lansing butcher shop, was tarred and feathered for making a "bestial insult" to the American flag. A news account of the event clarifies the standard legal punishment for such an offense: "Michigan, as a state, protects the flag. A statute provides a fine of $5 to $25 and 30 days in jail, either or both, for those who 'publicly' defile the American flag" ("Saier, Tarred" 1). However, it is clear local citizens decided to form their own court and mete out their own punishment for the offense, as Saier was never formally charged.[6] Additional details provided by the *Detroit Free Press* note that Saier was taken to the "links of the Lansing Golf Club" the night of November 2nd, a location identical to Herrmann's fictional account, where he was "given a mock trial before a jury of 20 vigilantes, robed in white" ("Lansing Man" 1).[7] An account in the Port Huron, Michigan, newspaper describes the scene in a more detailed fashion: "The white sheeted figures found him guilty as charged and he was conducted to the pot of hot tar and the bag of feathers opened and the coating neatly and effectively applied. Waiting a few minutes for the coat to set, the party bundled the butcher into one of the automobiles and drove rapidly back to the city" ("Butcher Who Insulted" 1).

Shortly after the initial incident, Saier and his sons demanded a federal investigation regarding the tarring and feathering. They claimed, along with several community members, that Saier had unfairly been singled out. Among the claims in his defense were that his family was supporting the war effort in that several of his sons had enlisted or were planning to enlist, he owned liberty bonds, and the flag desecration event never occurred. Newspaper accounts of the time do not clarify if the federal investigation occurred or if it resulted in any prosecutions or vindication. In late 1919, Saier would file a $25,000 libel lawsuit against the *Lansing State Journal* for its coverage of his tarring and feathering, alleging that the stories published by the newspaper "deprived him of friendly relations with many and caused a decrease in trade that he says amounted to about $4,000

---

[6] The Saier coverage appeared the same day the *Lansing State Journal* printed the "Final Report of Vigilantes is Issued" mentioned earlier in this introduction, suggesting a high point in the Vigilance Committee's activities in Lansing.

[7] It is probably not a coincidence that this description of a white sheeted mob sounds reminiscent of the Ku Klux Klan.

depreciation in the value of his market" ("State Journal is Sued" 2). One of the issues relevant to the trial was a 2 November 1917 extra edition of the *Lansing State Journal* that was published just after the tarring and feathering took place: "Portions of that story and the one printed in the regular edition of the following day were set forth in the plaintiff's declaration as libelous" ("Saier Takes Stand" 13). Even this detail makes its way into *Foreign Born*, as Roger Bartlett comments to Ernst, "Meisel wasn't in the hospital when that extra came out. He wasn't there. Do you know what that means? Well it means the *Journal* knew all about it before it ever happened," suggesting a conspiracy around the event both in fiction and in reality (177).

The trial would eventually determine that Saier had no claim to costs related to his business diminishing, as he had already sold the business to his son. Regarding the libel accusations, ultimately the jury deadlocked, although newspaper accounts of the trial explained that the jury was leaning heavily, split 10-2, toward a "no cause" verdict freeing the *Lansing State Journal* of responsibility ("Jury Disagrees" 1). In reviewing coverage of the 1920 trial, there are significant inconsistencies that call into question the judiciousness of the Vigilance Committee's actions back in 1917. Witnesses present at the tar and feathering testified to Saier's admission of guilt, but there was conflicting testimony from community figures as to Saier's un-American statements. Notably, the sole witness to Saier's flag desecration would not return for the trial and claimed he wanted nothing to do with the case ("Saier Takes Stand" 13). A bank manager also testified that Saier was paid up on all of his Liberty Loan bonds and owned several hundred dollars' worth. In *Foreign Born*, Herrmann glosses over some of these other details, opting for the more dramatic outcome of Ernst "learn[ing] that Meisel had gone half insane and couldn't talk and was near death in the hospital" (178).

There are other references in the novel that bear real world parallels to circumstances surrounding World War I. Ernst reads German American publications that were prominent at the time and that also faced scrutiny for their pro-German views. The most notable of those is *The Fatherland*, a national pro-German publication edited by George Sylvester Viereck. Phyllis Keller describes the focus of the periodical, particularly prior to U.S.

involvement in the conflict: "It frequently identified the fate of German Americans with that of the 'beleaguered' German nation. But, under Viereck's guidance, the paper increasingly focused upon three leit-motifs: anti-English propaganda, German American pride and political power, and the 'proper' policy and practice of American neutrality" (80).[8] These ideas are all expressed by Ernst in *Foreign Born* prior to the United States entering World War I as he reads the publication. *The Fatherland* later changed its name a few times in the face of criticism for its pro-German views; the *American Monthly* was one of its later revised titles, and that title also appears in the novel, corresponding with that similar passage of time. Ernst and other German Americans in the novel also receive warnings from the American Protective League in a nod to the real-world organization that spawned the work of many Vigilance Committees and other community surveillance efforts during World War I. The League was a group of "more than 200,000 untrained, volunteer detectives" who functioned as a "semi-official auxiliary of the Bureau of Investigation" [which would eventually become the Federal Bureau of Investigation or FBI in 1935] (Luebke 211). According to Frederick C. Luebke, the League "supplied its members with oaths of office, badges, and imposing certificates. Its agents conducted many hundreds of thousands of investigations during the course of the war. First they spied on enemy aliens, but soon the web spread to entrap any citizen who held dissenting views" (211). The vigilante prosecution of dissent is clear in the fictional examples Herrmann presents in *Foreign Born*.

Beyond the historical facts, Herrmann's novel is significant for the subtle social commentary interwoven throughout the discussions of patriotism. There are many places where Herrmann uses character dialogue or description to show that professions of patriotism or flag displays are false systems of measurement for loyalty to the United States. For example, Dick Miles and Ernst's

---

[8] In the 1930s and during World War II, Viereck's pro-German beliefs would lead to his employment in spreading Nazi propaganda in the United States. He would eventually go to jail for these efforts. See Phyllis Keller's "George Sylvester Viereck: The Psychology of a German-American Militant" for more details about this period of his life.

son, both barely eighteen years old, run away to enlist and join the war effort. Henry Miles, a strong member of the local Vigilance Committee and a participant in Wilhelm Meisel's tarring and feathering, wavers in his support of the war once his son becomes involved. While Ernst is far from happy about his own son's participation, he notes the irony in Miles's inconsistent attitudes toward the war. Henry Miles was perfectly willing to support the war effort as long as he didn't have to make any real sacrifice: "Now Ernst you know very well he's too young and there are plenty of men to go to war, and besides with all the work I've been doing here there wasn't any need for my son to go away" (189). Herrmann's commentary encourages the scrutiny of how sincere the local patriotism really is: "Ernst was thinking lots of things about Henry Miles and the whole lot of the Vigilance Committee, American Protective League fellows in the town. They were just a bunch of coward slackers, he was thinking" (190).

With a son enlisted in the war, Ernst's behavior shifts more in support of his son than the war effort as a whole. He hangs a service flag in the window of his shoe store to show support for his son, and this small effort, along with news of his son's enlistment, changes the city's whole attitude toward him. Ernst notes continually that his behavior is not very different from what it was before his son enlisted, and his attitude is still pro-German, but the cosmetic appearances create an immediate and substantial reaction:

> Ernst fell to thinking that it was easy to make these
> people think that you were patriotic. And he got
> to thinking that he wasn't a bit more patriotic than
> he ever had been before but he was a little proud of
> Charley for having the guts and courage to run to war
> but he did still think that Charley had been foolish
> and brainless when it came to being reasonable about
> the war. He was still hoping that Germany might win
> the victory before his boy had a chance to get across
> the water and in the war. But he was determined
> he would let people think that he was patriotic and
> wanted to see the Allies win the war. (201–202)

Ernst slowly transforms his store into the most patriotic business in Fairbanks, all while maintaining the same beliefs he had before his son enlisted. While acting patriotic, he still supports his German homeland and his sympathy for the German people. Almost everyone in the community measures Ernst's behavior by the surface appearance of his actions. As flags appear in his store and as he commits to the war effort by offering to send shoes to the Belgians, everyone applauds his new behavior without much questioning of his quick conversion. He is welcomed back to the businessmen's club and gives a speech there that even causes his own feelings about Germany to waver a bit amidst the strong profession of American allegiance. The original draft of the novel finishes, however, with his reading of the *American Monthly*, a nod to the idea that Ernst's support of Germany is still strong despite his overt appearance of American patriotism. He continues to walk the fine line between trying to support both countries he loves.

At some point, Herrmann added additional material to the end of *Foreign Born*. The complete version of the novel in the files at the Harry Ransom Center ends with a clearly written "The End" on the last page of the typescript, finishing the manuscript with Ernst's reading of the *American Monthly*, and the plot summaries of early reader reports confirm that ending. "The End" was eventually crossed out. Any remaining material at the Ransom Center related to *Foreign Born* is fragmentary, so there is no way to trace a timeline for any added material or to gain a sense of what it looked like. An August 1928 reader's report from Simon & Schuster reflects a different ending, showing that a revision was complete by then, describing a conclusion involving Ernst's "visit to Germany after the war to fetch home his enlisted son and his German girl-wife and his disgust with Germany and admiration of America" (C.P.F.). While answers cannot be found in the archives, Herrmann's bibliography provides a clue to the missing material, as a story titled "Charley Weiman" appeared in 1932 in a little magazine titled *Contact: An American Quarterly Review*, edited by William Carlos Williams, and the story's plot covers the material mentioned in that 1928 reader's report.

The story in *Contact* is the only portion of *Foreign Born* to ever previously appear in print. Williams and Herrmann were friends, having met sometime in the mid-1920s, and were knowledgeable about each other's literary work. Williams apologized to Herrmann in early 1928 that he had still not read the copy of *Foreign Born* John left with him. In October 1931, Williams wrote to Herrmann seeking material for his new magazine.[9] In December of that same year, Williams wrote, "I read over a good bit of Foreign Born. It's not too peppy but it has something good in it so I lifted a slice from it—and then didn't use it after all." Herrmann's story was dropped from that issue over concerns about the publication's length. It would eventually appear in volume three of *Contact* in October 1932, the last issue of the revived magazine to be published, alongside work by authors such as Williams, Nathanael West, Erskine Caldwell, Louis Zukofsky, and James T. Farrell.

"Charley Weiman" is indeed an alternate ending to *Foreign Born*, as it contrasts significantly with the context of the original ending. By the end of the story, Ernst makes a significant shift away from his affection for Germany to the 100% Americanism he had previously mocked. The story begins by describing his son's experience in the U.S. Army. Charley is stationed stateside for the beginning of his service and chafes at the safety of that assignment. On a visit home to see his parents shortly before finally getting sent overseas, Herrmann starts to suggest that Charley's service has slowly changed Ernst's perspective: "Ernst felt a little as though he himself were on his way abroad to fight for democracy and to preserve America. He was beginning to be really patriotic and was less interested in the American Monthly and the Nation" (244). The war ends two weeks after Charley arrives in France, and he eventually ends up with some troops joining the army of occupation in Germany. Charley enjoys his time in Germany far more than his experiences in France. He finds the people friendlier and meets up with distant relatives. In the process, his perspective on the war changes as well: "He grew sentimental about the people and wanted to help them and he began to be sure the Allies were more to blame than Germany for the war" (249). Charley's sympathy for his German relations and German heritage, once

---

[9] *Contact* had originally been created and edited by William Carlos Williams and Robert McAlmon in the mid-1920s and was revived in 1932, largely through the efforts of Williams.

faced with it directly, is similar to the conflicting feelings that his father has been experiencing all along. He even becomes enamored with a young German woman, and after being discharged from the army, he eventually becomes engaged to her. However, increasing poverty makes daily life in Germany difficult, especially as Charley seems extremely wealthy by contrast. He prepares to move back to America with his new fiancée, but not before Ernst and Helen Weiman travel to Germany to meet the young woman. Ernst initially looks forward to returning to Germany, but in the face of postwar conditions, his estimation of his German homeland changes drastically. The story concludes with Ernst's declaration, "I am glad I'm an American. My father was the wisest man in the world to come to America when he did" (261).

Herrmann may have added the section that became "Charley Weiman" to the manuscript of *Foreign Born* to try and appeal to publishers since so many were passing on the manuscript. He may have thought the pro-American ending to be more popular in the post-war era. As with much of the rest of the novel, this section is likely based on personal knowledge or experience, as much of it is set in Munich, where Herrmann himself spent time during 1922–1924. He would have witnessed firsthand the weakness of the currency there and the impact that had on the German people. Personally, I find the wholehearted conversion of Ernst at the end of "Charley Weiman" to be disappointing, as the critique of blind or insincere patriotism in the earlier sections of *Foreign Born* is more subtly crafted and involves deeper social analysis. The contrast between the two endings, however, is one of the aspects that make this novel and its composition interesting to consider, as it presents an opportunity for readers to weigh the characters, their behavior, and expectations regarding nationalism and patriotism and draw conclusions on how we might measure the sincerity of those alignments.

At a time when we still contemplate quite frequently what it is to be "American" or what national allegiance looks like in an increasingly global society, *Foreign Born* and its portrayal of the past provide an opportunity to reflect on our present. This novel may have indeed been ahead of its time—the wounds from World War I were likely still too fresh for it to have a large appeal to audiences of its time—but to rediscover the novel now, amidst continued discussions of assimilation and how to measure sincere allegiance to one's country, can potentially provide new perspective and perhaps suggestions on how to better approach our national and international future.

Works Cited

"Butcher Who Insulted U.S. Flag Mobbed." *The Times Herald,* 3 Nov. 1917, p. 1.

"City in Brief." *Lansing State Journal,* 19 June 1922, p. 2.

C.P.F. "Simon and Schuster: Editorial Department Report." 23 Aug. 1928. Container 3.1. John Herrmann Collection. The University of Texas at Austin, Harry Ransom Center.

"Final Report of Vigilantes Is Issued." *Lansing State Journal,* 3 Nov. 1917, pp. 1–2.

Herrmann, John. "Foreign Born (Part 3 of 3)." Container 2.2. John Herrmann Collection. The University of Texas at Austin, Harry Ransom Center.

———. Letter to Josephine Herbst. 9 Dec. 1924. Box 13. Josephine Herbst Papers. Yale Collection of American Literature. Beinecke Rare Book and Manuscript Library, New Haven, CT.

———. Letter to Josephine Herbst. 21 Jan. 1925. Box 14. Josephine Herbst Papers. Yale Collection of American Literature. Beinecke Rare Book and Manuscript Library, New Haven, CT.

H.M.W. "Reader's Report of 'Foreign Born.'" 30 Aug. 1926. Container 3.1. John Herrmann Collection. The University of Texas at Austin, Harry Ransom Center.

"John T. Herrmann Dead." *Lansing Journal,* 24 June 1898, n.p.

"Jury Disagrees in Libel Suit." *Lansing State Journal,* 2 Dec. 1920, pp. 1–2.

Keller, Phyllis. "George Sylvester Viereck: The Psychology of a German-American Militant." *The Journal of Interdisciplinary History,* vol. 2, no. 1, Summer 1971, pp. 59–108. *JSTOR,* http://www.jstor.org.libproxy.troy.edu/stable/202443

Kilar, Jeremy W. *Germans in Michigan.* Michigan State UP, 2002.

"Lansing Man Gets Tar Coat." *Detroit Free Press,* 3 Nov. 1917, p. 1.

Liveright, Horace. Letter to Genevieve Taggard. 16 Sept. 1925. Box 19. Genevieve Taggard Papers. Manuscripts and Archives Division. New York Public Library.

Luebke, Frederick C. *Bonds of Loyalty: German Americans and World War I*. Northern Illinois UP, 1974.

MacLean, James, and Craig A. Whitford. *Lansing, City on the Grand: 1836–1939*. Arcadia, 2003.

"Merchant Tailor Firm Here Business Pioneer." *Lansing State Journal*, 1 Jan. 1929, p. 51.

Perkins, Maxwell. Letter to John Herrmann. 29 Jan. 1927. Container 3.3. John Hermann Collection. The University of Texas at Austin, Harry Ransom Center.

"Saier Takes Stand Today." *Lansing State Journal*, 24 Nov. 1920, pp. 1, 13.

"Saier, Tarred Makes Threat." *Lansing State Journal*, 3 Nov. 1917, pp. 1.

"State Journal is Sued by Wm. Saier." *Lansing State Journal*, 31 Oct. 1919, p. 2.

"Theater Added to City List." *Lansing State Journal*, 25 Sept. 1919, p. 2.

"Three Years Silent, Plan Liederkranz Concert." *Lansing State Journal*, 8 Dec. 1924, p. 12.

"Vigilantes to Renew Activity." *Lansing State Journal*, 24 Jan. 1918, p. 1.

Williams, William Carlos. Letter to John Herrmann. 8 Dec. 1931. Container 3.5. John Hermann Collection. The University of Texas at Austin, Harry Ransom Center.

———

Sara Kosiba is Associate Professor of English at Troy University. Her research primarily focuses on writers from the American Midwest, including Ernest Hemingway, F. Scott Fitzgerald, Josephine Herbst, Dawn Powell, and John Herrmann. Her work on Herrmann includes an introduction to the first American edition of his first novel, *What Happens* (Hastings College Press, 2015), and she is currently at work on his biography. She is a past president of the Society for the Study of Midwestern Literature (SSML) and serves on the editorial boards of SSML and *Middle West Review*.

Editorial Note

Ross K. Tangedal[1]

This edition has been prepared from an unpublished, corrected typescript housed in the John Herrmann Collection at the Harry Ransom Center at the University of Texas at Austin as copy-text. Notes, annotations, deletions, and revisions in Herrmann's hand have been integrated into the text; accidentals (spelling and punctuation) have been regularized where appropriate, using Herrmann's *What Happens* (Hastings College Press, 2015) as a guide to the author's preferred style; and substantive emendations have been accepted only where the editor deemed them products of Herrmann's direct intervention. Herrmann's spare, removed style has been kept, along with his idiosyncratic spelling of certain words such as "highschool" and "proGerman." These and other eccentricities mark the text (even in typescript) as markedly modernist, as Herrmann experimented with form and structure.

In 1925, Herrmann began circulating *Foreign Born* to publishers, but by 1928 he was including the material that became the published story "Charley Weiman" as part of his submission. The material serves as an alternate ending to *Foreign Born*, showing what may have been had Herrmann completed the book. The story was published in *Contact* (October 1932) with multiple errors in grammar, punctuation, and spelling. No full version of the manuscript exists with the story material inserted, and there is no evidence that addresses how the material may have been

[1] Work on this edition was supported by a faculty research grant from the College of Letters and Science at the University of Wisconsin—Stevens Point. The editor wishes to thank Associate Dean Todd Good and Interim Dean Eric Yonke for their support.

incorporated into a revised manuscript. Therefore, a corrected version of the story as it appeared in *Contact* is included in this edition as a supplemental item rather than part of the novel.[2]

Editing a book from so early a draft is complicated. We are not privy to Herrmann's potential revisions, additions, or emendations had he been given the opportunity to see his book through to final publication. However, in its current state, the text provides a telling narrative of wartime anxiety crucial to understanding the American response to the Great War. It is this narrative that the editor has attempted to amplify.

Ross K. Tangedal is Assistant Professor of English at the University of Wisconsin—Stevens Point. He specializes in twentieth-century American print & publishing culture, textual editing, and book history, with emphases on Ernest Hemingway, F. Scott Fitzgerald, and Midwestern literature. His articles have appeared (or are forthcoming) in the *Hemingway Review*, *South Atlantic Review*, *F. Scott Fitzgerald Review*, *Authorship*, *MidAmerica*, and *Midwestern Miscellany*. He has also published essays in the *Teaching Hemingway* series (Kent State UP) and the *Rediscovering the American Midwest* series (Hastings College Press). He is a contributing editor for the Hemingway Letters Project (Cambridge University Press) and publisher-in-chief of the Cornerstone Press at UWSP. He serves on the executive advisory board of the Society for the Study of Midwestern Literature and on the Advisory Council of Younger Scholars of the Ernest Hemingway Society.

---

[2] See Sara Kosiba's Introduction to this edition for more on "Charley Weiman."

Foreign Born

Book I

1

Back in 1880, old man Weiman brought his wife and son to America and set himself up as a shoemaker. Fairbanks was then a town of only fifteen thousand people. The old man did good repair work and he could make a good strong wearing sort of shoe. He found himself with a fairly steady business and laid by money year by year. His shop was two blocks below the center of town where Ralph Miller had his high class shoe store and catered to the real best people of the town.

In 1890 Fairbanks was favored by a wagon works moving there and setting up in business. The population grew in numbers. The center of business moved southward toward the wagon works and stopped right by the Weiman shoe store. Ernst was wiser than his father, he was business through and through.

—Now is the time papa when we should do something here to the store and make it better. We got the best place in the town now, papa. Let's fix the store up and get the business.

The old man sitting at his bench just nodded.

—No, I guess we are all right now. We make money. What else you want?

—Oh papa use your head a little. If we fix up, put some new stocks in, then we get more business. We can get more than Miller easy.

Finally the old man gave in. The changes in the store were put in Ernst's hands. When the thing was finished it was without a doubt one of the finest shoe stores in the country. The old man was so bewildered he didn't want to work any more. Ernst told him to stay home, he could as well as not. They would hire a shoe repairman.

The new store made a good deal of difference to Weiman, both the old man and young one. It also made a lot of difference to Ralph Miller. All the new business coming to the growing town went to Weiman's. The old customers of Miller soon began to buy their shoes at Weiman's because of its central location and its really high class appearance.

Ernst didn't stop with his improvements, he just kept right on improving until he had one of the best shoe stores in the country. Naturally the best people in Fairbanks bought their shoes at Weiman's.

Old man Weiman died in 1895 and left the store and all of his property to Ernst, with the exception of some stocks left in his wife's name. In addition to the store, Ernst inherited a fair sized block of stock in the wagon works which was now yielding a profit of ten to fifteen percent a year. Then there was a little bank stock and two houses the old man had got for almost nothing but which were worth a neat sum at the time. Ernst Weiman found himself worth over three hundred thousand dollars.

At the time the store was remodelled the old man lost heart for working. He found it hard to sit around the house all day and talk to his meek-mannered German wife. He got to thinking of the cash money he had been saving in the bank. Then he talked to Charles Ross, the banker. He bought some wagon works stock, and later he bought the two houses. A few times he loaned out money on the quiet and made a good sized interest. Then he talked some more with Ross and bought more stock in the wagon factory.

This was better than the shoe store. Things had changed too much to suit him. Ernst had bought new machines for repair work and he had two clerks in the store to help. A fellow who, it was plain to see, knew nothing about shoes was doing the repair work on those machines Ernst had bought. One time old Weiman helped Ross out of a difficulty and he acquired some bank stock doing this. The old man was by no means idle during those last few years before he died.

———————

And Ernst was not idle in the shoe store. He was making money and making himself to be a figure of the town. In the first days of the business he had waited on the customers because he spoke much better English than his father ever learned to speak. He went up through the third year in highschool before he settled down for good in business. Now that he was doing well in business he was liked by the successful men of the town.

One night not long after his father had been buried Ernst was sitting talking with his mother. He knew that she didn't exactly approve of all the changes he had made in the store. She had liked the old way better. Her man had been much better when they first came to the country. America had spoiled nearly everything that seemed good to her. Her son was not like she had wanted him to be, not like the boys at home in Germany. Life was too fast moving here in this country. She dreamed now of her fatherland.

—Mamma we should build a new house for us to live in.

—No Ernst, we should not spend all that money. I wonder sometimes your poor father left you any money after all you spent on that store. He worked hard for you, Ernst. Now you should save your money. Someday you will be getting married and maybe have some babies.

—But mamma, listen here, we have a good business in the store and make lots of money and we should have a good house to live in. I think I will have Mr. Wetzel make us a real swell house like that house he made for the Johnsons, only different. You will like it, mamma, living like a Koenigin in a swell house. Then business only gets better mamma. Look at the new front on the store. The more you put up on something the more comes out. That is always true of everything. I think I will have Mr. Wetzel make us a new house.

—Ernst you should save your money. Frieda Schweitzer makes funny eyes at you I notice sometimes. You will someday want to marry. Maybe someday we can go back to Germany when we get the money.

—Don't joke with me always mamma. We can go for a visit to Germany when you want to. When I can get away from business. But who would ever think they wanted to live in Germany mamma? And please don't be talking to me about Frieda.

I never liked Frieda from the time I was a boy. I think I'll have the new house made for us. I will have them build it out there near the Ross's and the Johnson's and then we will get out of this part of town into the real swell part mamma. Then you will have a big house for yourself.

—I don't know, sometimes I think it would be better maybe if we lived in Germany again.

The new house was built for the Weimans in the best section of the town. Business grew better and better. Ernst was becoming a figure in the town. He joined the business men's club, which was organized to help the interests of the town. The men all liked him. He was a pleasant, easy man to get along with. He seemed to know how to make money.

At home he talked with his mother in English, more than in German, but he never dropped his slight German accent. It stuck and as the years went on seemed to grow more and more pronounced. This was why the men in the club took to calling him Dutch. As Americans they thought that Dutch was German and Ernst thought he was being called a son of Germany. He liked to have them call him by a nickname.

Ernst had about him a way of perfect politeness and a German way of raising his hat when greeting men about the town. His manners did not fail to make the women think him charming. The men were proud to have Ernst raise his hat to greet them though he was sometimes said to be too much affected.

———————————

Old man Weiman had known all of the old German settlers in the town of Fairbanks and they were all very friendly toward him.

Before Ernst took over the store the old fellow had done some singing in the Liederkranz society. He seldom missed a Saturday night of quiet beer drinking in the garden between the hall and the river. There he talked with his cronies, smoked a long cherry stemmed pipe, and discussed the old country and the new.

These men all liked old man Weiman but Ernst was too up and coming for them to understand. However, when the old man died, they asked the young one to join their song society. They sent him a sympathetic letter praising his old father.

Well I don't know, Ernst thought, I guess maybe if I get the time I'll join. But these fellows, they don't do anything. All the Germans that are doing things don't go there. I guess it's better not to. Besides people sometimes laugh at these fellows. It might be a little bad for business, things moving now the way they are. I better stick to the business club boys, maybe, but I might go to one of their meetings, it doesn't cost much to join and I don't have to go there all the time.

Saturday night he went to hear the song fest. The old Germans there were jolly fellows. They told him how much he had grown to be like his father. What a fine man he was becoming. But the young men, most of whom had gone to the little German school near the old Weiman home, were all suspicious of Ernst. He was an outsider from the day he started going to public highschool. He dressed much better than they did. And he had a look about him that meant money. He was just a swell in the town, putting on airs, that was all. Because he had a little money he thought that he was better. The young German fellows didn't like Ernst.

Old man Schweitzer asked him to come out and sit at the table with him where they would drink some beer. Then three other old cronies of his father sat down with Ernst and Schweitzer. Ernst was no great hand for drinking, he sipped his beer slowly. They all talked in German and Ernst found it grated on his ears somehow.

We all ought to learn to speak English when we come here, he thought. That's the way to make the money.

—Well Ernst, your father was a fine man. Hard worker, he was. You're coming right along in his feet.

Schweitzer was very proud of Ernst. The men all fell to talking about Ernst's father and Ernst got tired listening. Then they talked about the songs that had been sung.

—This was a sure fine evening tonight. Went off like a clock wheel, just as smooth, one man said.

Ernst had not found himself much impressed by the music but agreed that it was a very fine evening. It was good to get among these real people, so he said. All his father's friends. He was careful in what he said to these people, he didn't want to hurt their feelings. But he knew that he was in the wrong place. The business club was the best thing in the town. There the real men were. There, there was something doing, good fellowship, jokes, first names and lots of fun. Yes, these old fellows maybe got a lot of fun out of this kind of thing, but he couldn't see how it did them any good.

The young fellows of his age were sitting around talking, some of them were sitting with their girls.

They ought to be out doing something like I've been doing, he thought. Wasting time drinking beer is not going to get a man ahead. These young men had been his first playmates, but he hardly knew them now. One or two of them had been his closest boyhood friends. But now he must go on with the times, he thought. He turned to the men and begged their leave to go. He had to get home fairly early, his mother waited for him there alone.

—I'll drive you home with my horse Ernst, said old man Schweitzer.

—No, I guess a little walk will do me good. Thanks. I'll see you all again. I had a good time tonight all right.

—Auf wiedersehen.

———————

After service was over at the Lutheran church the next Sunday, Mrs. Weiman said good bye to Ernst. She was going to Mrs. Friedmann's house for dinner.

—You'll find everything laid out for you in the kitchen Ernst, I got things all ready.

Schweitzer heard her say this, then walked up to Ernst and spoke to him.

—Oh Ernst, why don't you come with us for dinner. We will be very glad to have you. And Frieda will be glad. And my husband told me he would like to have you come to see us. It has been so long since you have been to see us. Since you moved away I don't believe that you have ever been around to see us.

Ernst was undecided. He didn't want to eat his dinner at the Schweitzers, but he couldn't find words to use in order to refuse them.

Before he answered up walked Frieda and her father. They insisted that he come to dinner. So he went along with them.

Frieda, big and tall and smiling, looked at Ernst. She thought of what a handsome man he had become. She had known him when he first came to Fairbanks and had liked him then. Now she liked him in a different way. He was such a fine man and he was getting rich. He was good looking and never made eyes at girls. Frieda reserved Ernst for herself. She thought of the big house he had built and how he now had the finest shoe store she had ever heard of. He seemed much better than any of the other boys of German families in the town. She knew he went around with the best people and she thought that that was something pretty fine. Young Johnson had been taking him to parties now and then. She had seen the two men walking down the street together. Johnson was among the best names in the town.

Frieda and her mother never talked about Ernst together but the mother had her eye out all the time.

Old Schweitzer was a florist. He had a good business, but he didn't make the money Ernst was making. He wasn't the progressive kind. He had had his eye on Ernst too. He thought that such a fine young man would make a good mate for his daughter when the time came for her to think of marriage.

Ernst had not thought much about marriage. He was too busy in the shoe store. Besides, when it came to marriage he would pick out somebody on the other side of town. He was getting along so well now, someday, maybe he would marry somebody, but not Frieda Schweitzer.

At the dinner table it was suggested that Ernst and Frieda might take the horse and carriage and go out for a drive together. Ernst was not sure he wanted to go driving but he let them make the plans

Frieda was very happy sitting, riding with Ernst in the carriage. Ernst began to feel her there beside him, feel her body pressing, jolting against his. It seemed to him slightly indecent that her legs and haunches should roll against him when the carriage jolted. His education in such matters was of the back fence kind. He had heard dirty stories and tales of girls and men together. He knew how babies were made but he never before in his twenty-six years had felt just the feelings that he then felt. He had been excited by thoughts of sex but he had been a boy and knew what to do about these thoughts. The feeling sitting in the carriage was not a night time feeling but something more alive and real and happening to him then. It even made him wonder if he was really there at all and if that thing was happening to him sitting there. Why should Frieda, who did not seem to him attractive, she was so big and strong and manlike, make him so uneasy? It was sin to feel that way.

Frieda was very happy. She felt this same excitement, but it did not make her conscious of her body, it just made her very happy. She felt more like talking so she told him what a fine man he was becoming. Then she stopped and said, —But I'll get your head swelled way up telling you those things. You have done lots though Ernst. Papa says that you are a great business man all right. I'm so glad you are doing so well Ernst.

—Well I have to work right along Frieda. I like it though.

Ernst didn't feel like talking but he wanted to get his mind off Frieda and her legs that jolted with the carriage touching his and making him excited. He was quiet for a minute.

Frieda, waiting, listening, hoping he would have some more to say. Sitting, waiting she was thinking. Thinking she grew conscious and she quivered and drew back her legs and looked down at the floor. She was thinking that she loved him, she would like to have that man to marry, and she mustn't have her leg against his leg that way.

Ernst missed the pressure of her leg and thought what Frieda had been thinking and felt guilty because they both knew what they had been thinking. He began to blush a little and he jerked the reins a little and he twisted his necktie just a little to the left.

—Maybe we better be turning back again, do you think so Frieda?

—Oh no Ernst let's drive further, let's go to Jones crossing and come back through the woods road by the river.

Now that Ernst was missing the feeling of the leg of Frieda he began to want to feel it rubbing on his leg again.

Going back toward Fairbanks on the woods road along the river Ernst was wanting the feel of Frieda so much that he suddenly put out his arm and put it around her. Then he was embarrassed. So was she and neither spoke. He felt like a fool for a minute. Why had he done that? It looked silly. Neither spoke. How could he draw his arm away, he wondered. He must do more than that, he thought.

—Frieda give me a kiss, will you Frieda?

—Oh Ernst really I can't do that, you shouldn't ask me. We shouldn't be riding along this way.

Ernst drew his arm away from Frieda, sulked and looked ahead.

—Ernst you don't love me, let's not be silly. Let's just be good good friends. The best friends. Shall we Ernst?

—Maybe that is better, Ernst was quick to answer. He didn't want to kiss her, he had only asked her for a kiss because he had to do something. He couldn't have stayed there sitting like a fool.

Frieda wondered why he didn't answer more, why he didn't kiss her. She would kiss him if he kissed her. She should have let him kiss her. Maybe he would never ask again.

They did very little talking after this until they were back home again.

—You must come again and see us Ernst, please do. Come oftener Ernst to see us won't you?

—Thanks a lot Frieda, yes I will, of course.

I will not, he was thinking as he left her at the door. I don't like her, I don't care a bit about her. I was a fool. I never made such a fool of myself in my whole life before.

Frieda was sometimes happy during the night and sometimes very unhappy. Sometimes she thought that maybe Ernst loved her and then she thought again coldly and knew that he didn't care for her at all. And when it came to her finally that she was certain he didn't care for her she was very very unhappy. I should have kissed him, yes I should, she kept repeating. She was so unhappy.

2

A few days after Ernst had been for his drive with Frieda, Harry
Johnson came walking beaming into the store saying, —Well
Dutch old boy I'm through with college. Got the old diploma right
where my mother can put it on the wall. I'm going to get a few of
the boys together and we'll have a little jamboree.

Ernst would have liked a little less noise in the shoe store
when customers were being waited on, but this was Harry Johnson
and when he came back from college that was different. Old man
Johnson's son could do about what he wanted, the customers
wouldn't have cared how far he went.

—Well let me congratulate you Harry. That's fine getting all
through college. So you're going to have a little spree?

—You bet. And say Dutch tonight we'll all go to the lake
with rigs and you go along with me and I got lots of liquor out at
the cottage and we'll have a rare time Dutch. I got a keg of beer
from Jerry's and some wine and some swell scotch. We can all go

swimming if we want to, build a fire, have a damn good time. I'll
pick you up tonight at seven, we ought to be out there by nine at
least, because I told the rest to get there then and we want to be
there a bit before.

—I'll be waiting for you Harry then at seven.

Ernst went back proud into his office barred with little brass
rails running up and down. Having Harry Johnson, the son of old
man Johnson, call you Dutch in front of everybody in the store
and ask you on a party, there was something pretty good in that.
Ernst was getting in with the right people true enough. The fellows
that Harry Johnson would ask to the party wouldn't be the kind of
fellows that hung around the Liederkranz Hall. He would be asking
Miles and Winters, Stone and Henderson and others from the best
families in the town. That was pretty good all right. Frieda and her
people weren't the people these folks were at all.

That night riding out to the lake with Johnson in his carriage Ernst
felt very important. Young Miles was riding out with them. The
three young men were talking all about the girls in Fairbanks.

—Why don't you get a girl Ernst? My God any girl in town
would like to go with you. Margaret Haynes likes you, I heard her
say she did.

—Well really fellows I don't feel now that I want to get
married just yet so what's the use?

Johnson told him he should get in good with Helen Ross,
she was the best bet in the town. They didn't mention Hazel
Warren or Rosemonde Darlington, Johnson and Miles were gently
following these two young things up themselves. But they did go

on to mention Florence Armstrong, Willis Bulkley, Esther Shields and Helen Freeman.

Ernst had to answer them with something.

—Well really I don't know these girls so very well. I go around so much with fellows and I don't do much dancing, and I never thought of getting a girl. I don't want to marry right away anyway.

—Well you don't have to marry to call on a girl, said Harry Johnson. —You would have a better time that way. All the girls were anxious to get dances with you at the last party. Next time talk it up to one of them strong and go and see her.

Ernst was glad to have the conversation stop at the opening of a bottle and he took a little swig of wine with the two boys.

The horse clopped along gaily, swinging right and left, and soon they came to the Johnson cottage on the lake. They got out and hitched the horse and lit the lamps inside the cottage, gathered wood to make a fire and got the beer bunged. Other fellows now began to come and the drinking started and young Johnson got many toasts on finishing college and his future in Fairbanks.

Ernst, because he had never gone in much for drinking, didn't drink as much as most of the young fellows. But he was very happy to be here with all the live young fellows in the town. He was Dutch to all of them. They all liked Ernst.

Johnson took occasion every now and then to talk to Ernst and tell him what a good business man he was. He told him that his father thought Ernst would someday be one of the biggest men in the town.

—I heard you got some bank stock, don't sell it, dad said it was going to multiply. I thought I'd tell you Dutch because they are trying hard to get it in. Don't sell it even if my dad should try to buy it, do you hear?

Young Johnson really was very fond of Ernst. The young Johnson was now playing off his old man in cold blood.

—He's going to try and get it in, and so is Charley Ross. Don't let them do it. I'm with you Dutch. And say Dutch don't forget to come to the dance as my guest next Friday. You ought to join our little dance club, will you?

—Yes, I guess I'd like to. No I won't sell that bank stock. Really are they going to buy it in? I won't sell it. My dad bought it, I won't sell it, say, thanks a whole lot Harry.

—Never mind Dutch old boy. Only don't you breathe a word I told you. My dad would raise all kinds of hell if he ever guessed I told you.

Ernst was very grateful for the news young Johnson gave him but more grateful for the friendship that had caused the news to be given.

—I would stand by Johnson till the last hair of my head, said Ernst.

—Huh, what you talking about Dutch, you drunk.

—I didn't say anything at all. You're dreaming.

These were the fellows sure enough. They all liked him too. A great bunch of fellows and a fine bunch of friends to have. Ernst got to be so happy that he took a little bit more liquor even though he had never gone in much for drinking and he got to be almost as drunk as the other fellows at the party.

When Johnson came around near him again he called him over.

—Say Harry a funny thing happened to me last Sunday. I went over to the Schweitzers' for dinner, they were close up friends of my father and mother and can you beat it, I had to take the Schweitzer girl Frieda out riding in their rig. And do you know what, she tried to make me make love to her there, can you beat that?

—Say Dutch, leave those folks alone. They're all right where they belong. You're not one of them Dutch. Now don't you run around with that girl. Why in highschool she was nothing. But you know that's just like a girl like that. You ought to go around with Margaret Haynes. She's the girl for you. Say she had her nerve, what did she try to do?

—Well it wasn't quite as bad as that, she just kinda rubbed her leg up against mine, you know, and I, why I couldn't do anything. But I finally had to tell her I guess we better not do any monkey business.

—Don't you monkey around with that girl Dutch, I tell you she's not the kind for you.

Johnson then started thinking that maybe Frieda Schweitzer might not be so bad after all. If she acted that way he might take her out some time when nobody knew about it and maybe there might be something doing. Never do to tell anybody about it though, just do it on the sly sometime and see.

—No, you leave her alone Dutch. If she ever tried that with me I'd show her.

I'd have done it, Johnson thought. But he couldn't help but think that Ernst was a hero for turning her down that way. Johnson was not so simple in his nature as Ernst. He was always on the lookout for a female, though the times he got them were mighty few compared with the looks he gave them.

By the time the party got really lively Ernst was singing songs in German and the boys all quieted to listen to him. They all praised him for the songs he sang and hit him on the back and told him he was a good fellow. They all liked Ernst. Every one of them liked Ernst.

———————

Ernst became a member of the Black and White club which was a group of these young Fairbanks fellows who had organized to have a dancing party every Friday night. It was the select social club of the city and Ernst was now in with all the real best people. He had been to their dances several times as Johnson's guest, but now to be a member was a feeling much better than being there without being a member.

Johnson urged Ernst to dance with different girls and get to know them better and Ernst needed all the urging he could get.

He danced with Margaret Haynes three times and she was very nice to him and tried to make him have a good time at the party. He danced with a few other girls too but he also did a lot of sitting out between the dances. Once he danced with Helen Ross. She was the best one but it was funny she was a little hard to talk to and Margaret Haynes always seemed to make it easy to talk.

Ernst decided he didn't want to have a girl to go around with. They were too hard to talk with, most of them. The young men were a lot different than the young ladies.

3

Margaret Haynes's mother invited Ernst to come to their house for dinner. Ernst accepted the invitation because he was glad to have the chance to visit the home of these fine Fairbanks people and he liked Margaret well enough to think it would be fun to see her in her house and talk to her again.

Margaret was just as old as Ernst was and her mother had begun to worry just a little about getting her a husband of the right kind. Ernst had a real good business and some bank stock and some stock in the wagon works which was yielding quite big profits and he was a good looking hard working type of young man. And the mother of Margaret felt quite sure that Ernst would someday be a big man in town.

At the Hayneses' home Ernst was made to feel very much at home. Mr. Haynes sat stiffly talking to this young man about the weather and the prospects for more business in the fall. He talked to Ernst in a different way than when they met at luncheon in the business men's club. He was now much more like the father of a family and he was trying hard to please Ernst. He was in the game all right, though it was quite unconscious.

Mrs. Haynes was very nice and saw that Margaret sat where she would show off to most advantage and she gave Margaret little caressing looks and made Ernst think them a very affectionate almost perfect family. And she didn't hesitate to tell Ernst what a great deal of good he had done in the town of Fairbanks. And how hard he worked.

He would have been uncomfortable if they had not made everything so easy for him. After dinner he and Margaret sat in the parlor near the fireplace and talked about the dances and the Black and White club and about the young men in the town.

—You're a great friend of Harry Johnson, Ernst, said Margaret.

—Yes, I like Johnson and I guess he likes me quite well.

Everybody in the town had begun to notice that Ernst was a friend of Harry Johnson, it had been a help to Ernst to have Johnson for a good friend.

Margaret tried to switch the conversation to something more personal in its nature, so she went back to the dances.

—I love to dance with you Ernst.

—Do you, well I like to dance with you. I like to dance with you better because you and I always do quite a lot of talking. And we always have a good time dancing.

—Yes we always do don't we? You must be sure and ask me for dances at the party Friday evening.

The conversation carried on with no direction and they seemed to get no nearer to the point that she was seeking. Finally Ernst thanked the Hayneses' for their dinner and the good time of the evening and started to go. Margaret walked with him to the door. She took his hand and held it a little tighter than she had held it ever before when she had met him or was bidding him good bye. Ernst felt the pressure going all over his body and he squeezed her hand the harder, then he turned and left the house and tipped his hat and said again good night.

He felt all excited and very happy but the thought went through his mind that maybe after all he didn't want to make love to Margaret. Maybe he wouldn't be wanting her only for dancing and talking. His thoughts went to Helen Ross. She was something more remote and better. Margaret was too apparently trying to make him like her. Now that he had left the house he saw a lot of things he hadn't seen before. He saw that Mrs. Haynes had been a little bit too anxious to make him be pleased with Margaret and the father had been funny, stiff and different than he ever was at the business club luncheon and Margaret had been too good and smiling. Helen Ross was different. Thinking of these things Ernst began to take Margaret all to pieces in his mind.

She's too big and not too good looking and she hasn't anything in her head. She hasn't got the go that Helen Ross has got, not by any means. I don't think I like her very well. I didn't have such a good time at her house for dinner.

The next day Ernst forgot about the girls and thought about his business and planned to do some more advertising in the paper and make a few more improvements in the store.

Old man Johnson and Charles Ross walked in the store and told him they would like to speak to him on business.

—It's just a little matter Dutch. We're making a few changes in the bank and in order to make them we want to keep the stock all in the hands of the directors. We thought you might sell your stock to us. We will give you twice its value even if we are to lose on it because the policy is to have the stock all in and we want to do that even if we lose by doing it. Of course you'll make a lot of money on the deal and have some good cash to use for investing. It is all your gain you see. But we don't care if we do lose.

Charles Ross did all the talking. Old man Johnson stood behind him listening looking now at him and now at Ernst.

—Well really Ross, I'll tell you how it is with me. I don't want to sell that stock. My father told me never to sell it till I had to. It pays a good dividend and I don't want to sell it.

—Well don't you see Dutch you are making more money this way than you could by holding it ever.

—That's all right I think I'll hold it even if I lose.

They talked on for a few minutes but Ernst hung tight and kept his stock and wouldn't sell it. Then the men shook hands with him in a very friendly fashion and Johnson turned and spoke to Ross.

—I knew Dutch didn't want to sell, Charley, and sometimes when I see the things his father did I think whatever he does is about the proper thing to do. I really think you'll be glad you held it maybe Ernst. Of course we had to come and see you and maybe it would be better if you didn't do any talking about this for a while.

—Oh I never talk about my business. I won't say a thing about it.

Ernst was happy when the men had left the store. Young Johnson had been a fine friend to tell him not to sell his bank stock. If he hadn't told him he would have sold it out for twice its value in a minute.

In just a few months Ernst was happier than ever because he hadn't sold his bank stock. His money was by that time worth almost double. He would hold on to the bank stock now for good, he thought.

And he couldn't keep from thinking what a big man he was becoming in the town. He was quite sure by this time that Margaret Haynes had her eye out for him and then to have these two big men come to him on business and make it so important seemed to make him bigger than ever in his mind. He felt that he was really becoming a figure of importance in the town of Fairbanks.

He neglected the old German friends of his father and didn't bother any more to go to the Liederkranz Hall. He was moving now in better circles.

———————————

One day old man Schweitzer came to him in the store. He looked angry, hot and excited and he called Ernst to talk to him in the office.

—Ernst Weiman that young fellow Johnson is a friend of yours isn't he? Well it's too bad you have any thing to do with such people.

—Why what are you talking about Mr. Schweitzer?

—Well young Johnson asked Frieda to ride home with him from a church social last night and he tried to be bad with her and she came home all mussed up and crying and I have got half a notion to give him a good sound beating. He's no good, no good at all. Why does he pick on Frieda?

—Why that is awful Mr. Schweitzer. I can hardly believe that can be true. Ernst suddenly began to feel real nervous and excited and a little frightened.

—Well it's true all right and if that is the kind of friends you've got, well you needn't come around to see us. You shouldn't go around with such people Ernst. They are no good. And you can tell that young fellow for me that if he ever comes around my daughter again I'll fix him. Good for nothing fellow, that's all he is.

Ernst was getting very frightened. He remembered telling Johnson that Frieda had tried to get him for herself and now he knew that he had been the cause of Harry Johnson trying to get Frieda Schweitzer. He had made it seem quite plain that she was just a bad sort of girl.

—Mr. Schweitzer if I see that fellow Johnson I will certainly tell him what I think of him for doing such a thing. Why this is terrible. I hope Frieda is not all too upset about the thing. Why that was awful for Johnson to do. I'm sorry and I'm glad you told me. I never thought that he was that kind of fellow.

—Well Ernst I thought I better tell you. You should not be always going around with such people. Your father would not have liked it. You are getting too much money and getting on too well. You never had to work enough, that's the trouble.

When old man Schweitzer left the store Ernst felt very bad and thought of Frieda and now he began to hate her. He felt very guilty and the fact that Johnson had tried to get Frieda for himself made Ernst dislike her and think she was really a bad sort of girl. But he liked Johnson just as well as ever only he was sorry too because he had told him all that about the buggy ride and that Frieda had tried to make him make love to her. He knew that he was to blame for the thing Johnson had done and it made him dislike Frieda more than ever. He would have to talk to Johnson, he thought. But he knew he never would be able to say anything to him about the matter.

Ernst didn't speak to young Johnson about the matter and he decided that he wouldn't bother any more with the Schweitzers. He went to all the dances at the Black and White club and kept his store in top notch order and spent his evenings fixing things up around the new house he had built. Life seemed fine and beautiful and rosy and Ernst felt himself to be an important figure in the city.

4

Ernst was really becoming a figure to be a noticed in the town. His shoe store was by all odds the best in Fairbanks and he had a way of getting always mixed in some new schemes which the business men of the town got into to make money and make themselves to be figures in the town.

Charles Ross, the cashier of the First National bank, had recently been made president of a new concern organized to manufacture automobiles and he was anxious to have the thing become a big success and be an important industry in the growing town of Fairbanks. He was anxious to have all of the solid businessmen of Fairbanks join together and take an interest in this new industry. Ernst received Charles Ross one day while he was sitting looking over bills in the delicately brass barred office that was set aside for him in his new and model shoe store.

—Come in Charley, take a seat, I'm glad to see you here today. What can I do for you this fine morning?

—Well Dutch old fellow sterling times are coming for dear old Fairbanks. I've got a gilt edged proposition that I'm going to make to you. Only a few of us are in. It's limited you see. It's automobiles run by gasoline, just like a buggy. There's no reason why a buggy should not run by gasoline just like a train runs. Half the time of horses, expenses cut all up to pieces, cheaper as I said in every way, and Dutch the thing is this, it's coming sooner or later and you'll live to see the day when all the people will ride around in automobiles without their horses. I'm no dreamer Dutch, believe me. I'm a hard cold man of business. I can give you a list of names that might surprise you. Men who know their business Dutch, the kind of men you put your faith in. Harry Miles, Bill Winters, even old man Johnson, they have put down their names to back it.

—I don't know Charley. What you say is all all right I know. But what are you going to do to make people buy these things? Horses are good enough for everybody. Isn't that so? I never yet heard of any automobile that could run more than a few miles without stopping.

—But Dutch you never stop to think of the improvements that are being made every day. Now the automobile that we plan to make is no ordinary thing at all. It's got gears that make it so it can go up any kind of hill. And loaded too Dutch, heavy. This is no fly by night or fool's game, this is business. Far seeing men are seeing what I've been trying to tell you now. The automobile will be run on gasoline for power and it is without a doubt as I have said the coming thing. Now Dutch I don't ask you to be a fool or throw away money, all I ask is that you look it over, talk to the men who know about it, and get in the thing while the chance is ripe. You'll be damned awfully happy some day I can tell you now.

Now Ernst was not so sure of this plan that Ross was talking about. He wanted to be shown. When he put the new front in his store against his father's and his mother's wishes he was sure that he was doing something that was going to be a help to his business but when he thought of putting money in a gasoline contrivance to replace the horse and buggy he wasn't sure at all. But he felt flattered to have Charles Ross come to him long before the plan had been made known to the public and offer him a chance to get in on the ground floor.

—Well Charley I will tell you now just how I stand on this whole thing. I believe in you and Johnson, I know that you two men are not doing things that may turn out someday to be foolish. I'll listen to what the proposition is and I think I may do some business in it myself. You talk about forward looking, there was never any fellow more that way than me. I knew the town was going to move this way and I had the old store all built over and people thought I was putting things on too thick I guess, but you can see for yourself that all the time I saw what was coming. I got a property here that is worth as much as any in the town and lots of people have been asking me how would I like to rent it. Just the other day I got the wind that some fellow from some chain store was looking for a place and that he thought of coming up to me. Do you think they're really going to come here to Fairbanks with that chain store business? I don't like it taking all the money out of the town that way. I am going to hold on fast to my business. *Help the old home town* is always the motto, am I right?

—That's the way to talk Dutch. That's the very reason I have come here to see you. You are without a doubt one of the forward lookers in this burg. With you in on this thing it can't fail because

I never yet have known a Dutchman to get in on anything that wasn't a sure go. We're all together Dutch. We are the men who are making this town. Why, I think when we were boys. And now look at us Dutch. I'm glad to see what you are doing. I knew your father well and I told the people here that someday they were going to see you Germans right up among the first people of the place. You and your dad sure put the thing across all right Dutch, you are both to be commended, and again I say I'm glad to see that you are with us in this thing.

Ernst was made to feel very happy by the flow of pleasant talk that Ross kept pouring. It was nice to feel that you were one of the best men in the town. One with Ross and one with Johnson, Miles and all the others. All the big men in the town.

—Yes I believe in you Ross. You have always been a model here to me and what you say is probably true. If you say that the automobile is going to be the thing I'm with you from the start.

The two men put their heads together and talked about the business and about the glorious chances to make themselves more money. They were close together in the office just like brothers. Ernst felt very happy with his shoulder touching Ross's. He would be a big man of business, respected, looked up to in the town. Maybe, well the chance was better, maybe he would someday marry Ross's daughter, maybe he would get in with the Rossess, maybe he would get to be as big a man as Ross was. As he thought about the daughter he decided that he could spend more money and he raised the amount he had offered to a sum that made him third in holdings.

—That's right Dutch, Ross was saying. —When I see you put that much in I have got more faith than ever. You are without a doubt a man who knows what should be done with money. Now it's you and I and Johnson. We're the three, and you'll be made an officer of some kind, I am going to see to that.

Ross was so delighted he felt sure that the scheme was going to be of profit. He was going to be much richer and a captain of finances. This young fellow Ernst is sure a hummer. He'll be one of the richest men in town. These Germans never seem to fail. They come with nothing. Look at his father. And then they just make more money than anyone else can make. In three years he'll be laughing at the shoe store. He'll be a big man of finance. Uncanny head he's got.

———————

That night at home Ross was speaking to his daughter and he told her that Ernst Weiman was one of the biggest young fellows he had ever come across.

—Yes but listen pap, Ernst is so funny. He doesn't look so bad but when he talks you know right off that he's a German and he doesn't dance as nicely as most of the young men in our set. I'm surprised that they all like him these young fellows. He is always arm in arm with young Miles and now that Harry Johnson is through with college you would think they had been school chums the way they stick around together. He was nothing, I remember. In highschool no one even thought of him. Why just a few years ago his dad was just a poor old shoemaker. Then suddenly they get their place all fixed up and now they are right in everything. His mother though, I notice, knows enough not to put her foot in. They wouldn't think much of her down at the club. They are just new rich people, that is all they are.

—Yes but daughter listen. Stop and think so are we all only not quite so new? That doesn't matter in this country daughter. If a man has got the stuff young Weiman's got why he's all right. He's bound to go much farther than these other young fellows. Why to tell you frankly he is one of the biggest stockholders in this new company you have heard me talk about. His father left him money and his credit is like gold. We would loan him all the money in our place just on his face. He's a crackerjack that fellow. No one like him. If I had a son I couldn't want him to be much better than young Weiman.

Father doesn't understand things, Helen Ross was thinking. He thinks Ernst is the best thing that ever came along. Still if Ernst makes all that money, and he isn't a bit bad looking, and he seems so strong and, well, he's something like a baby. When he talks at least he is. I like him all right, but he is different. No it doesn't matter maybe that his father was a poor old stooped man and his mother is just a plain old German woman. Still I wouldn't like to see her sitting here.

—They built a fine house father. It looks about the best in town in many ways. It is I guess what you would say quite tasty in the way it's built and the way it stands back from the sidewalk. Imagine Ernst and his mother living in that house alone. She must feel funny in such a fine house father. Ernst would fit it better.

—What is that you say? Oh yes, of course dear, there has never been a doubt in my mind that young Weiman will surprise the whole city. He has already. And he is just beginning. When I think how at his age I was nothing much to speak of. Well getting on all right but nothing the way he is. It is marvelous. The business men may someday make him president of the club. Everybody has confidence in Dutch.

—Don't call him Dutch father. That's not his name. And besides, well I don't like to hear it spoken. I notice that Mrs. Haynes has been asking him over there for dinner, more than once I guess, if what I hear is true. She probably thinks that he will take a shine to Margaret but I notice at the club he doesn't ask her much for dances. Come to think he doesn't seem to ask anybody much, just goes here and there from one to another. I danced with him once or twice, yes twice, last Friday.

Charles Ross read on in his paper, hearing only faintly what his daughter said.

—Yes he is quite a fellow, Ross said sighing as he turned the paper.

I wonder if he likes that Margaret Haynes, Helen wondered. She is not the type of girl for him. But he is so very funny. I think of a fellow having no one practically to bring him up and then turn out as father says. I don't really like him, yet when I think about him I guess he is all right and all of that. I would have a better chance than Margaret. In fact I never even thought about it. Why there would really be almost nothing to it. I could marry Ernst, I know that that would be quite easy. Margaret is not especially good looking, though I guess the men like girls like that.

———————

The next day when Helen was downtown she walked into Weiman's shoe store and Ernst smiling broad and happy said,

—Good morning, it's a fine day is it not?

The clerks stood back against the shelves of white cardboard shoeboxes all with hands behind their backs. Ernst was walking toward Helen smiling ready to do what he could to make her happy in his place of business.

—Well Ernst and how are you this morning? Not so busy are you now. I need some shoes Ernst, dancing shoes, pumps.

—Oh just a minute Helen. Jim go down and get those new dancing slippers from that box that came this morning. We have got some new New York shoes in this morning. There is one pair among them that I picked out just especially thinking they would be the very shoes for you. Your father came to see me yesterday, just business.

—Yes, he told me all about it Ernst, I think it's fine.

—Here they are, the shoes. Aren't they fine, good looking?

Ernst, in trying on the shoes for Helen Ross, could not keep himself from looking at her legs and hips and thinking of the difference between the big heavy animal haunches of Frieda Schweitzer and he felt a feeling of excitement going over him while he was trying on her shoes. He would like to have her legs rub against his in a buggy the way the legs of Frieda Schweitzer had done that Sunday afternoon they went out driving. He thought it would be good to go out driving with Helen Ross in a horse and buggy.

—Oh they are very good looking Ernst. I wonder do you think they fit all right? They mustn't be too small for dancing, but I want them to look nice too. Are they really new? I think that they are very lovely. I think that I will take them. They feel all right, I guess they'll do all right. They are nice looking Ernst. I'm glad I came. I hope nobody else gets the same things.

—They won't, I'll see to that. I really will I mean it. At least not for a while yet.

—Will I see you at the club this Friday? I'll be wearing the pumps on Friday for sure.

—Yes I'll be there with the bells on, can I have a dance that night? Don't forget.

No it's funny, Helen thought when she left the shoe store, he isn't like a husband. He is nice all right but sitting there and putting on those pumps he looked absurd. I don't want a man to put my shoes on. No I don't. I wonder if he really is as great a hand at business as father said. Put on shoes and be a big man, well look at Lincoln. And his store is certainly a fine one. Like New York almost. Those clerks all stand back before him. He is different now than when I knew him in highschool. He only waits on people that are good customers though I'm sure. I never saw him wait on anybody else before did I? No, except on me last month when I got those brown suedes with the ribbons. But he used to, well but father says himself he did lots of things, that's nothing really. Ernst is to be respected for all the things he's done.

———————

Friday night they danced together, Ernst and Helen, and he felt he was her equal, and he felt that he could make a few advances. Helen watched Margaret and knew that Margaret was after this young man so she was very good to Ernst and talked to him and joked and took his arm when they walked from the dance floor after they had danced together. She suggested that they sit and talk a while and sitting there she eyed him very closely and considered in her mind how he would be for kissing. They danced again

together and once more before the evening was finished and they
came to like each other very much for dancing and for talking and
Ernst thought now that maybe he might get her for marriage. He
thought of her in highschool. She was different, or she seemed
much different anyhow. She had been just an unattainable
something beyond his reach and yet desired. Now she was where
he could touch her, talk to her and maybe someday marry her if he
could only make her see it as he did.

———————

The next day he talked with his mother in their fine new home in
the best part of the town.

—Ernst you should now once in a while think of marriage.
There is Frieda Schweitzer, I noticed that she always looks at you
funny sometimes in church when we are there. She would make a
fine wife Ernst. Her mother and her father, your papa and I knew
from a long time ago when we first came to Fairbanks. She is a fine
girl for you to marry, don't you think? I bet she can cook a schnitzel
or make those knoedels you like so well Ernst.

—Why mamma you are talking absurd about Frieda. I never
cared for Frieda. I liked her all right but not that way. I am now
quite a business man mamma and I have no time for foolishness
like Frieda. I may marry though. I sometimes think that maybe
Helen Ross has got a little liking for me. She would make a fine
wife mamma. I don't know if I love her but I like her an awful lot.
And then her father and I are good friends and business partners in
this new business I spoke to you about.

—Ernst you are maybe very foolish about that new business.
I am afraid with that Ross and all his people. You will lose all

the money that papa made for you. You should not have done it maybe.

—Now mamma remember what I did about the store and the new front that I put on, you didn't want me to and now you see that this is just the thing that made us such good business. It is sure to be the same with this. When Ross and Johnson get into some business it is no monkey business mamma.

—And Ernst I don't think that Helen Ross is for you to marry. She is snobby and I never thought that she was such a nice girl as Frieda. You should marry a nice girl that is good and German and can cook for you and is able to do work around the house.

—Well now you know I never said a word about marrying Helen Ross. She probably wouldn't marry me if I asked her and I never asked her did I? When the time comes for that I will do it mamma never worry and it will be somebody that I love enough to marry.

—Well my boy I think sometimes your ideas are funny and I don't think all these new ideas are for much good. You are sometimes so headfirst with everything that I never think that I can tell you advice any more since your father died. I think that you have got it in your head to marry that Ross girl and I don't like for you to do it. I sometimes wish now that we had always stayed back in Germany where things are different. We have the shoe store and this new house which I am sure your father would not have built because it is too big and people think we are showing off. At the church I notice that the women there don't like me like they did before, not all of them anyway. And when they come here to see me once they always talk about the house and what you are doing in your business and how much money you have made and I don't think we should act so rich. They don't come here so often to see me, all of them as they did in the old house before. And you go out so much to parties that it seems that everything is different than before papa died. I sometimes wish I could go back to Germany again. There everything is wonderful, beautiful, and the people nice and the fields and wood and the hill back of our old house in Germany every spring is beautiful and in the town too. Sometime Ernst we will go back and see it and maybe Ernst that is where I should like to die in Germany. I have been here in this country too long already.

—We might take a trip to Europe sometime mamma if we can get away for long enough from the business.

5

Ernst began to think that what he needed was a horse and buggy. With a horse and buggy he might get to know Helen Ross much better and in a shorter time than he could get to know her in another way. So he told his mother he thought they ought to be buying a horse and buggy and then they could go out riding on Sunday.

Mrs. Weiman didn't want Ernst to buy the horse and buggy.

—You don't need a horse Ernst. You have only a little way to work to go in the mornings. And I don't care to go riding. I have plenty of invitations to go out riding and I don't care much about it. You should think of saving your money and not about all the ways you can to spend it and besides if you get a horse and buggy you will just be going out riding more than is good for you. All you want is to take some girls out riding. I guess that's all it is with you. You think you take that Helen Ross out riding maybe. Well she has got a horse and buggy, she doesn't need you to get one.

—Now see here mamma, I never said a word about Helen Ross and you know very well I don't want to take her out riding. I never even go to make a call on her. Why are you always talking to me about Helen Ross?

—Now Ernst don't get on your high horse, I was only making a little joke with you, don't get so all excited.

—Well we ought to have a horse, I think that I will get one.

—Your father never needed one while he was here with us and I don't know what I'm going to do. You just go your own way always. When you get a horse what do you want next? We were much better off when we were in the old house before you got all of your big ideas Ernst. It is not much good in living any more with everything so upside down.

—Now mamma don't get all excited, we are much better off than we ever were before and everything is getting better. You should be very happy now mamma that everything is going so well with us.

Ernst bought the horse and buggy. But it was quite a struggle for him to get up the courage to buy it when he knew his mother didn't want him to. He felt a little sneaky going against his mother's wishes and he almost didn't have the nerve to go ahead and buy the horse and buggy.

———————

Because Ernst knew his mother would be angry he didn't tell her that he took Helen Ross out riding in the horse and buggy. And Helen didn't do much talking with her father about Ernst and the way the two had been going out riding in the buggy. So the people in the town knew that Ernst was courting Helen Ross before the old folks knew a thing about it.

—I am going to take Harry Johnson for a ride in the buggy, Ernst told his mother.

Then he met Helen and the two went for a ride out in the country. It was a pleasant sunny Sunday and they stopped and got out to look at the river and they talked and laughed and had a very jolly afternoon together. Ernst knew that he liked Helen well enough for marriage but Helen liked Ernst in a different way and thought that he was very nice. She knew that if she wanted him for marriage she could get him easy. But she wasn't thinking much about marriage. It was nice for her to have his attention and know that he liked her and know that she was much better liked than Margaret Haynes.

—Ernst, do you like Margaret Haynes? she asked him.

—Yes I like her very much. You know what I mean. She is a fine girl all right. I don't like her maybe the way I like some others but I like her.

—What do you mean, the way you like others?

—Well the way I like you for instance.

—Do you really like me Ernst? I like you too.

Their conversation got to be quite dangerous and Helen steered it to the danger point and Ernst followed where she led him.

—Yes I like you Helen, I wish you liked me as much.

—Well Ernst you would have to tell me how much that was before I'd know. How do you know maybe I like you more than you like me?

It was lots of fun for Helen, she had the situation so in hand, but Ernst felt uncomfortable and wanted to feel more comfortable and wanted to tell Helen that he loved her and have her say she loved him.

—I love you Helen, really.

—Do you Ernst? I didn't know that. Do you really think you love me?

—Yes I do. I want to kiss you Helen. Can I?

—Oh, Ernst you mustn't give me all these surprises. We can't do that Ernst. No we must wait and see if we both are going to always like each other.

Now that Ernst had committed himself he had to stand his ground. He walked right up close to Helen, put his arms around her and drew her to him and kissed her on the cheek. Then he asked her for her lips and she was now quite silent and she looked up at him fearing just a little and she shrunk a little in his arms and closed her eyes and then he kissed her on the mouth. It wasn't a long kiss or a kiss of great passion but it was as filled with passion as Ernst knew how to make it.

He called her his Liebling and his Schaetzchen and he held her tight and said that he had always loved her. She didn't talk to him, he had made her silent, but she held him tight up to her and she hung her head a little and she began to think of lots of things that began to trouble her a little. She was not sure she loved him, that he was the man she always wanted for a husband or a sweetheart. She thought of the days in highschool when he had been so far beneath her and she thought of his mother, the poor old broken German woman. She was very much afraid she should not have kissed Ernst after all. But he was good and strong and made her feel so trembling and weak and nice all over. She would see.

Ernst was very happy. He found it easy to talk and laugh and he felt himself strong and powerful and a big man without a shadow of a doubt. To win the love of Helen Ross was quite a thing all right. There were few men who were able to do the things he could do. And then he began to trouble himself with thoughts of his mother. She would be very angry, she would make it very uncomfortable for him at home if he told her about Helen. He tried hard to forget his mother and talked to Helen.

—Helen we can be so very happy you and I together.

Helen was afraid when he spoke about her this way. It made her think of marriage and being a wife to him.

—We must know each other much better Ernst. I like you very much, you know I do, I guess, but we must know each other better.

—We will darling, we will get to know each other better and you will get to know how much I love you.

—Oh you are so nice Ernst but we mustn't let people know about it, will we? I like you so much Ernst. You are so nice Ernst.

—We have got a lot of time to know each other. Let me kiss you once more Helen.

—Not now Ernst. Let's not now Ernst. Let's wait a little while.

—Please Helen. Then he kissed her and she was glad to have him kissing her and felt that she must love him but she was still not sure she did.

Riding home in the evening they didn't do much talking but they sat and held each other by the hand and now and then Ernst drew her to him and he kissed her and called her darling. They agreed to keep it a secret until the day when they would make it known to everybody in the town.

Ernst thought that was better because then his mother would not know about it and she couldn't then get angry. And Helen was glad because she was unsure and didn't want to be too fast about the thing.

6

Ernst began to spend a lot of time thinking about Helen and his love for her. His mother noticed that he was not the same and seemed now much more preoccupied and nervous and she began to think that he was in love or that something had gone wrong in the business.

—Ernst why is it you are so quiet and sit so quiet now and don't talk much. Is it with the business? Something is the matter?

—No things could not be better mamma. I am not quiet. You imagine that I'm quieter than I used to be. Things are really just the same as always.

—I think maybe you are in love with somebody. What about that Ernst, is it that Ross girl? I guess maybe that must be it, you are in love with somebody.

—Now mamma please don't always be talking about me being in love. And Helen Ross is all right isn't she? If I was in love with her. But can't you see I'm not in love with anybody? If I was in love I guess now I am old enough to be thinking a little bit about getting married. Sometimes I think maybe it would be a good thing for the business. And they say when you are married then you really begin to do something with yourself.

—I think you love that Ross girl.

—Now look here please mamma, I don't. But say I did love her or somebody, that would be all right wouldn't it mamma? She will make a fine wife for somebody someday.

—I don't want you to be having anything to do with snobbish people like that Ross girl and I hope you don't begin to be silly with her. If you want a girl to marry why don't you marry Frieda Schweitzer or some girl like that and have a good wife? You don't want to have a girl like that Ross girl for a wife Ernst do you?

—I never said anything at all about that mamma. I was just talking, and I don't see why you get so excited about it.

—You must always be sensible about things Ernst and don't be silly about things.

Ernst made the conversation take another turn. It was too uncomfortable for him talking with his mother. If he could tell her that he loved Helen Ross and would someday marry her his mother would be angry and he could not make her angry. He was worried because he didn't know how he would ever be able to tell his mother that he loved Helen Ross. And someday he must surely tell her.

Charles Ross came to see Ernst at the store and told him how the new automobile venture was working out. He was all excited and radiant and happy and full of enthusiasm.

—We got the old Thomas property down by the wagon works and we are going to make a machine Dutch that will be something like the one that fellow Haynes made down in Indiana and we can make one that will run more than his runs. Voss, the man that came to Johnson and me with the plans and all the details, says that they are going to start to making automobiles up in Lansing. Now that fellow down in Indiana has been selling some of his and ours is much better. It won't take long to be making them and we can sell them and someday we will be making lots of money. To start with we will make one a week and later two and then someday we can be making one a day he says. Then we will be making money. It will be easy to sell them. Johnson is going to get the first one and I am going to get the next and you can get one if you want to Dutch and I know other people that will want them. And we can sell them in Detroit all right to quite a few people. Johnson and I saw the one Voss made but it isn't very good because he made it himself and it is not like the ones we will make here. Only I can see from that that we are going to have a fine thing of it.

—I don't think I want to ride in one of those things Charley. I hope we get good business from them but I don't think I would like to ride in one. I don't think I will buy one but if you and Johnson get one then other people will get them and I can see that they will be selling all right enough.

—Oh we'll sell lots of them. You ought to come and see the place we're going to make them in.

Ernst and Ross rode in the Ross carriage driven by a negro coachman down to the old Thomas mill near the wagon works. Ernst met Voss and heard again the plans for making automobiles. Voss talked all about the way the things would be put together and showed some sketches of the finished product and talked about the machinery that was being installed in the old mill. Ernst didn't understand much that was told him but with Charley Ross and old man Johnson in the business it was bound to be a solid proposition. He asked them when the first automobile would be ready and they told him that it would be two or three weeks at the most.

—The wagon works are doing good business, Ernst told Ross. —I guess that is a good business all right. They will always do good business probably because an automobile will only take the place of the finest buggies and you couldn't use one of them all the time the way you can a horse.

—If they could be made cheaper then you could, and then the wagon company wouldn't sell many fine carriages for driving. Oh Dutch, wouldn't you come to our house tomorrow for dinner? Helen told me I should ask you. We would like to have you come to dinner.

—I would like to very much Charley. That is nice of you to ask me.

Helen had told her father that he should have Ernst there for dinner since they were such good friends and were both so interested in this new business.

When Ernst was at the Rosses' he began to imagine himself married to Helen Ross and he found himself hoping that they could soon be married. He liked the way the servants acted and the graceful way which Helen and her father had about them in their fine big house. He tried in every way he could to copy their manners and decided that they knew that way to live much better than he did.

After dinner Charles Ross left the room for a few minutes and Ernst took his chance to kiss Helen and tell her that he loved her. They were just light kisses and hurried, for any minute he might come back and see them, and Helen was afraid.

—Do you love me Helen? Ernst asked her.

—Yes I do Ernst. I have thought about you. Do you love me too, really? We must be careful, don't kiss me again. Sit down, father will be here any minute.

Helen was beginning to know that she loved Ernst and she was no longer afraid that she only liked him. Now she began to want him for marriage.

Charles Ross came back and sat down and started talking about the automobile and then he told Ernst that maybe it was a good thing he hadn't sold his bank stock. It might take a jump before very long because they were thinking a little of delivering a big dividend. He said he was glad Ernst had held onto his stock, although he assured Ernst he had never dreamed before that he would ever say that. He had thought before that Ernst was silly not to sell his stock.

—But, he said, —you German fellows never do the wrong thing. You can depend upon it, when you fellows do a thing it is all right. Your father was a great head for business. If he had lived a little longer he would have made a fortune. But you'll get there Dutch old fellow, you'll get there all right enough.

Helen sat and listened to their talk of business and she smiled every little while at Ernst who looked at her whenever he could do it without attracting Ross's attention. She thought Ernst

was a wonderful man when she heard her father say these things
about his business judgment. He was an all around man all right.
Margaret Haynes would never get him. She would show Margaret
Haynes who could have him. Then she started thinking what
would happen when they married. Where would she go to live?
She didn't like the idea of living with his mother. He would have
to come and live with them at their house. Or maybe his mother
would go live somewhere else. That would be the best way to do it.

When Ernst left their house that evening she went with him
to the door and he kissed her good night and told her again he
loved her and she told him she loved him. Then they decided they
would soon go driving again together.

Charles Ross didn't see a thing that was happening between
Ernst and Helen, but if he had known he would have been quite
contented. Within him was always the feeling that Helen could
do as she liked and when she found the man she loved she could
marry him. He was in no hurry to have her marry. Since his wife
died Helen had been a comfort to him and had in many ways
replaced the vacancy left by his wife's death. But if she was going to
marry there was no one he would rather have her marry than Ernst
Weiman, who was to him the most promising young business man
in the town. But he didn't think that she was thinking of getting
married to anyone just then.

7

On a Sunday while they were out driving Ernst and Helen decided
that they would be married in the fall. They thought it would
be better not to tell the town about it but just to wait until a
short time before the marriage and then announce that they were
engaged to one another.

—My mother will not like to have me getting married, Ernst
told Helen, —she will not like to hear about it. It is too bad she
feels the way she does.

—Oh Ernst you mustn't let your mother always treat you like
a little boy. You love me more than you do your mother don't you?
I know your mother doesn't like me.

—Why of course Helen. She can't say anything about it.
She will get to love you the way I do. She is just a little funny,
that's all.

Helen felt in her a dislike for Ernst's mother and she felt that
it would be a battle between the two women for the man and she

was going to win the battle. She had more right to Ernst than his mother had. But all the time she felt a little afraid of the influence Ernst's mother had over him and felt that Ernst might love his mother more than he loved her.

At home that night Ernst told his mother what he thought of Helen Ross and he would be getting married someday.

—Ernst I will not have you marry that Ross girl. I will leave the house. I do not like it. There are lots of nice girls for you to marry without marrying Helen Ross. She can never come here to this house with me. I will go or she will not come here.

Ernst tried his best to reason with his mother and he tried to make her see that Helen Ross was the best girl in the world for him to marry. He told her that they would all be very happy in the house together.

—I will not have you marry that girl and I will not stay here if you do. I will go back to Germany or live with Mrs. Friedmann.

Ernst felt very unhappy and undecided. He wanted so to marry Helen and he felt so bad to see his mother feeling hurt and angry with him. He wanted them to like each other. He would marry Helen, that was sure, and his mother would have to put up with it. If there was only some way to keep her from being angry? She mustn't talk of leaving the house and going to Mrs. Friedmann's, or of going back to Germany.

—Well mamma don't you get all excited because we haven't thought of being married right away and you will get to like Helen before we are married.

—I don't want you to go around with her Ernst.

—Now mamma that is not fair for you to talk that way. We should have her here to dinner.

—Not when I am in the house we will not. Why don't you marry somebody like Frieda Schweitzer?

Mrs. Weiman began to cry a little and Ernst felt very bad and decided it would be better for him to leave his mother and go to his room and go to bed and think about it.

She can go and live with Mrs. Friedmann, he was thinking, but everyone will know that she is angry with me. I don't know what to do about it. She has no right to feel the way she does about Helen. Maybe we had better wait a while to get married. Mamma will not live forever. We had better wait a while.

He went downstairs and found his mother crying and he felt so bad he went up to her and put his arm around her shoulder.

—Now mamma please don't you be crying. I will not marry Helen now, so don't be worried mamma. Please don't cry and be worried like that. If you don't want me to I won't marry her now mamma.

His mother cried a little more and stopped and looked at him and looked away.

—Oh Ernst you should not marry her and leave your mother alone like that. I could never stand it to have you marry her. You are too young Ernst. You should wait till you are thirty and the business is better and you have saved more money.

Ernst went to bed feeling worried and unhappy. He didn't know what he would tell Helen and he wasn't sure he would be wanting to wait to marry. He wanted to marry just as soon as possible and not be waiting. He thought a lot during the night and didn't do much sleeping.

His mother was no longer crying in the morning but she acted nervous and she looked at Ernst with strange fugitive glances

and she gave him a better breakfast than she usually made for him.
She cautioned him not to work too hard and to be home for supper
in the evening.

He was quiet and didn't feel like talking and when he left
the house he felt a little sulky and began to dislike his mother
because she was interfering with his happiness. He began to wish
that his father was still alive so he could leave his mother and be
married and then he began to wish that his mother would go back
to Germany and he even wished that she would die, but when he
wished this he felt a creepy feeling and knew that it was wrong to
wish her dead. He was afraid Helen would hate him if he told her
about the way he felt about his mother.

In the afternoon he went to see Helen and found her at the
house alone.

—You seem funny Ernst dear, what can be the matter with
you? Don't you feel well?

—I don't know Helen. I was talking last night with my
mother and well, she is old now and I don't know, sometimes I
think maybe we should wait to be married a little longer.

—You don't have to marry me at all. If that's the kind of man
you are. I thought you loved me. I can't be expected to love that
kind of man. You love your mother. Never be afraid that I would
be a person to interfere with your happiness.

—Oh Helen I didn't mean that at all. I want to marry you
today. I do darling. Please don't be that way.

—Oh never mind I know how you feel.

—Helen I will not have you say that. We will be married
tomorrow. I only thought I ought to tell you so you would know
that it will not be so easy for us with my mother. But I never said

I didn't love you or didn't want to marry you. We will get married right away. I could never live without you Helen. Please don't think the things you think.

—I'm sorry Ernst. I thought, oh well what's the difference.

Then she walked up to him and they kissed and he told her about his mother and that he cared only for Helen and that his mother could do what she wanted to do because he loved only Helen.

———————

His mother stayed at home and brooded and grew nervous and unhappy and before long she was sick in bed and had the doctor and the doctor couldn't find out what was the matter and things just got worse and worse. Ernst went out nights to visit Helen and he took her to the dances and one night they told Charley Ross that they were going to get married. He was glad to hear about it. But it made him for a little while quite serious and sad looking and not a little lonely looking.

—I am glad and hope you will both be very happy. When I get Dutch for a son-in-law I'll surely put him to work for me making money. We'll have this business genius in the family and we sure will use him Helen.

While he was joking he was thinking that the arrangement would be a good one and he thought that together with his son-in-law he might do some big business in the city.

———————

Mrs. Friedmann's sister had married Mrs. Weiman's first cousin in Germany so the two old women were in a way related and this brought them together and made them good friends, and their good friendship was the cause of Mrs. Friedmann getting the invalid Mrs. Weiman to stay at her house where she could be taken care of better while Ernst was away at work. Ernst was living all alone in the big house and his mother had gone to live with Mrs. Friedmann and Ernst began to think that she could just stay there and he could get married and everything would be all right. He went each evening to see his mother and she seemed to get no better and her health did not seem to be failing. They talked about everything but Helen Ross and marriage. Mrs. Weiman never broached the subject of his marriage.

Finally he decided he would tell her.

She said that she had known it all along and she very quietly told him that Mrs. Friedmann would be glad to have her stay and live with her.

—You are doing wrong my boy to marry her but if you will do it all right, I will stay here with Mrs. Friedmann.

She was so good about it that his heart warmed to her and when he left that night he felt a great deal of love for his mother.

Going out the door Mrs. Friedmann told him that his mother had told her about Helen Ross.

—You should not make your mother so unhappy, she said. —But if you do that your mother can live with Karl and me. I don't think you have been as good a son to your mother as you should have been. I think it is you that has made her sick the way she is.

Ernst thought going home that Mrs. Friedmann was probably right in what she said about him making his mother sick, but he couldn't help but feel that she no longer held it against him that he loved Helen Ross. He thought his mother was beginning to see the matter the way he did. But he was uneasy and unsure and a little afraid that he was doing wrong to marry Helen Ross.

8

It was four weeks after Ernst had been with Charles Ross to see the automobile factory that the first machine was ready for running. There was only room for two in this high wheeled automobile so old man Johnson and Voss were chosen to give it its first run through the city. It caused a great sensation. The people in the town had seen two or three automobiles made by a man down in Indiana but there was great excitement at seeing this product of Fairbanks running down the street with old man Johnson sitting in it with Voss to turn the steering handle.

The one cylinder was panting when they got back to the old mill which was now the factory, and Voss said he would have to do some more work on it before it would be finally ready. Johnson was excited and so was Charles Ross and Ernst was too, only he seemed to sense that it would never be the big success the men had thought it would be.

A few weeks later Ross came in again to see Ernst and he was looking a little bit downhearted.

—I'm afraid the thing is not going to work so well Dutch. I don't know. We spent a lot of money on it but that darned thing don't go the way it ought to. It goes so slow and stops and the other day he couldn't get it started running. It costs us more to make them than we can ever get out of the things. I don't know Dutch. I think sometimes we ought to try and get our money out.

—Don't you think it's going to go? I don't think anybody wants one of those things when they got horses. But Charley, we will lose a lot of money.

—No we won't Dutch. Listen here. I'm going to start a campaign and sell the stock out to small buyers and we can unload a lot of it that way and we can make it worth more. We can enlarge the mill and put in new machinery. I got a scheme here all worked out. And we can unload our stock. I'm strong for wagon works stock Dutch.

—It's good stuff Charley. We should have put our cash in that. I don't like that fellow Voss. He doesn't know his business. His machine is not as good as that fellow Haynes made, is it?

—Haynes hasn't been making any money Dutch. I know that. He hasn't sold enough to make any money. You got to put one thing on a commercial basis if you want to make any money. I'm afraid it can't be done. He can't turn out more than one of those things in a week. I'll see that we get our money out Dutch, we are just the same as relations now I guess. We've got to work together Dutch. Are you coming out tonight to see Helen? I'll let you know about the plan I got then. I think we'll get out of the mess all right. I'm sorry I was such a fool, and then to get you all tied up too. I don't want to be a laughing stock here in the town.

When Ross left, Ernst didn't find himself feeling very bad
about the matter, he was sure Ross would get them out, and
certainly if he could sell the stock to small investors they would
find their way out. He decided he wouldn't feel so bad if he lost the
money. The best men make mistakes.

Why the more money a man makes the more mistakes he
makes, he thought. You wouldn't be doing anything if you didn't
make mistakes. And after all if it wasn't for the automobile he
might not have gotten in so well with the Rosses and he wouldn't
have gotten Helen for marriage.

Mrs. Weiman didn't get any better from her illness and when fall
came and the time for the marriage she was still living with the
Friedmanns and Ernst was going to see her less and less often.
Before the time for the marriage came Charles Ross had found
it possible to make a trade of most of his own holdings in the
automobile firm and most of Ernst's holdings for some stock in
the wagon works which was making good steady money. Voss had
become president of the automobile firm and Johnson had been
slowly backing out so it was practically a new concern and most of
the money was in the hands of small business men in Fairbanks and
a few backers from Detroit who had chosen to take a flyer on the
thing.

Helen Ross had seen to it that Ernst should leave the Lutheran
church and join up with the Presbyterians, and he had been quite
willing, for most of the best people in Fairbanks were Presbyterians.

It was the thing in Fairbanks to be a Presbyterian. Ernst leaving the Lutheran church had made his mother feel very bad and very lonely and deserted. Her husband was dead and her son was almost dead to her now.

The Friedmanns were very good to her. When Mrs. Friedmann heard she had a few stocks in her own name she decided it would be well to be very good to Mrs. Weiman. Especially when she considered that Mrs. Weiman's son had been such a great disappointment to her. She was welcome staying there living with them.

The wedding of Ernst and Helen was a big social event for Fairbanks. Helen had chosen Margaret Haynes to be one of the bridesmaids. It gave her a great feeling of satisfaction. Harry Johnson was best man. The best people in the town of Fairbanks were invited to the wedding. The Mileses and Winters, Stones and Hendersons were there. Mrs. Weiman was too ill to be there but the Friedmanns, who had been invited because Ernst thought he ought to invite them, decided they would have to go and see the thing. They were curious and said to each other that they were going only because they felt it was their duty.

Things went off very smoothly at the wedding and when the married couple left to take the train for New York, Johnson and his cronies saw that plenty of rice and tin cans and shoes were used to speed the parting couple on their matrimonial journey. They had thought New York would be a fine place for a honeymoon. So few people went there and it was far away. It would be much better than a trip to Niagara Falls or to Chicago.

In their state room on the train they both felt quite bashful and very nervous and they hurried to put the lights out. Helen felt she knew why her father had been nervous when she said good bye to him.

In New York, Ernst was more in love with Helen than he had been, and Helen, though she loved Ernst dearly, found herself disappointed just a little bit with marriage. It was not exactly what she had always thought it.

They went to the theater and Ernst looked through some Fifth Avenue shoe stores and planned to make his store a better one than ever. They dined in the best places and were always making love and looking newly married. When they were back in Fairbanks, Helen decided that she was not disappointed. She decided that love was what it was and now that she knew what marriage was she was ready to settle down and live a quiet respectable married life.

To all outward appearance things were going very well with the Weimans. People thought that they were an ideal young married couple.

But as much as Helen loved Ernst she did not really like to have him making love to her. She believed in moderation and certain days for lovemaking and when she could she was glad to miss the lovemaking. She was not really happy making love to Ernst, though she really knew she loved him.

Ernst had always known that it was best not to make love too often so he was not disgruntled with the arrangements they had made. But he thought that God was funny not to make Helen feel as much happiness in making love as he felt. It chilled his love for

Helen to know that she did not find as much pleasure in their love
as he found.

———————

They soon began to have a circle of young married friends to call
on and to have at their house for entertainment. Harry Johnson
married Hazel Warren in the winter and he and his wife became the
best friends of the Weimans. There were four or five other couples
that made up the circle and these people were together once or
twice a week for cards and talking. They were the best people in the
town of Fairbanks and Ernst now felt that he was without a doubt
a figure in the town of Fairbanks.

———————

A few days after they came back to Fairbanks, Ernst and Helen
went to call on Ernst's mother. She was sitting up in bed and
waiting and she took Helen's hand and drew her down to her and
kissed Helen on the forehead and a tear formed in her eye.

    —Ernst I hope you will be happy. I hope you will be happy
with Helen. Both of you.

    —We are very happy aren't we Helen? Ernst replied.

    Mrs. Weiman then began to tell Helen where she would
find things in the house and about the peculiarities of the water
system and the care that must be taken with the gas lamps in the
front room. Helen listened and answered her from time to time.
She wanted to get out of the Friedmann house and away from Mrs.
Weiman. She felt now that she had got her son away from her that
she pitied Mrs. Weiman and did not really like her. Ernst was a little
like his mother, she thought, as she sat there watching both of them.

—I am going to stay here with the Friedmanns, but I will be to see you some day when I can be out again.

When they were gone she felt much weaker and alone and miserable. That girl will never be good for my boy, she thought. And she thought how Ernst seemed so happy with Helen and it made her feel very bad to know that he loved Helen. She began to feel herself much weaker and really ill and she began to wish that she might die quietly and alone and then he would be very sorry that he had married Helen Ross. And she thought of Ernst walking on top of her grave out there beside her husband and thinking that he had not been as thoughtful of his mother as he could have been. She felt weaker and in a way happy and began to hope she would die. The world had no need of her, she thought. I am all alone now and my boy is not my boy like he used to be.

Mrs. Friedmann tried in little ways to make Mrs. Weiman dislike her son and not just feel hopeless and forlorn because he had deserted her for marriage. But she could not make Mrs. Weiman hate her son.

One day Mrs. Friedmann told her she should not leave her money with Ernst. He had too much already and it was bad for a young man to get rich the way Ernst was getting. Mrs. Friedmann said it would be better to leave it to somebody that cared more for her than Ernst did, or perhaps with some charity, she added as an afterthought.

Mrs. Weiman began to see that Mrs. Friedmann was thinking of her money and thinking she would like to have it. It made her feel angry toward Mrs. Friedmann but she didn't want

to show her anger so she told her she thought she would make a
will. Mrs. Friedmann was glad to hear this and on her suggestion a
lawyer came to see Mrs. Weiman about her will.

When the lawyer and the old lady were in the room alone
together she told him, —I will give all my money to my boy Ernst.

—Then you don't have to have a will Mrs. Weiman.

—Well I don't want people to know about it, so you just let
them think we did the business, will you? I don't want you to say
that we didn't do any business.

—Why of course Mrs. Weiman, that's all right with me.
Only you didn't have to call me to do that. It's a little funny, but of
course I won't say anything, if you don't want me to.

—Well just you charge me the same as it would be to make a
will and that's all right with me.

She thought that her son would feel bad when he knew how
his mother had gone on loving him after he had left her to die
alone and she was glad that she was able to leave him her money
just to let him know so he would feel bad thinking that his old
mother loved him so very much.

Until old Mrs. Weiman died the Friedmanns thought that
they would be getting her money when she died.

———————————

Ernst living in his big house with Helen thought that things were
all right with his mother and he didn't know of all the thoughts
that were always going through her mind. He thought that she was
now content to leave him married. He was happy being married
and living the life of the best people of Fairbanks. Helen now had
servants in the big house to do her housework and she called on

her friends in the afternoons and had them come over to her house. Ernst worked at the shoe store every day and tried in every way he could to keep it always a high class place of business and one of the best stores in the town.

Charles Ross came to see him often and they were always talking business and planning some new schemes to make more money. Ernst went in strong for wagon works stock and when a stove plant started in the city he bought some stock in that. He decided it was best to spread his money out in different things and always stay strong in wagon works because it yielded such good interest on the money and now and then declared a dividend in stock.

————————

Harry Johnson, who had been going from one job to another since he got out of college, settled down in the new stove company and became an officer through the influence of his father and he was glad to have Ernst put some money in the firm on this account. Harry and Ernst were the same good friends, though with both of them marriage had made them seem years older to each other and they talked more gravely with one another about the things they had for conversation.

Ernst had always wanted to ask about the affair Harry had been mixed up in with the Schweitzer girl.

—Say Harry, I don't know as I ought to say anything about it, but I wondered about that time that you went out with Frieda Schweitzer. Her father came in here and told me you were out one night and tried to do something with her.

—Say Dutch, why that old fellow is all off his head. Why, of course, it was just like the thing you told me about. I took her home and she started getting fresh the way she did with you. But say you mustn't ever let Hazel know about that or anybody Dutch, will you?

—I just wondered Harry. No of course I won't say anything at all.

This started the two young men talking about love and they began to get personal and do a little talking about their wives. Each one of them was reticent when it came to speaking about his own wife but each was eager to hear about the other fellow's wife.

Harry Johnson was first to start telling things about his marriage and the things he told made Ernst feel that Harry was either lying or else he and Helen were not getting all the happiness there was for them to be gotten. He was made to say that things were with him much as they were with Harry but he tried to stop the conversation as soon as he could. He felt that he must never tell Harry about all the things that Harry had been telling him.

He felt that Harry and Hazel were making love too much but he felt that he was in some way missing happiness that Harry seemed to be getting from his marriage. He couldn't make himself say anything about his lovemaking with Helen. He thought Harry was being wrong to say the things he had been saying about himself and his wife. He knew that Harry should not talk about such things to another man.

———————

Charles Ross married a good looking Presbyterian widow because he had been so lonely since his daughter married and he knew that he was too young to go to seed. Their marriage, because they both were wiser, was a very quiet marriage, but for days and weeks the tongues of the best people were wagging about the marriage and saying that Charles Ross was a doddering old fool to go and marry again when he had a married daughter and was old enough to know better. And they said that this Presbyterian widow was trying to be like a little highschool girl.

He and his new wife did act like a young couple and they started entertaining and giving expensive parties and the tongues were soon stopped from wagging and people soon began to think that it was the best thing for a man like Charles Ross to marry a woman like the Presbyterian widow. They ceased to think of Charles Ross and his wife as a sinful old couple and they allotted them their place in the best society of Fairbanks.

Ross felt much younger, and he and Ernst became closer and better friends. The Johnsons were the last to get over the idea that Ross should not have married the widow, but when Harry Johnson and Ross and Ernst got together, and with a few others of the younger men of the city played some games of poker in a friendly way and Harry and Ross became good friends with each other, then the older Johnsons began to think that it was not so bad for Ross to marry the widow.

And when Ross called on the Johnsons, bringing his wife with him, he made old man Johnson feel much younger and made the old man like him as he had always liked him before. Then he had won the best people in town to his side and his marriage was sanctioned by all of the best people in Fairbanks.

Helen had not taken it so well when she first heard that he would marry, but she felt so sorry for her father living all alone that soon she began to be glad he had married and she began to like her new mother, for she didn't feel jealous because her real mother had died when she was still a young girl. Ernst thought it was fine to have him marry. He thought it was about the best thing that could have happened to Charles Ross.

9

The automobile factory failed in the winter and Ernst and Charles Ross and Johnson found themselves glad to be out of it. The small stockholders lost their money and still have their stocks with gold seals on them, which are worth much more than the stock can ever be worth. Voss hated to see the firm go to pot the way it had. He knew that pretty soon things would have been in order and the automobile could be made cheap and good enough to make money for the maker. But he couldn't get any more money and so the firm had to go into bankruptcy.

  —It's a good thing we got ourselves out of that, Ernst said to Charles Ross.

  —That automobile isn't any good for making money Dutch. They never can get a thing like that to really be a good thing.

  Charles Ross was blamed by some people for the failure but he had so much money and such good standing in the city and besides they thought that he had also lost some money, so they soon began to take the blame from Ross's shoulders and it settled all on Voss, who left the town of Fairbanks and wasn't heard of for some time to come.

———————

In the summer Helen found herself with child and in the fall following the marriage a baby boy was born to the young Weiman couple.

Ernst had told Helen they should call it Friederick if the baby was to be a boy.

—No Ernst in America you should call your baby by some names that are not so German.

—Well that's a good name, Ernst had told her, —but why don't we call him Charley if he should be a boy. If he is a girl then we will call him Helen.

—No if the baby is a girl we will call her Mildred, that is better, and I never cared for Helen, and my mother's name was Mildred.

The baby was named Charles and his grandfather was proud and promised he would see that little Charley got what was coming to him in this world.

———————

Giving birth to the baby had not been easy for Helen and she was sick for several months as a result of the hard time she had had. She had been afraid before the baby came and the doctor told her that was the reason she had had such a bad time of it having the baby.

The young married women in the set the Weimans went in came in regularly to see Helen and see how she was getting on after having had a baby. They all thought they would like to have babies and thought that any babies they would have would be better babies than the little Weiman baby.

Hazel Johnson had not yet had time to have a baby and she wasn't sure she wanted one, although she said if the Lord wanted her to have one she would welcome it with open arms. She had heard so many stories about having babies and had heard a woman could always tell when she was conceiving.

—Theresa Hamlin told me she could tell by the way she felt, Hazel told Helen. —She said she never had so nearly come to fainting away completely and she said she knew right away that she was going to have a baby. And she had a baby, Helen. Could you tell that way? Did you find it any different? It seems to me by that way of telling I would have had lots of babies already.

—I never felt a thing like fainting Hazel. I never even felt I liked to have Ernst making love to me except a little sometimes but mostly it is nothing the way you say it is.

—Well you are funny. You might just as well not be married than to be that way Helen.

—Oh that is so unimportant and I don't like to talk about it and I think it is something people should never mention. If it wasn't for the men there wouldn't be that.

Hazel Johnson told her husband Harry Johnson that she didn't think Ernst and Helen had such a happy time of being married as they had with each other.

———————

Ernst was very proud to have a son and receive all the congratulations of his friends, the business men of the town. At the business men's club luncheon he was joked with and congratulated and he felt proud to have so much attention and know that he was the father of a baby son. He decided he would see that his son would be one of the biggest men in Fairbanks the way he was becoming. Now that he had a son he felt himself becoming a bigger man than ever in the town and his politeness and his dignity became more marked and he assumed a position among the very best people and was looked up to as one of the biggest men in the town of Fairbanks. Rumors all around the town were that he was really much richer than he let people think he was. He had attained a position in the town right up with the Johnsons and his father-in-law Charles Ross. Ernst Weiman was beginning to be pointed out as one of the biggest figures in Fairbanks.

The old German friends of his father and his mother were jealous to see Ernst in so high a position and they considered him a snob and none of them bought shoes at his shoe store except when they were very curious to see and talk to this man and confirm their opinion that he was just snobbish. He remained polite as he had always been but they thought it was only his way of mocking them and they thought him too affected in his manner.

Frieda Schweitzer was one of the Germans of the city who saw him most clearly as a snob and not a good type of man. She felt very sorry for his mother and went to call on her and tried to console her in her illness. The other Germans felt sorry for old Mrs. Weiman and her old friends came back to her to console her and watch her in her misery which had seemed to come about when she lost her only son. They came to console her but more than that to watch her in her misery and to tell her they were sorry. But they were not really very sorry for her.

When she died Helen was too sick to have the funeral at their house so the funeral services were held at the Friedmanns'. Ernst made all the arrangements for the funeral and had things done in the best way possible.

He had gone more often to see her in her last days of illness, and he found himself loving his old mother and not liking to see her suffering.

The best people of Fairbanks, with the exception of Charles Ross and old man Johnson and his son Harry, did not turn out for the funeral but the whole German element of the city tried to get in the house to hear the service and those that couldn't went to the church and waited, for after the service in the house there was a service in the church which all of them attended. Then the procession to the graveyard and the burial of old Mrs. Weiman was over.

Mrs. Friedmann waited anxiously to hear about the will the old lady had made.

Ernst got his mother's stocks, which were turned over to him by the bank after his mother's death, and he didn't say anything about them to people because it was to him a private matter.

Mrs. Friedmann waited and wondered when the will was to be read.

Finally Mrs. Friedmann could not wait any longer and went downtown to see Ernst and find out about the will.

—Oh good morning Ernst. You must bear up after your poor mother's death. You must feel very sorry, she was always so lonely and she loved you so much.

—I always loved my mother very much. No one could have had a better mother. She is happy there with father I guess.

—I wondered, I don't know, but she told me she had a will made out. I suppose the thing has been taken care of. I thought though, she was going to leave some money to the church. She used to talk about it. I wondered if the church was going to get some money from her will?

—Why no Mrs. Friedmann, mamma didn't make out any will at all that I know of. She had a few stocks but she didn't make out any will that I know of.

—Didn't Mr. Haesler the lawyer ever tell you anything about the will she made out? I know she made it out. She made it out when she was sick at my house.

—No I am sure she didn't have a will made out Mrs. Friedmann.

Mrs. Friedmann said good bye shortly and left the store and began thinking that Ernst had done some cheating some way. He probably got hold of the will and tore it up and I'll bet she left those stocks to us after all we did for her. After all we did if she didn't leave us anything she would be awful. She surely must have left us something from those stocks of hers. Ernst never did anything the way we did for her. He has no right to that money. It is our money, every bit of it.

She went to see her husband.

—I think Ernst got those stocks. I think her will has been torn up by Ernst, papa. He said there is no will. I know she made a will. Mr. Haesler came and she made a will when he was there. I was in the house when she did it. We ought to get something for all we did for her.

—Now maybe she didn't make a will and maybe she wanted Ernst to have the money for his baby. We only did what was decent. We shouldn't expect to be paid because we had her come to live with us. We asked her to and she was always good to the children and at Christmas all she gave us was more than board would have cost her. And Ernst gave us things too, mamma. You mustn't think that we should get her money. It is for Ernst because he was the oldest son and he should get the money.

—Now see here papa, I tell you she wanted us to have that money for all the things we had done for her. Ernst has got more money than he needs. I heard it said that he was as rich as any man in the town and maybe he has got a million dollars somebody said once. I think I will go see the lawyer and find out. That Ernst was never good to his mother and it would be like him to do some trick on us who need the money.

—You better not go see the lawyer and get all mixed up in this. She went to see the lawyer, Mr. Haesler.

—I wondered, Mr. Haesler, if maybe Mrs. Weiman left some money to the church? She always talked about leaving some money to the church and I wondered if she left it in the will she made out? I haven't heard anything about it and I was down this way this morning and I thought you wouldn't mind if I dropped up here to see you for a minute. She was such a fine old woman. It was too bad her son was always treating her the way he did.

—Why Mrs. Friedmann, Mrs. Weiman didn't make out any will. She didn't make out any will at all.

—You came there to see her to make a will. She sent me to get you to come and make a will for her.

—But she didn't want a will, she said she only wanted Ernst to get the money and I told her she didn't need to have a will to do that.

Mrs. Friedmann turned white in her face and got angry and choked a little and began to mutter.

—That's the treatment that you get when you do everything for anybody. If I had known she wouldn't have stayed in my house. Ungrateful I call it. And that Ernst gets everything and he never did anything. He is just dishonest.

—Why Mrs. Friedmann you are surely wrong in what you say.

—I didn't say a thing to you Kurt Haesler, but I want to tell you that the Weiman family is a bunch of ungrateful people. Ernst Weiman and his father and mother. They are crooks. How did they make their money? We came here when they did, to this country, and how do you think they got so rich? I want to know. They are no good, and that Ernst Weiman putting on those airs.

—Why the Weimans are good people Mrs. Friedmann, you are wrong about the Weimans. Ernst is one of the most respected people in the town and he does a lot of good for the town.

—For himself more I guess, Kurt Haesler. You're as bad as anybody. You can't trust nobody anymore. Who would have thought she would be that way?

Mrs. Friedmann made life uncomfortable for her family. She was so angry and she started in to make the Germans in the city, who had all been friends of the Weimans, see that the Weimans were not good people. And she tried to make Ernst out to be a bad sort of man when he was really very honest and ambitious and one of the best people in the town of Fairbanks. The older people couldn't see that Mrs. Friedmann was right when she said the old Weimans were not good people, but they were half willing to admit that Ernst had not turned out the kind of man his father would have liked to make him.

She had been clever in the way she said these things about the Weimans that the people didn't know her hatred of the Weimans came from being left without the stocks when Mrs. Weiman died.

———————

One day Ernst passed Mrs. Friedmann on the street and took his hat off and circled it out forward in a graceful arc and said, —Well how are you today Mrs. Friedmann?

She turned her head away and walked on fast with little short steps and Ernst wondered what was the matter with her.

The other old German friends of his father and his mother, when he met them on the street, spoke to him politely but now he saw that their politeness was not friendliness at all. Mrs. Friedmann was the first to let him know that for some reason he was not well liked by the Germans in the town. From then on he noticed that they were just polite to him and not friendly anymore the way they had been when he was a boy and his father was alive.

I guess they just are jealous of me, he thought. Because I have gone on working and doing things here they are jealous and because they haven't gotten in with the same people I have gotten in with they are jealous. Well I guess the Johnsons and the Mileses and the Winters and the Stones and such people are better people anyway. I don't care if they don't want to like me, only I don't see why they don't like me just because I have got ahead a little. And Mrs. Friedmann has no business to be acting so funny.

One day he met Haesler and they started talking and Ernst began to see that Mrs. Friedmann had been angry because his mother had not left her any money when she died.

He felt bad when he knew this and went to his store and sent the Friedmanns a letter and a check for two thousand dollars to repay them. He said in the letter the money was to help repay them for all they had done for his dear departed mother.

Mr. Friedmann would not let his wife keep the money and sent it back with a letter telling Ernst they had been more than repaid for the little they had done to make her last days easy, and he didn't want Ernst to feel they didn't feel the way he said they felt about it. We want you to know that we liked your mother and father and we like you and want you to be successful in the things you do, he wrote to Ernst.

10

The place the Weiman couple occupied in the society of Fairbanks
remained among the best people and Ernst saw his fortune
increasing slowly and steadily and he saw his son growing up and
going to grammar school with the children of the other best people
of the city. The Germans in the city slowly began to regard him
much as they regarded Charles Ross, the Mileses and Stones and
Winters. They allotted him his place on the other side of the city
among the best people and were forgetting that he had once been
one of them.

The married life of the Weimans was apparently smooth
and unruffled. They demanded very little of each other, these two
people, and sex played a minor role in their lives. Ernst knew that
it was distasteful to Helen and he grew to be able to live without
demanding much of her in this way. The thought of it became
an irritation to her, and she loved Ernst more because he did not
demand much from her.

In 1906, after the Olds Motor Works in Lansing had begun to market automobiles on a commercial basis, the Fairbanks Wagon Works changed their name and became the Fairbanks Motor Company and Voss came back to Fairbanks and became one of the leading engineers in the company. Ernst and Charles Ross found their stock taking on more value and found themselves now in a money making automobile company.

—I knew it would come someday Ernst, but when we tried before the thing wasn't yet ready. They didn't know how to make the things the way they do now.

—It's a good thing we stuck in this wagon works Charley. My father always used to say that it was good stock to have.

Helen Weiman gave her son a great deal of her love and she tried very hard to make him grow up to be a fine man in the town. She was very anxious to keep him from ever being a bad boy and tried to keep him always among playmates who would be a good influence for him.

Ernst was very proud of his son and thought that there was nothing his son would not someday be able to do. He dreamed of the future of his son and planned to leave him a great deal of money so that he might find the very best in life for himself and not ever have a time of being poor the way Ernst had been when he was a young boy. He was glad to see that his son was growing up with the best children of the town. Little Charley had a golden career mapped all out for him by both his mother and his father.

—Ernst, I think it would be a good thing to send Charley off to a private school somewhere in the east.

—Well it might be, Helen, but it is good for him to be among the people here in Fairbanks. He has all of the best boys here for his playmates and that is a good thing for him. Away at school he would be among only strangers.

—That is right Ernst. It would be too bad for him to have to go away and be with strangers. I think it will be better for the boy to have him here where we can always be with him and see to him and he has so many nice friends among the boys here.

She thought of little Charley away among strangers and felt sure he was better off right here where she was.

In Fairbanks the best people sent their children to public schools and the highschool and the children of the best people found a way to make the schools exclusive by having clubs for the boys and girls made up of only the children of the best people except when now and then a real good athlete in the school proved to be not unacceptable and found his social position raised by being invited to join a club. Even in grammar school where there were no sororities and fraternities for the pupils, they found themselves always being joined together at parties and at playtime.

Little Charley Weiman was a child of one of the best families, and not only was his father one of the most respected men in Fairbanks, but his grandfather Charles Ross was too.

Charley found his place already made for him in the society of the town of Fairbanks.

And because the place was made and he was put in it he wanted to look around and see the other side of life in Fairbanks. His curiosity brought him into contact with boys who were not from the best people, and he had some friends among them that he was wise enough not to let his parents know about. This was not as important to little Charley as his parents would have thought it had they known about it. Little Charley learned more bad things from the boys of the best families than he learned from these other boys.

He had heard more about the mysteries of marriage when he was ten than his mother had ever learned, or his father either. And he could smoke a cigarette with manlike assurance and he knew how to swear and pilfer pennies from his mother's dresser drawer.

But even with all his boy knowledge he was still a good example of one of the boys of the best families in Fairbanks. He was fond of his father and his mother, but his knowledge made him more or less remote from either of them, even when he was a boy of only ten years old.

Book II

11

Though Ernst was growing wealthy daily, the shoe store remained his main interest, though if it were figured out on paper it would be seen that it was but a small share of his total wealth. His pride was in his shoe store and his home and family and his position in the society of Fairbanks.

The regular course that life took as it carried Ernst along was not interrupted until 1914 when the war started between Germany and the Allied Nations. And even then this course was not abruptly interrupted.

The Johnson family, having in some way come over on the Mayflower, were inclined from the start to favor England and France. But they were not strong on that point, for there was some German blood mixed in them in a diluted manner and it kept them saying they were neutral in the matter though they did think it might be better if England were to win the victory.

Harry Johnson spent a lot of time arguing on the matter.

—Now Ernst, you know yourself that for this country it will be better to have England win the war. If Germany had not gone through Belgium I wouldn't feel that way.

—How could Germany have gone any other way? Didn't they tell them they were going to do it? Didn't the Belgians fire guns out of the churches? Well? And if they had gone through Alsace then England would have been there and France would have had them licked right from the start. No Harry, you are wrong.

—No Ernst, you're wrong there. They invaded a neutral helpless country and England had to go to the aid of Belgium to keep her treaties and keep the integrity of Belgium from the Germans. That's all there is to it.

—Please, Harry, don't get things all wrong that way. It wasn't like that. Germany warned them didn't they? Well there.

—But look at the raping? The Germans are great fellows for that stuff I guess. That's what German blood does. Makes them all for the women. How about it Ernst?

—There never was a more decent people, you know that very well. You have got no right to say such things about the Germans. They are good people.

—Now Ernst don't get sore about it. We don't care who wins the damn war. What does it matter if we keep our noses out of it? We ought to be thankful we're not in it. I don't care a bit about it.

—Well, I don't know, sometimes I think most of the people here in Fairbanks are not fair with Germany.

Charles Ross was inclined to favor Germany in the struggle but he was not caring much who won just so America kept out of things.

He and Ernst found it more pleasant talking and with Ross for a listener Ernst talked so much about the war he got to be a regular German patriot, and he got to know about everything that was going on in the war. He took to reading papers that were biased in favor of Germany and he pooh-poohed the local paper which he insisted was proBritish.

Whenever he met any of the former German friends of his boyhood he stopped and chatted with them about the way things were going.

—They will soon be up to Paris, he told Karl Wagner, the druggist who had gone to the little German school with Ernst when they were boys.

—Yes it won't be long, Ernst. They certainly are the warriors. The Germans. Think of it all alone the way they are, they could beat the whole world. Even with America in it they could beat them all. That's a wonderful machine, that German army.

—You bet it is. Nothing can stop them. They got the stuff all right Wagner.

One day when Germany had suffered a few losses he found himself near old man Schweitzer's flower store. He stopped in for a minute and Schweitzer seemed honestly glad to see him. They had talked to each other so seldom since Ernst had been married.

—Well Ernst, things are not going so well today. But it will not be long before things are all right again I guess. Did you hear about that blockade business that the British put around Germany? We can't send anything over there now to our relations.

—Yes we can, I sent some stuff through Norway, it will get there that way. It's too bad things didn't go so well in today's paper. But I'll bet you it won't be very long before things will be

all right again with the Germans. The British pigs just want to get
the colonies away from Germany, that is all they want. And France
is after that African territory. It is nothing but a great big swindle.
They forced Germany to go to war. They made her.

—Sure they did.

—America ought to go with Germany and they would end
it. There are more Germans here than anything else in this country.
America should be with Germany.

—Well Charley Ross thinks we better stay out and Germany
will beat them pretty soon anyway and maybe Charley is right
about that. But if we did go with Germany the way we ought to we
could beat them all in no time. Say Ernst, why do you never come
down to the Liederkranz Hall any more? Come down on Saturday
night and I will see you there. They will take a collection to be
sent to Germany in some way and if you are there then the people
will be freer with their money I think and they will give more. The
way they are shut off there in Germany they need things because
they can't get them so easy. I see that they are stopping ships, the
British, and taking mail off when they can get it. That is against the
international law.

—I know it, Mr. Schweitzer, that is against the international
law. American ships and things like that should be protected. But
I notice you don't read much about it in the paper. I don't know
about going down to the Hall. I haven't been there in a long time
I guess. Well yes I guess I will go there. We all ought to send some
money to help them if we can do it.

At the business club luncheons the men all talked about the war
and about remaining neutral, and some of them liked to talk with
Ernst in favor of Germany and others kidded him good naturedly
and none of them held it against him that he was so decidedly
proGerman excepting one or two who were just as decidedly
proBritish.

—Well Dutch, old fellow, the Germans are getting pushed
back now I guess. They will get pushed back, because no country
single-handed can keep it up against the whole world the way they
are trying to do. They bit off too big a hunk.

—I don't know. I'm not so sure as you are, Henry Miles old
fellow. That's a great organization, that army Germany has got. The
blame isn't all on her shoulders.

—Well but of course Dutch, when you think of Belgium.
You see that was their mistake. They shouldn't have gone into
Belgium. That got the British against them.

—They had to, and besides the British wanted to get their
commerce, that was it. Germany was getting ahead too fast for
them.

—Like you German fellows in America. Nothing can hold
you back. Well there is something to be said for Germany no
doubt.

Charles Ross came up to these two men and put a word in.

—Well Dutch, old fellow, are you at it again? Always talking
about the war and the old fatherland. Just keep old Uncle Sam out
and I'm satisfied. You can argue all you want to about it, we just
better keep our noses out.

—Well we won't be getting in, the president will see to that,
Miles said.

—But we ought to quit sending over ammunition and stuff
to the British to use against Germany. That is against international
law isn't it? And for humanity we have no right to send things to
kill our own relations. I don't like that at all, Ernst told them.

The conversation with these good old friends that Ernst
had at the business club luncheons was always good natured and
they never got into heated arguments. Ernst didn't like to argue
when they said things about the rape of Belgium. He just felt like
saying bah, and sometimes said it. But he always tried to keep the
arguments from getting heated, and he tried to keep them down on
the ground and sensible and not too personal.

The men all liked Ernst, even those who found they could
not agree with him liked him. He was a successful man and a
pleasant polite creature who never offended them and made them
continue to respect him and like him as they had always liked him.
Some of them thought that he was off his head on the subject of
war but he was not offensive to them and he did not antagonize
them too much.

When he argued in favor of Germany with some man who
favored all the Allies he was quiet talking and polite mannered
and he qualified his statements just enough to leave a loophole for
the other fellow's ideas on the subject to find themselves somehow
agreeing in a way with Ernst's ideas. It was really just his good
politeness and good manners and somewhat obsequious manners
that made the other fellow think that Ernst and he had not been
really arguing.

When he left such an argument he thought, my God those
fellows can't see anything. They think that Germany is worse than
any other people when we are really all alike. They have got the

same God we have got. It is the French to blame even more than the English. But the English had no business to get in it except to make a steal from Germany. These fellows are too proBritish. They have no right to be proBritish.

Ernst would sit around his house in the evenings with his brows knitted, reading the *Fatherland* and the *Nation* and some German papers that he had sent to him from Milwaukee. He liked the attitude of that man Viereck in the *Fatherland*. He certainly would not think of missing an issue of the *Fatherland*. And the *Nation* said some things he liked to read.

1 2

Helen Weiman, seeing Ernst so interested in the war, began to feel
within herself a certain irritation, and she began to think that he
was very biased in his opinions when he thought that Germany was
in the right and the Allies were in the wrong.

Ernst is just like all those Germans in the city, she thought.
He is more a German than an American. He shouldn't be so silly
about the matter. I never could think much of the Germans and I
guess they were as much to blame or more so, when you think of
Belgium. Just because he was born in Germany and had German
parents he thinks he is living there in Germany. It isn't good to be
looked upon by people as being so proGerman.

She spoke to Ernst, who was sitting and reading.

—You shouldn't read those German papers all the time
Ernst. You ought to get both sides of the matter. I guess some of
the people who think about it differently than you are just as apt to
be right as you are.

—This is the only way you can get the truth. The other papers are all British owned, most of them at least.

—Well then that is German owned I guess.

—No it isn't, it is all for America and doesn't hold up Great Britain. Great Britain has always been the natural enemy of this country and there is no reason now why we should not realize that the interests of Germany are the interests of us.

—You are just a regular German, Ernst, and you only see one side of the matter. You ought to be neutral. And anyway you ought to quit talking so much with those Germans around town all the time. It doesn't help you any to be talking with such people and hobnobbing with them the way you have been doing.

—They are good people, Helen.

—Well you are tiresome always talking about the war the way you do. I get mighty tired of it.

Helen said this in a voice that showed Ernst her irritation, and he felt bad to see her show this irritation, but he kept on reading his paper and didn't answer her for awhile.

She sat looking at him reading and she was wondering if he wasn't a little bit crazy on the subject of the war. It made her feel more irritated to see him go on reading his paper.

—Ernst you have simply got to have those lights fixed in the kitchen.

—Well you only told me about it today. I haven't had the time to see about it.

—You have time for the German nonsense though I notice.

—I'll see about it in the morning, Helen.

She thought about other things with which she might reproach him.

—Charley should not be out so late with those highschool boys. Those feeds they have should be over earlier.

—It's not very late yet.

—Well it is time that he was home. You never seem to take any interest in the way we bring up Charley. You leave everything for me to do. Why don't you take more interest in your son and less in all that truck?

—Oh now see here Helen, you know very well I take an interest in him and do all I can for him. Everything is all right with him. He is going along fine. I don't like it the way you act about things, Helen. My relatives are all over in Germany and I know that they are good people. Why I remember little Fransel, he was a fine little fellow. He would be in the war and lots of other boys I knew and sons of people there I knew. They are good people.

—Well good people wouldn't have done what they did in Belgium.

—Look at England and France. Don't tell me one is any worse than the other. Unless maybe it's France.

—Well it's Germany all right, and I hope Germany gets beat all to pieces. I hope they kill them all off.

—Helen you should not say that, you don't mean it surely. You are as bad as Harry Miles.

—As bad? Well I should say as good. It's too bad you're not that sensible, the way some other people are. Just because you are nothing but a German you think everybody else hasn't any rights. I hope Germany gets good and licked. Harry Miles has got some sense.

—Don't talk Helen, you don't know anything about it and you haven't any right to be talking.

Ernst by this time was feeling irritation at his wife and feeling irritation that had been gathering in him for years when he had never known it, and he began to know now that Helen irritated him and had been irritating him for a long time. He thought that they had never gotten along together the way married people should get along, and he began to half realize that he had been missing something all the time since his marriage, and he began to feel resentment toward Helen.

She, in sitting looking at him as he was reading, saw in him only the side of him that came to her at night and wanted things that she did not want. And she thought of him as coarse and to be feared and as a burden to her which she had borne a long time and must go on bearing. She felt that she would never never be so weak as to let him make love to her again. She did not want that, it was something that was almost revolting for her to think about. She found that there was not pleasure in it. Marriage was for her a good thing only for the home and Charley and the position that it gave her in the society of the town. How women could talk about the pleasures of being married as such exquisite pleasures was more than she could understand. She had never found marriage or in the lovemaking any great exquisite pleasure. Only her boy had been a pleasure to her and he had been much more to her than Ernst had been. Her before-marriage curiosity had never been satisfied and she knew nothing about real, happy marriage. She thought of Ernst coming to her in the night for kisses and caresses and thought how she was never feeling eager to give them and how when she had given them she always felt a little bit disgusted with herself for having done it. Ernst seemed to like so well what she disliked so much.

He sat there holding his paper but not reading, only thinking, and he thought of the way Helen tried to avoid his lovemaking and of how she was never really happy when they were making love and he knew that she did not like him to be making love to her and this made him very irritated.

Charley walked into the house.

—Say father, why you are all wrong about the French starting the war. I heard the Germans did it and they went through Belgium. And they did a lot of destroying of the things there and that is why England went in it. It was Germany's fault. You always talked about it being the other way. Dick Miles argued with me about it and I finally had to say that he is right. He said the reason you said that was because you were born in Germany. You ought to talk to him about it, then you would see what is right.

—Charley you are too young to know it. You don't understand and the talk they fill you with is all lies.

—No it is not, Ernst, and you shouldn't talk to Charley that way, Helen said.

—Well all right then, I don't care but neither of you know the facts about it. If you would read the papers you would see how things are.

—Oh you're just proGerman father, that's all, Dick Miles said that was all the trouble. How about it mother, he's just proGerman all right isn't he?

—Of course he is Charley. Saying all those silly things.

Ernst was getting hot under the collar and anxious to put a stop to the talk. He knew he could not reason with his wife and son about the matter. They wouldn't understand a thing, he said.

—Well you'll see. I tell you that. You'll see who's right about it. It just seems to be the popular thing to talk against the Germans. But they'll show the world what's what, just wait and see.

Helen was happy having her son with her against her husband and she smiled at him with appreciation and said, —I guess we know, don't we Charley? Your father has got his head all full of proGerman business. He ought to go and fight with them instead of doing all this talking. If you love your dear old Germany so much why don't you just go over there and fight instead of doing all this talking.

—It would be better to fight for England, said Charley.

—Oh you two better run along to bed, you don't know anything about it.

—Oh we don't, don't we? Well you'll see old Mr. proGerman when Germany gets good and licked. I wish America would go in and lick them.

—If they did I'd fight the Germans.

—Don't be silly, Charley. You are too young to know anything about it. And Helen you shouldn't go filling his head with those kind of ideas. You shouldn't encourage him to have silly ideas like that.

—Well I'm not going to sit and listen to all this proGerman truck of yours. I'm going to bed. You better go to bed too Charley.

—Yes I'll be up there pretty soon mother. I'm going to look at the paper.

Ernst and Charley started talking and now that Helen had gone upstairs Ernst tried to talk real seriously to his son about the war and tried to make his son see his way of thinking and think the way he did about the war.

Charley listened to him but he said he didn't think his father was right about the things he was talking about.

—Miles told me and he knows all about it. His father told him.

—Well Charley, I guess I know as much about it as Dick Miles's father and he is just a Britisher through and through. I've talked with him myself and I know. You shouldn't believe all those things Charley.

—Well they sound just as good as the stuff you talk about father. I would rather have America go in the war for the Allies than for Germany. These Germans here in Fairbanks aren't very much. Look at that little German school you went to. Why those Dutchies there are a bunch of sad eggs. The English are better people than the Germans here in Fairbanks.

—I guess you are too much like your mother is. You don't understand, and I want to tell you there are some fine boys at that German school. They are better in lots of ways than these young fellows who go about gadding all night. I'll bet the Wagner boy doesn't traipse around the way you do to parties and feeds. Highschool boys should be home nights.

—I don't know the Wagner kid, but most of them are funny looking guys. And he doesn't go to feeds because he's not in any frat. I got home early father, it isn't even half past ten yet. I stay home almost every night anyway. The best fellows I know in town are for the Allies not the Germans, and it's pretty safe to bet that they are right.

—Well you had better go to bed. There's no use talking to you and your mother. But I don't want to hear you saying anything against those boys at the German school. They are just as good as you are and you want to remember that. And some of them are pretty hard working, steady fellows. Germany is not such a bad country as you seem to think it is. There are some pretty good people there, I'll tell you that.

13

At the Liederkranz Hall on Saturday night Ernst met old man
Schweitzer and Wagner and many others of his old German
acquaintances and he found himself being looked up to by people
all around him and he found that the people were taking a pride in
the shaking of his hand and the greetings that they exchanged with
him. He found that he was being more of a figure in this colony of
Germans than he had ever been before in any group of people. He
found that he was very happy to cut such a fine figure.

  —Well Ernst, said old man Schweitzer, —we all are tickled
to see you here with us and we miss your good old father. We are
glad to have you here with us Ernst.

  —It seems mighty good to be here Mr. Schweitzer and see
the people that I used to know so well when I was a boy. I am sorry
I haven't kept in touch with all these people Mr. Schweitzer.

  —Well we're all friends Ernst and mighty glad to have you
with us. Come on, the singing is going to begin pretty soon now
and we don't want to miss it.

They went to their chairs to sit and listen to the singing of the Maennerchor that was made up of the best singing Germans in the town of Fairbanks. Ernst found himself enjoying the music more than he ever felt that he enjoyed music before and he found himself applauding and he found that the German music had a sweetness to the ear when these men were singing that made him sentimental and made him think about his boyhood back in Germany. And he thought about the little friends of his boyhood in Germany who would by now be grown men and probably fighting for their country and he grew sad and then he became quite angry that there was war and that these people must be fighting to save themselves from the Allies. His heart grew warm inside him for the German people in Germany and the Germans in the hall there sitting with him. His heart in growing warm toward these people cooled toward the self-assured and self-sufficient men that he met daily in his business. There was not in his set or circle the genuineness of these people, the realness and the good solid human kindness that he found in the German people. He began to feel sorry that he had not always felt as he was feeling then. He was sorry that he had not spent more of his time with his German friends.

There was very little war talk. These German people felt so much alike on the subject of the war that they found very little reason for talking about it. There was instead much pleasant chatter about life in Fairbanks and there was also much chatter about the presence of Mr. Ernst Weiman in the hall, for Ernst Weiman was by this time a figure in the town of Fairbanks and he was looked up to and respected and held to be and was one of the richest men in the town and one of the men most to be looked up to.

It was a pleasure for the German women that he had known in childhood to come up to him and introduce him to their children. It was a pleasure for them to have their children know Ernst Weiman and shake hands with him.

Frieda Schweitzer, still unmarried, came to the hall with her father and she took pleasure in speaking to Ernst and in thinking of a time far back when she had gone with him out driving. Since her mother's death she had kept house for her father and the years had made the jealousy of Ernst and the inner hating of him almost vanish, and she now felt proud that she had been one to know him very well. But when she looked at him she felt a little sorry for him, for she was sure that he was not happy in his life with Helen and in his set of the best people. She could see the look about him of happiness in the hall that made her sure he was not happy in his other life with his wife and family and the people in his circle. She could see that he would have been happier with her perhaps, and then perhaps he wouldn't have been so happy.

—Well Ernst you are looking very well, she told him.

—Yes Frieda, I feel quite well now, only I think it is awful about the war and everything the way it is.

—We are going to do our best here to do relief work and they are planning on having a big bazaar to raise some money. Have you heard about it yet Ernst?

—Just a little. When will they have it?

—We will hear tonight, they are going to have a meeting. How is your family and your wife, is she well? I saw your boy Charley on the street the other day. He is a fine boy Ernst.

—He is a good boy. We are all quite well now.

Wagner walked up to them.

—Well we ought to get in the other room for the meeting. Come on in Ernst. You going in too aren't you Frieda?

They went in the room where the meeting to plan for the bazaar was being held.

The plans were made to hold a bazaar in the hall and sell all kinds of things to make money and have a regular good time and then send the money to Germany by way of Norway. Ernst was called upon to give a speech, and he talked to them in the German-American language that all of these old Germans spoke and urged them to help all they could to save the fatherland from destruction, and he pledged a good sized amount, which turned out to be two thousand dollars.

—We have all got to help in every way we can, he told them. —We have got to help because without our help it will be a losing fight for Germany. I will do all I can and every man should feel the same way about it. We have got to show them that they have our moral support in this time of dire need in Germany.

—That was a fine speech you made Ernst, Frieda told him. —It was a fine speech and everybody was glad to have you speak. Everybody looks up to you Ernst. You have done so much and it is a great help to our cause for you to be helping us.

—That was a great speech you made, Frieda's father told him.

Ernst could not help feeling that he had made a great speech to these people and it made him feel his closeness to them and it made him feel a certain love for them. He knew that they looked up to him as being one above their station. He was a figure in the town of Fairbanks and a man of money and a man of power. He was a man of more power among these people than he was among other people in the town but he was a figure of importance for the whole town. Here he felt his importance very much, and he was happy.

He thought of his childhood in Germany and in Fairbanks and thought that he had always held these people in respect and liked them. He began to wish he could bring his son to the hall and have him learn to know these people. He would like to have his son grow up knowing the influence of these fine German people. But he knew that his son would not mix with them and he knew that it was better not to take him to the hall. He didn't think about bringing Helen to meet these people, he knew that that was out of the question and he didn't even stop to give it thought. He loved Helen now in a far off manner and loved her only because she was his wife and the mother of his son and because they had been living together for a long time. The thought of her did not fill him with emotion or desire. She was there as his wife, and he admitted that he loved her but he didn't really love her. She irritated him in some ways and she didn't understand much about life and she didn't understand much about the war and the things he thought. She was his wife though, and that was why he felt he loved her.

He looked at Frieda Schweitzer and felt that she would not have been a good wife for him. Helen had been a good wife for him to have. If he had married Frieda he wouldn't be where he was after having married Helen. But he felt he would enjoy Frieda in some ways that he didn't enjoy his wife in. If Frieda was Helen, or if they were in some way mixed up to be both, he would think that they were perfect. Frieda made him think of lovemaking and he wondered if Frieda was like his wife in lovemaking. He thought that she would be different and maybe would be happier and make him happier. But he wouldn't have wanted to be married to Frieda except for that one thing. In that way he felt sure she would be better than his wife was.

—Frieda do you ever think about the time when we were young here in Fairbanks? I do. We had good times when we were young here. I remember.

—Oh yes, it was nice then when we were young. I used to have cases on you then all the time, Ernst. I can still remember. It is a long time ago isn't it now Ernst?

—I remember I had cases on you too Frieda. Isn't it funny how things go in this world with people? Everything changed and moving, going ahead, that's the way life is, and memories. They are sometimes perhaps the best thing in life because when we look back everything looks so fine. I remember when my father died and I started in the business and everything kept getting on and I worked hard and got ahead and made lots of friends and had a boy and, well yes memories are a lot to think about in life Frieda. Especially when you get to be along a little bit in years the way I am.

—Why anyone would think that you were ancient. You are a young man Ernst. You shouldn't talk about getting old the way these old fellows do.

Frieda thought about the way the years were going on and she thought about the way she was getting older and she couldn't help but feel sentimental when she remembered Ernst as a boy before he married.

—I wonder if you are as happy as you would have been, well say, if you had not been so successful. Sometimes success makes people unhappy.

—I don't know, life moves along Frieda and I guess I have been as happy as I could expect to be, but some days I guess not.

—Your wife doesn't like to come here does she?

—No, she doesn't feel the way I do about some things I guess.

Frieda was sure now that Ernst was unhappy and she began to think that she could have made him happy and she felt very sorry for Ernst and for herself. But she knew that she mustn't let him know what she was feeling and she knew that life must go on the way it was going but she did feel sorry because she had not had it in her power to make Ernst happy in his life. She thought that Helen was a bad wife for him and she never had liked her but now she knew she had a reason for this not liking her.

Some people had been trying to get over to the table where Ernst and Frieda were sitting in order that they might speak to Ernst and be seen speaking with him.

Frieda felt uneasy seeing people lurking just a little way from the table trying to get a chance to speak to Ernst but not wishing to break in on the serious, almost solemn, conversation that they could see was going on.

—Well Ernst you will do a lot of good for the fatherland and I am glad to have talked with you so long. It has been a long time since we talked together. I will see you at the bazaar and you should come here Saturday nights for the singing. It was nice tonight.

—It was awfully fine to talk to you Frieda. I enjoyed talking to you and thinking about the old days and going over them this way. I will see you soon again surely.

She left the table and went in the garden and her father asked her what she had been talking all that time to Ernst about.

—Oh just about the old days papa when we were kids together. It makes me feel funny to think about so long ago.

—You and Ernst were good friends then, Frieda. I always thought it was too bad he got in that crowd of people he goes around with, the swells there. But he is a real fine fellow and I think he deserves all the things he has got in life. He worked hard and so did his father, and Ernst is today, I should say, one of the richest men. It is good for us to have him come around. It will help to get more money from the bazaar. I think I will go in and have a little talk with him. You two had your heads so close together I thought I wouldn't say anything to him about coming out here and sitting in the garden.

After Frieda left, Ernst half rose to leave his seat and find new people to talk to but they were there and started talking to him before he had time to move away from where he was sitting.

The people stood around him in an admiring circle and talked and chatted and tried to joke and talk about the old days when they were kids in the little German school. Each tried to make himself a familiar of Ernst in order that people might see how they stood. Wagner, seeing the conversation going on, walked up and slapped him on the back and reminded him of some stunts the two had pulled off when they were kids in school together.

Ernst enjoyed all of this and liked the feeling that he was being sought out to be a friend of these people. He liked the taste of fame it gave him to be looked up to by these Germans. And the familiarity he found pleasant and encouraging.

—Let's have some beer Ernst, Wagner said almost demanding.

A few of the less timid men sat down at the table and one woman who had been listening to the conversation and smiling and acting as if she knew what it was all about sat down at the table and said she would have a kleines beer. It was Mrs. Friedmann's daughter and she felt that she was in a way related to Ernst and wanted the relationship to be known to the people.

She started talking about the time when she was quite a young girl and Mrs. Weiman had lived with them and had died at their house.

—I can remember you coming there to see her and I remember how she gave us things at Christmas and candies and got ice cream for us quite often. She was a fine mother.

—Yes she was indeed, Ernst answered.

Wagner changed the conversation and Mrs. Friedman's daughter, seeing that she was not wanted, drank her beer and left the table. All of the timid people had spread away from the table and left only six people sitting there together drinking and looking at Ernst with admiration and trying to get a word in. Old man Schweitzer walked up and joined the group.

The conversation of the men now went to the war and they all grew serious. They talked first about their friends and relations in the old country and then they fell to talking of ways to be a help to Germany in this country.

—We can send them money and food and clothing and we can try to keep America from ever getting in the war against Germany. The stories they tell of the atrocities in Belgium are lies and we should show them. We should all stick together. We should talk to people and try to make them feel right about it. The British fill the papers with nonsense and people swallow it whole. This damned paper here in Fairbanks is just a British paper. It is always full of lies. They say every day almost that Germany is being pushed back and you find out when you read the *Staatszeitung* that they are all lies. They have got to quit stopping American boats with mail in them because that is against the international law and we should make a kick about it to the congressmen. That is the way to do it, write lots of letters to the congressmen.

The talk of the men ranged over matters of the war as it affected them at that time and they were all very serious minded and when they drank their beer they gave a toast to the Kaiser and to Germany and to the brave German army. The found themselves making many toasts and drinking quite a lot of beer and getting all more or less optimistic about the war. When the group broke up at summons from their wives and daughters who were ready then to go home to bed the men were all feeling quite optimistic about the outcome of the war.

14

When Ernst got back home from the Liederkranz Hall, Helen
was waiting nervously sitting in her chair. She had been irritated
by Ernst and the thought that he was with those German people
talking all the war stuff that he liked to talk so well, and she
thought that he had no right to mingle with those people who were
far below his social station. She was getting mighty tired of seeing
Ernst so interested in the war news and the gains and losses that
his fatherland was making in the war. She thought that Ernst was
making a fool of himself to be so interested.

Other people are not so wrapped up in the war, she thought.
If he was sensible he wouldn't be so foolish. Anyone would think he
was a regular German. I wish he would tend to business and quit
going around with those German people. It doesn't help us much
in other people's eyes for him to be so proGerman.

Ernst walked into the room and saw Helen sitting there
biting at her fingernails and looking tense and irritated.

—Why you up this late Helen? It's time you were in bed. Is Charley in yet?

—Yes he's in all right. It's you that stays out late. I suppose you like it in company with those German people. I'm surprised that you would be finding so much pleasure in their company. As if you didn't know enough good people without going around with a bunch of German butchers.

—Don't you say anything about these people Helen, they are all right, all of them. They are real people and they know what they are talking about and they know a little about what is going on too.

—Well if that's the kind of people you like it's too bad I ever married you. You should have stayed over with those people. You used to have some sense but ever since this war started you have been acting foolish. I don't like it. I don't like it at all and it doesn't look very well for you to be going around with such people. Hazel Johnson said tonight that she saw you were quite interested in Germany and the German people and she wondered if you were working for the German government.

—Oh let those people talk. If Hazel wants to talk that way all right, I don't care. I only want to see what is right, that's all I want.

—What's right? Why how you talk. And just today I read that a German submarine had sunk one of our merchant ships. I guess the Germans are right are they?

—Now see here, haven't they got a right to sink a ship carrying ammunition that is intended to kill their own people? If we send ammunition over there we've got to expect to have our ships sunk. It's war, that's all it is.

—Well this ship didn't have munitions, it had food for the starving Belgians.

—Food maybe, yes, and also ammunitions. Any time you see a ship go over there like that it has got ammunition. I can read you what it says in the *Staatszeitung*.

—Oh you and your German papers make me tired and I won't have you litter up the downstairs with them. You can take them to your room. Do you think I want people coming here and seeing the stuff you read? The *Fatherland?* Why that is nothing but a German paper full of foolishness. I looked at it. It is full of lies. And you shouldn't be trying to fill Charley's head with all that truck and nonsense.

—You better go to bed Helen. You don't know anything about it. And I don't want you talking the way you do. I don't like it.

—Well you know what you can do. Good night, Mr. proGerman.

Ernst sat a while in the room and tried to read the paper but he kept thinking about Helen and thinking that he didn't really like her after all. She made him so irritated.

What do I care what those people think about me? I guess I've got a right to stand up for the country I was born in. I guess it's not so foolish to stand up for Germany. And those German people are fine people. I remember when I first knew Helen and she was different and things were better because we were able to understand each other and now it is as if I don't even know her. They were nice people at the hall. Helen was nice when I first knew her. Before Charley was born and when we came here to live and in New York together. She has just been getting this way slowly from the start.

She doesn't love me much, the way she acts. There is no reason she should act the way she does about the war and then there's Charley. He is just as bad almost as his mother.

———————

Harry Johnson walked smiling into Weiman's shoe store and spoke to Ernst sitting back in the brass barred office. He came in smiling and he sat there with a look of importance and of mystery.

—Well Dutch, we just landed a fine big contract at the stove works and we are going to start in making real money. Your stocks are going to be worth a damn sight more than they are now. We got a contract to make shell casings, I don't know who they are for but it is probably England. Now that is going to make us lots of money. We have got to enlarge the factory and put in new machinery, but the money will all be gotten easy and I thought I would tip you off to get some more stock before it gets too high. You'll make lots of money from it I can assure you of that. It's a damn fine proposition.

—You going to make shell casings at the stove works for the British? By God Harry I wouldn't have anything to do with making things to fight against Germany. I wouldn't buy any stock to help get shells to fight against Germany with. I should say not. If America would quit doing such things the war would stop right away. It is America that is making the war go on by sending over war supplies to the Allies. You shouldn't be doing that Henry.

—Well Ernst if we don't somebody else does and I sometimes think it would be better for us to see the Germans get beat than the English or else the Germans will just come over here and take America too. I read that in the paper. That is what the Germans are planning.

—Oh Harry I didn't think you were so foolish. Germany never had any such idea. How could she come way over here? My God people say some funny things about the Germans. What do they want coming here?

—They want to rule the whole world just like Napoleon. That's what I think and if you weren't born in Germany you would be able to see it that way too. You are biased.

—So are you Harry, just the other way though. Biased that's it.

—Well tell me Ernst do you want to get some stock? If you do I'll see about it for you. If you don't all right.

—I don't want to have anything to do with that kind of murder business.

—Well if that's the way you feel maybe you want to sell the stock you got. You have got quite the lot already. I'll buy it. Do you want to sell it? You can if you want to.

Ernst thought a while and puckered up his forehead and considered whether it would be the right thing for him to sell his stock. If I sell it, he was thinking, then somebody else will just buy and they will be making the money instead of me. If I don't I will make money and then I can send the money to Germany to help them that way. I can send them money and that will be better than selling my stock. And if I don't buy some more it's the same way.

—Say Harry, maybe I will take some of that stock in your company. Get me some. I might as well make the money. And it won't be hurting Germany because as you say somebody else will buy it if I don't. I'll buy some Harry.

—Well you don't have to if you don't want to. I thought I was doing you a favor.

—Well who said you weren't Harry? Only I didn't see it the way you meant there at first. I'll take some. Put me down for, well I can handle maybe twenty thousand. I got a little money on hand now and can handle that much.

Ernst thought, it will be good money, getting in that business and what I make I can use for help for Germany and that way can do more than I can any other way and there isn't any way to make as much money as there is in war stuff. I will give all I make to the Hall and let them send it over and that should be quite a lot.

—Yes, come to think about it I would like to have some of that stock Harry, because you have got a good company and with a contract everything should be fine with the stock.

—Now you're talking sense. You want to forget all that sentimental business about Germany and the fatherland? You will just get to be a nut. People will think you are crazy. What do you care as long as we have got the good old USA and we are not mixed up in the mess? I say stay out of it and keep neutral but there isn't any use in being so much for Germany as you are. Germany doesn't mean anything to you living here in this country. Why you wouldn't like to be living there, you ought to forget about it. America is the only country in the world for me, I'll tell you that. You wouldn't stay in Germany five minutes.

—Well I don't know about all that Harry but I'll take the stock. I don't know, all I want is justice and not a lot of lies.

—Well I'll send the stock around Dutch, or bring it myself perhaps.

Ernst had felt in talking to Harry Johnson that he could not talk as freely about the things he believed in as he could have talked with his German friends or as he did talk with his wife and son at home. He had felt that he did not dare talk to Harry the way he talked with some other people because he knew that Harry would have no sympathy with him in his beliefs. He had restrained himself when talking to Harry but now that Harry was gone he went out and spoke to one of his clerks and told him of all the injustice that was being done to Germany. The clerk had to listen respectfully to his employer and he heard of all the outrages against the German people and he heard Ernst growing excited about the subject and damning France and England and praising Germany and the Kaiser. When Ernst had let off his steam in this way, talking to the clerk, he went back to the office and picked up a copy of the *Fatherland* and wrote out a check and sent it to a German relief organization that was advertised in the magazine.

———————

At home one night Charley announced to his father and his mother that he was not going to take German in the highschool in the next semester.

—Nobody but a bunch of farmers and Dutchies study German there. I'm not going to be in any class with that kind of people any more. You don't see any of the boys in our frat taking German and none of the other fellows that are any good at all.

—You had better decide to take German, Ernst told him. —I want you to learn German. It is more useful to you than anything else there.

—Spanish is the only language, or French. That's how they do business, in Spanish. That is the best language when you think of South America. What is German anyway? Who wants to speak

German? You never hear anybody but a bunch of hunkies speaking German.

—Now see here Charley, Ernst told him, —you had better stay right in that German class and tend to business.

Helen decided it was time for her to break in on the conversation.

—Charley can take what he likes and Spanish is as good as German, or French would be good too for that matter. What does anybody want to speak German for? I guess I got along without it and you would be better off if you never heard it. If it makes people crazy the way you act I guess it's better for Charley to take something else. What does Dick Miles take for language Charley?

—He takes French.

—Well you just take it too.

—Now don't you two get acting silly. Charley will study German, that is all there is to that. He's got to study German and learn it, do you hear Charley? Don't go getting any ideas in your head that way, you just stay in that German class.

—Oh dad, see here, I'm not going to stay in that class. I guess mother knows what's right.

—We won't have any talk about it. I don't want you getting silly. What do you want French for? It's all right but after you learn German then learn French or Spanish. You have got a lot of good things to read in German: Goethe, Heine, Schiller and those other fellows. That's what you should do.

Helen, hearing Ernst speak about those German writers, put a word in.

—Well I'd like to see you reading something sometime that was good. All you read is that German paper. Why don't you read

Goatee and those other fellows you talk about. Telling Charley about things you don't know anything about.

—Well I guess in school I had to read them and the Bible too I'll tell you. When I was a boy there wasn't all this gadding around the way there is now. There isn't any religion any more and when I was a boy I got a licking from my father if I talked the way Charley talks. He ought to get his hide tanned good and proper. You take that German now, do you hear? I don't want you cutting out that German. Now no monkeyshines about it. Do you hear me? You take that German. I got half a notion to send you over to that German school. You might learn something.

—Don't listen to him Charley, he is off his head a little about the war. You and I will talk this over, your father isn't able to see things any more. Ernst do you want your boy hanging around with a lot of ruffians? I won't have him taking things in school there where he gets in with that kind of people.

—Those people are good people and I don't want to hear this talking and you take that German Charley or I'll take care of you.

—Don't answer him Charley, Helen said, —he doesn't know what he is talking about at all.

—You better both get off to bed. I want to read and not be bothered and you are both being silly and I want you to know who is, well who has got anything to say in this house.

—Well good night you old proGerman.

Ernst was boiling mad by this time but he didn't say any more to his wife or to his son and when they left the room he got to feeling very sad about the way things were going in his family. He got to feeling that he was all alone in his family and he didn't really even have a family anymore. He was alone and they both

were against him and he felt unhappy and hot under the collar
and wanted to be able to show both Helen and Charley that he
was the boss in the family. But he couldn't, he felt unable to show
them, they left him outside of everything and he couldn't get up to
them enough to show them. His father would never have stood for
the things he had been standing for from his family. His mother
would never have acted toward her husband the way Helen had
been acting. It was a mistake to have ever had such a family when
everything could have been so much better if he had had another
kind of family. He didn't feel that he would be wanting to even
speak to his wife Helen any more after the way she had acted and
he felt that he would just like to turn Charley up and give him a
good spanking the way he had been spanked when he was a boy.
He would like to give Charley a spanking and not speak to Helen
any more and just let them both know that they didn't know a
thing about what was going on and that they were both just simply
silly about everything and had no sense at all.

15

Roger Bartlett was getting along in years and he had once been a rector in the Episcopal church in Fairbanks and had lost his position because he began to get funny ideas. His ideas got to be so funny that he was very seldom asked to preach in any of the Episcopal churches and he never got a permanent position preaching but he was asked to fill in now and then for some rector who was out of town on his vacation. He got to see a lot of the country filling in for rectors who were not preaching and who had gotten him to take their places temporarily while they were away from their parishes. He got to meet a lot of people in this way and found other people who also had funny ideas. He had some ideas about spiritism which were not the ideas of the Church of England and he had other ideas that were very radical. He was not the kind of man to have a permanent position preaching in a parish of his own. He had funny ideas, but as people said, he was a nice funny old fellow and they couldn't help but like him but he did have very funny ideas about some things that was sure.

Bartlett was never referred to as the Reverend Bartlett but mostly just as Roj Bartlett. His mother had left him sufficient income when she died to keep him going without working, and he chose to live an easy life in his old fashioned house in Fairbanks, with a meager income that was just enough for him to live on.

Ernst used to pass Roj Bartlett's house when he was walking from his home down to the shoe store and the two men began to expect meeting each other in the mornings and the evenings when Ernst was walking to and from his work. They stopped and talked about the war and about the Germans and Ernst found out that Bartlett was decidedly proGerman even if he was almost pure English in his blood and in his upbringing. Ernst began to like Roj Bartlett and like the talks they had together. He began to think that Roj Bartlett was not such a funny old fellow after all but a real fine brainy sort of man.

—Good morning Roj, he said, —how are things this morning?

—They are fine Ernst, say stop in a minute, I have got a paper that I want to show you.

Bartlett had a paper published somewhere in the southwest where he had once preached while the regular rector was away on his vacation. In the paper was an account of all the main events of the war, and from the account it was plain for these two men to see that Germany was not at all to blame and was in every way in the right.

—I wish you would get me a copy of that paper Roj, I would like to have it to show it to some people that I know.

—I'll write and get you one. I guess it won't be long before the war is over, if the Germans just keep on going the way they are. Bah, the English and the French, bah, bah, I tell you, they haven't got a thing. So this is a Christian world. If people knew the things I know they would know something about it.

—What do you mean by that Roj?

—Oh it would take a long time for me to tell you and sometime you will have to come over here in the evening and we will talk it all over together.

—What is it, some of your funny ideas Roj? Well I tell you now it takes ideas to make a world and without them where would we be? You have got the spunk to stick up for your ideas and sometimes even if people think they are funny they are apt to be, well, not so funny as people may think they are.

—Stop in Ernst and see me some night and we will have a long talk together. I will tell you about the time I was in Germany. Nicht war. I guess I know a little of the language, only it's been a long time since I tried to speak it.

—Ja wohl my guter friend, we will stop and have a long talk sometime. It makes me sick all this talk about the war and the way the papers are so full of everything against Germany. I guess Germany is about as good a country as any country could be.

—Well I guess so, we will have a talk about it.

In the evening going home from work Ernst found Bartlett standing in front of his house in his shirt sleeves watering his lawn and smiling with a smile that made him seem to be real happy.

They stopped and had a talk and agreed that Germany should win the war and America should keep her nose out and not go sending ammunition and other things over to help the Allies and England and the French.

These little talks with Bartlett always gave Ernst a happy feeling, for in Bartlett he found a man who would agree with him and who was at the same time just as English as he was German, for Bartlett was almost pure English in his blood. Ernst felt happier after speaking with him and felt more like going home to his wife and family with whom he could not carry on a conversation on the war since they knew nothing about it and were only silly when it came to such things.

One night Ernst stopped in to see Bartlett for a while on his way home from the shoe store and he decided he would stay a little late and let them hold his dinner for him. He would rather stay a while and talk to Bartlett than go home and sit there with his wife and listen to her talk and have to answer her and know that she was irritating him.

The two men talked together but did not do very much talking about the war because Bartlett began talking about himself and his experiences and why he didn't care for women because they seemed to him too dirty really and what fun could any man see in that? He had had women try to get him when he had been preaching regularly and he always managed to slide out because he knew the women had good reason to want to get him but he never felt the slightest desire to go with them. Phui, phui. He told about the way he had once written poetry of a religious nature and he had won some prizes too and he wrote articles now and then and he went on talking about himself. Then he went on talking and told Ernst what a bunch of old fashioned stodgy people were in the church he belonged to and for that matter with the Presbyterians there were also many stodgy people. Religion had to have a good cathartic was what Roj Bartlett said about it, and he told how he could have gotten very high in the church if he hadn't wanted to believe more in the truth than in the Church of England.

Ernst found out that Roj Bartlett was really a funny fellow and not at all like a preacher should be but he was pretty sensible when it came to the subject of the war. And he didn't hesitate to tell anybody that he met exactly how he felt about the whole matter. Nobody minded having him tell them what he felt about the war and about Germany because everybody knew that he was almost pure English, and besides he had been a rector in the Episcopal church and was known to be a nice old funny fellow.

Bartlett and Ernst didn't talk about this thing that Bartlett knew that if other people knew would make things different. They talked mostly about Bartlett except when he tried to make Ernst tell him some things about himself and about his life at home and about his wife.

—Your wife is a fine woman Ernst. I guess you have a pretty good time together don't you?

Then he chuckled.

—Do you really like that side of life, Ernst? What is there in it? I could never see that there was anything in it. It never appealed much to me.

—Married life is a good life for a man. A man should be married, I guess.

—Have you always been happy and do you never get tired of it? I should think a man would get tired of it.

—Well Helen and I are pretty sensible. But now since the war started she talks so silly about the English and we don't have it quite so smooth as we used to have.

—You have a little trouble do you?

—Not much, but we argue about it and she doesn't know a thing about it and there isn't much use talking to a woman.

—I supposed not, no they are just to play with I guess. You German fellows, though, know how to act with women. Your old father was a fine old fellow. I remember when I got a pair of shoes from him that I wore, let me see, about eight years I guess, and I guess they are still up in the attic somewhere. Your father was a fine old man Ernst, and he knew how to do and bring up a family. The man has got to keep the upper hand all the time the way it says in the Bible.

Ernst wanted to tell Roj Bartlett all about his troubles and pretty soon he began to tell him all the trouble he and Helen had been having and he told about the way his son acted and he got to be real sorry for himself and made himself out to be very much abused and ill used at home by his wife and family.

This talking made Ernst feel better, and the remarks that Bartlett made added to his comfort and the two men parted better friends than ever.

Walking home Ernst thought, that Roj Bartlett is a fine man and even if he is funny he has got a lot of good sound common sense. He understands things better than most people ever could.

Bartlett thought about Ernst and thought that he was just suffering what was natural if a man would be tied up to a woman and he felt that it was too bad that Ernst was made to suffer as he was.

———————

Ernst found that more of the German people in Fairbanks were coming to his store to do their business and he welcomed them and always tried to get to have a little talk with them about the way things were. A few of his old steady customers did not like to see these German people coming there and talking about the war and damning England and the French.

Henry Miles did not like it. He was in the store one day talking to Ernst about other things than the war when Ernst left him and excused himself for a minute and went and spoke in German-American to a dowdy looking German who was wanting a pair of rubbers and a chance to talk to this man Weiman who was such a figure in the town of Fairbanks and who was so interested in the good of Germany. Ernst enjoyed talking to the old man because he felt that the old man felt honored in talking to him and because they were able to say some words for Germany and against the Allies.

Henry Miles did not like to see Ernst doing this, and knowing that Ernst was getting nutty on the subject of the war, and feeling a strong proBritish feeling in himself, he felt such a sudden animosity for Ernst that he left the store and decided he would buy a pair of shoes at Ralph Miller's, though he had already more shoes than he needed.

The bolder Germans in the town of Fairbanks dropped in to talk to Ernst from time to time and did not even buy a pair of rubbers, and Ernst was always glad to talk to them and always seemed to find time from his business for this talking.

Wagner, who owned the drug store three blocks down the street, was one of the Germans who most often stopped to chat with Ernst and who bought no shoes at all. They got together nearly every day after the war news had been read and discussed it and took to damning England and the Allies. They took to exchanging interesting articles from newspapers and magazines and Ernst gave Wagner the article Roj Bartlett had gotten for him.

Ernst became acquainted with Wilhelm Meisel, who was one of the German Catholics in Fairbanks, not one of the German Lutherans with whom Ernst mainly associated. He was somewhat of an outsider among the Germans with whom Ernst associated because he was a Catholic and there were very few Catholic Germans in the town of Fairbanks. But he was first of all a German and was perhaps the most German of all the Germans in Fairbanks. He would have been glad to get to Germany and fight for his fatherland if there was any way he could be sure of getting there. His butcher shop had German flags hung up in it and had a little box for taking contributions for the Germans' relief organizations and he was always talking of the glory and the good of Germany and he was always damning France and England and reviling them with ugly words and doing things like fingering his nose when he saw an Allied flag or a picture of some Allied general or anything almost that was Allied and of a nature he could finger his nose at.

Even people in the town who were a little bit proGerman thought that Meisel was a little bit too nutty on the war to be considered a very sensible person. And people who were a little bit proAllied took a violent dislike to Meisel and considered him to be a nuisance in the city and a very bad ungentlemanly sort of person and a vulgar sort of person and a worthless idiot and a damn fool. Why doesn't he go back to Germany instead of staying here in this free country?

But Meisel was not an idiot or a damn fool. He was just an awfully good German and he felt that everything he considered an injustice to Germany was an injustice to him as well and he would stand up for Germany no matter what anybody said about it.

Ernst was a little uncomfortable with him in the store because he knew that people did not like Meisel and he was afraid that it might hurt his reputation in the town to have this fellow hanging around his store and talking and reviling the Allies in a big tone of voice and sometimes taking cracks at America because America was sending so much ammunition to the Allies and not a bit to Germany. But this uncomfortable feeling did not keep Ernst from enjoying talking to Meisel, for the things Meisel said and did were the very things Ernst would have liked to do and would have done if he had not been so well mannered and polite and genteel in his manner. Ernst found it a great pleasure to stop in Meisel's meat market and talk to him there, where he was not in his own store with customers around that might be listening and might not like to hear the things being said.

———————

Ernst asked Helen if she would like to go with him to the bazaar at the Liederkranz Hall.

—There you will see some fine real people and some good spirit and lots of amusements, because it is going to be quite a thing the way they have got it planned.

—Don't be silly with me Ernst. If you want to go to that thing go alone, but you are silly to be so foolish about these German people and you are making such a fool of yourself. Everybody is talking about it and it isn't very nice for Charley and me to have to see you acting the way you are. I wouldn't go there for anything and you ought to know better than ask me. Go along you old proGerman, go along with your German friends. They are about all the friends you will have if you keep up this way.

—Oh don't talk so foolish. You don't have to go, there are plenty of good people there all right, if you don't want to go you don't have to.

———————

Ernst stopped and got Roger Bartlett to go along with him and they went together to the bazaar at the Liederkranz Hall. The hall was decorated with German flags and pennants and American flags and flowers and colored lights and there were booths with different things in them for sale and there was a space set aside for dancing and the hall for the speeches was all decorated and the garden between the hall and the river was strung with colored lights and everybody there seemed gay and happy and hurrying and anxious to make money for the cause of Germany.

Ernst and Roger Bartlett walked in the hall and looked around them and soon some Germans seeing Ernst came up and made a circle around him and all tried talking to him and he introduced Roger Bartlett to them and they didn't seem to like to see this man who was almost pure English in their hall but they were polite to him and looked at him now and then as they talked to Ernst.

—Well Mr. Weiman, you have got to walk around and see things and shake hands with the people and we want you to meet the speaker, Mr. Braun from Germany, who is here tonight to speak to us.

Ernst and Bartlett met Mr. Braun from Germany and learned that he was a real German who had found himself stranded in America when the war started and was still here making speeches around the country to get money and sympathy for Germany. He debated in some cities with movie actresses and other people on the question: Shall America join in the war for Germany or for the Allies? He always took the German side of the question and was more than often defeated by the movie actresses or the people who were debating against him.

Bartlett was keenly interested in Mr. Braun from Germany and the two men started a discussion which both seemed to be enjoying and which went above Ernst's head for the most part because both of these men were highly educated and were talking about things Ernst knew about only in a vague way.

So he took to talking with Mr. Schweitzer and his daughter Frieda and some other Germans who were very glad to be speaking to Mr. Weiman.

Ernst explained to Schweitzer, seeing him uneasy, that Bartlett was a great German sympathizer and fine man with a lot of good sound common sense. Schweitzer was not slow to spread the news that this old Episcopal rector was a strong German sympathizer and the people showed that they were glad to have him there when they began to know this.

From the hall where all the booths were located came noises of calls for people to buy and raffle and take chances on the candies and pick out lucky numbers and have their fortunes told and take home a baby doll and ring the ringer and do other things that were to be done there where the booths were located.

There was quiet in the hall where the booths were located when the time for speeches came, and Ernst found himself sitting on the platform and they had also asked Bartlett to sit there but he refused because he said he didn't feel that he had that right until finally they almost made him sit there and then he did. Ernst gave a

short two minute speech and the toastmaster called on Bartlett and
Bartlett gave a fine speech and then came the main speech of the
evening by Mr. Braun of Germany.

The whole audience was enthusiastic and liked to hear high
German being spoken and found themselves applauding and
proud to see what a fine cultured man they had for a speaker from
Germany. Enthusiasm for the cause of Germany was very high and
much money was taken in in cash and pledges that night.

Ernst found himself loosening up and giving more than he
had planned, and he thought about his stove works stock and didn't
hesitate to give a big amount. Bartlett didn't have the money to
be giving but he gave a little. After the speeches the booths started
running again and the tables in the garden filled up with people to
do beer drinking and talking and the hall where the speeches had
been made was cleared for dancing and an orchestra began to play
waltzes and one-steps and people started dancing. The evening
was very gay and happy and things looked bright for a victory for
Germany and the cause of right.

Braun and Ernst and Bartlett sat at a table in the garden and
Wagner and Schweitzer and some bolder members of the committee
came and sat there too to listen to the talk that these three big men
would be talking and to get in a word now and then if possible.

The beer made them feel like talking, and they had a good
time sitting and drinking.

Frieda came out in the garden and called to Ernst and said,
—Won't you come in and take a chance on some candy at my
booth in here? I don't think you're being very nice.

Ernst excused himself and went inside with Frieda and they
stood near her booth talking and she seemed to see again how

unhappy he was at home and she acted motherly toward him and asked him if he wouldn't dance a waltz and then they danced together.

—Isn't it a fine evening? We are taking in lots of money Ernst.

—It is a fine evening all right Frieda. I am having a good time all right. I am having a better time than I have had for a long time.

—Ernst I know you are unhappy and that is too bad. You ought to be happy, you have so much and all and I can see that you are unhappy. I would like to tell that Helen that she doesn't know how to treat a good husband.

—Oh Helen is all right, it isn't that, only sometimes Helen and I don't get along as well as we might about the subject of the war. You see she hasn't any German blood to speak of, though they say we all have some. The English, you see, from the time of the Anglos and the Saxons. Well Helen, of course, as you can see doesn't feel as strongly about the war as I do and it is sometimes kind of hard for us to agree on things like that.

—Yes of course it would be, I can see that. She should have more sympathy with you though. She's your wife and should see that things are the way they are. I really can't sympathize with her Ernst even if she is your wife. I really blame her very much.

—Oh you mustn't do that because she is all right. Oh let's not talk about that when everybody is having a good time.

—You work too hard Ernst and you will make yourself sick and you shouldn't worry about that war because everything will be all right.

The dance stopped and they walked out to the booths and loitered there among them and Ernst spent some money at various booths and he started thinking that Frieda was very sympathetic and really a fine woman and he wondered if he had married her whether things would have gone better than they were going with Helen. After what Bartlett had told him he supposed that things were about the same with all women. But he couldn't keep himself from feeling that Frieda would have been or would be better for lovemaking than Helen and he thought that she would enjoy lovemaking and make him care for it too.

As it grew late in the hall and in the garden, the people began to grow tired and the spirit of gaiety and noise and excitement slowly died away and people sitting and standing began to grow serious and it was almost as if they all knew that America was going to go into the war against Germany and people began to lower their voices and talked seriously and earnestly about the war and what would happen to the world and to Germany and how maybe they would all be in the war and suffering the way people in the poor fatherland were suffering and it was so hard to help them because it was hard to get money and food to them with the British blockade and the holding up of neutral vessels by the British.

Then people began to go home, and Braun went to his hotel and Ernst and Bartlett started slowly walking home and thinking without talking, and Ernst felt tired and thought that he should learn to drive his automobile because when only his son could drive it, or his wife, it made it necessary to do a lot of walking and he felt tired walking.

—They made a lot of money tonight Roj, it was successful, but did you notice how it suddenly got so still in there and people then quit laughing? That was funny and I felt a funny feeling go over me that something bad was going to happen.

—That's what I told you I would talk to you about. That sense you felt, that is the sense that man must cultivate. It's psychic and it is the real true sense. You have got strong mediumistic powers Ernst. We will have to have a long talk some time at my house.

—Well I don't think much of that stuff but I did think that I felt kinda sad and blue and as if something was going to happen.

—That's it Ernst, we will talk about it when we have time. It takes a long time to talk about it and I wouldn't be able to go into it the way I want to tonight, but sometime we will sit around and talk it over.

They said good night when they reached Bartlett's house, and Ernst walked home alone and sad and feeling a funny feeling in his spine as if something was about to happen.

<h1 style="text-align:center">16</h1>

The time for America to go in the war against Germany was
fast approaching and things in Fairbanks were beginning to get
exciting and people were beginning to feel a depressed feeling and
a hopeless cornered feeling and Ernst began to feel that all the
injustice in the world was turned against him. Germany had to
sink those ships to keep ammunition away from the Allies and how
could she help it if the ships didn't all happen to have ammunition
because without food the war could not be fought. You could not
blame Germany for sinking the *Lusitania* when they had airplanes
and ammunition and guns on board her and the people had been
warned before she sailed that she would never get to England. Sam
Rathburn, the shoe salesman, didn't sail but instead he cancelled
his passage when he heard these warnings and other people would
have been wise to have done the same thing. Just because Wilson
kept us out of war was not a sign he was always going to, it was
just a trick to get the votes. If the pacifists in Congress would only

hold to their guns the country might stay out of war. There was no reason why America should fight in the war in Europe which was none of her business because Germany had no idea of coming over to America. That idea was just plain damn foolishness.

Harry Johnson stopped in the store and told Ernst that it was time to give up that proGerman business of his and realize that his country was in danger. They would have to go to war against Germany to save the country. Harry told Ernst that the stove works had lost over sixty thousand dollars when a ship was sunk with some shell casing from the Fairbanks plant.

—Well Harry I don't care, you fellows are all wrong and for humanity and God it is wrong for us to talk of fighting. It is all a matter of money all the whole thing is. We loaned money to the Allies and not to Germany and that's the hitch.

—Well you had better get over your ideas because we are going to be going to war with Germany sooner or later. We can't have our citizens sunk on the high seas by the Germans. Our country is in danger.

—Well it was an English vessel, Germany doesn't feel anything against this country, when the submarine *Fatherland* came here you could see that they were friendly. That's what Germany will do to this country, send submarines if we stick our noses in somebody else's business where they don't belong.

—Take my advice, Ernst old fellow. I know how you feel and I like you as well as any man in this town and you know that but you have got to get over your proGerman business because you are just getting nutty on the subject.

————————————

At the business club meeting Ernst found the men not so friendly and he knew that his popularity with these men was waning. They spoke to him quietly and seriously but none of them held any lengthy conversations.

Henry Miles got up to make a motion.

—I move that we as the representative business men of the city send a telegram to the president urging the prosecution of war against Germany. It will be a good thing to show the people in Washington how we feel.

The motion was quickly seconded and then Ernst got on his feet to protest and he said a few words and then became embarrassed at the strained silence and sat down and there was very little applause and a lot of whispering and he could see that he was unpopular.

The motion went to a vote and only five men held out against it, and Ernst saw that these men were one a minister and one a college professor and one a jeweler and one a strong Christian department store owner. Henry Miles was appointed to a committee to draw up a telegram to send to the president.

These damn fools, Ernst was thinking, damn fools, just like little kids, they ought to get their bottoms spanked damn good and proper. Charles Ross and Harry Johnson had been with the other side and they both went up to Ernst and Charles Ross said, —Well Ernst it's time to give up this proGerman business, the thing is coming and I tell you you only get in bad when you speak about it. I am sorry you made that speech here, it just looks bad for you and it doesn't help Helen and with me related to you it looks kinda bad for me too. I'm getting old enough to not like things like that and I wish you would get more sensible on the matter.

—Listen here Charley and you too Harry, I don't give a damn what happens to anybody. I believe what I believe and I am a Christian and by God I'll say what I believe and you fellows doing such a thing and trying to make more bloodshed and the huns, well they're not over there in Germany. They don't want war, it's you fellows. By God what I say I say. I'm going back to the store.

Ernst left the meeting without many good byes and hurried to his store and sat down in his office and called Wagner on the phone and told him what had happened and Wagner told him what damn fools those fellows were and that Ernst should not mind but just leave them alone, that was the best thing for him to do.

———————

At home that night Ernst was feeling real cross and angry and his wife sat just smiling.

—Well what do you think of your Germans now and all the things they're doing?

—Why don't you keep quiet about things you don't know anything about Helen.

—Well dad, young Charley said, —I'm going to join up with the foreign legion in Canada and go to war.

—Don't talk silly there Charley, I won't have you making that kind of jokes.

—I mean, some of the other boys are going to do it and so am I.

—Helen are you going to sit and listen to your boy saying such rot?

—Now Charley, you shouldn't talk about joining the Canadian army. If America was in the war I would want my son to fight but not with a foreign country. It will be time enough for you to go in the army if America goes in the war.

—Well it will help America to fight for Canada. America ought to be in the war now. All the fellows in school feel that way about it. Our frat sent a letter to the president about it. We are all going to join the army together if America goes in, but I thought it would be better to try for the foreign legion in Canada now. It would be a wonderful experience all right.

—I won't have any foolishness and I hope you didn't have anything to do with that letter to the president. I won't have you having anything to do with such things. And you can talk about joining the army when you are grown up. But you are not going to join any army, do you hear me?

—Mother could I join the army if America went in the war?

—Of course you can, when you are old enough.

—Well I am old enough now.

—Well we will talk about it later.

———————————

At church the minister who had always been of a peaceful disposition and had always preached against going to war began to find texts to quote which made it seem almost necessary for America to go to war against Germany, and his sermon was a call to take up arms against the Germans.

Ernst was very angry listening to the sermon and he decided he would not go to a church any more that was as un-Christian as to preach in favor of war.

He had an argument with Helen about the sermon and Helen told him she was convinced it would be a good thing for America to go to war against Germany.

—And you better get over your proGerman business pretty quick too or else you'll find people saying you're a spy. I guess they think that about you already, people talk to me so funny. And it isn't much fun for me to have to have such a foolish husband and so un-American. It doesn't do me much good, I can tell you.

———

Ernst talked to Roger Bartlett, and the old ex-Rector got real excited and mad and profane and talked against America and the Allies and said that he would never do a thing to help the Allies if America went in the war.

Bartlett took a pleasure in stopping all the people he knew in the town and telling them what he thought about the war, and even if they thought him crazy they did not dislike him because he was only funny and eccentric and really didn't mean what he said. But they all knew Ernst Weiman was all the way through a German and probably a spy as well, and he was a person to be watched after. But Bartlett could say what he liked against his country and his president and the Allies. He remained always almost pure English and a funny old fellow and it was all right for him to be proGerman.

———

A few rotten eggs were thrown at the butcher shop of Wilhelm Meisel and he got madder than ever against the Allies and the Americans, who were just as bad as in the war.

———

A bunch of highschool boys, including Charley Weiman, got hold of Karl Wagner's son and gave him a good hazing and called him Dutchy, German, raper, Kaiser, half-assed crown prince. He went home all bruised and with clothes torn badly and told his mother and his father what had happened and he kept his lower jaw stiff and didn't whimper. He was just mad and would like to get each one of those fellows alone some time in order to show them what he could do to them.

Old Wagner got excited and frightened about the turn things were taking, and the beating his son had gotten made him afraid that maybe he might be getting such a beating if he wasn't careful. He decided he would begin to keep his mouth shut and not say too much from then on.

Wagner stopped in the store to talk to Ernst about the way things were going. He told him what had happened to his son.

—We have got to be careful Ernst because people are all going crazy about the war and we will get in awful bad. We better just not say too much to people and just talk to ourselves about it.

—Well Wagner I intend to say what I please and do as I please and I am not going to get crazy on this subject and be a damn fool. I am just as much for Germany now as I ever was and I mean to stay that way.

—But with people acting so crazy and the paper full of all this business it is better to be careful and not say too much.

—And you say my son was in that bunch of crazy fools? Well Charley is going to get a good licking I can tell you that. He and his mother have both gone crazy about this thing and I am not going to stand for it much longer.

—Well I guess Charley didn't do so much, but he was with these fellows, so my boy said.

—Well if he was with them he is going to get it I can tell you. And I don't care what people say, America has no right to go in the war.

———————

America declared war on Germany and the excitement that the people in the town of Fairbanks had been living under increased. Flags began to appear on the streets and people were all talking now about the war that they were in and about how they would soon make an end of Germany. And a great many of the young men of the town volunteered for the army and a great many others looked for excuses for not volunteering for the army. The young men of the best people in Fairbanks seemed to be first to volunteer because all the eyes of the town seemed to be on them, and it was expected that they would be the first to enlist because they were from the best people.

Charley Weiman was all excited and told his mother and his father that he wanted to go right off to war. Ernst was saddened and quiet at first, and he found it hard to tell his son that he could not go in the army. But Helen didn't want to see her son go away to fight or get killed in a foreign country, so she was also against Charley joining the army.

—No Charley, you are too young to go in the army and you ought to finish in highschool first anyway.

—Well I'm seventeen and I will finish highschool this year and if I go right now I can finish when I get back all right. Lots of the fellows are going to go. Lots of the fellows are going to go in an ambulance corps to do Red Cross work and some of them are going into other branches. There isn't any reason I shouldn't go.

—I will not have a son of mine fighting against Germany. We have got relations there fighting and we will not go fighting against them. How would you like to kill one of your cousins in Germany?

—Oh dad, if they are in the German army they aren't my cousins, that's all there is to it. I won't be related to a bunch of huns and bums like the Germans.

—You're right Charley, Helen told him. —They are not our relations, they may be your father's but they are not our relations because we are in America and we should be Americans. But I don't want you to go to war until you are old enough. Besides they won't let a seventeen year old boy in the army.

—Yes they will, all you got to do is sign a slip of paper and say that it's all right with you and then I can get in. I might go in the navy, I thought a little of that, or aviation maybe. I'll tell you now I'm going to get in it. What will people think of me if I don't go in it?

—They all know you are too young Charley, and don't be so silly, Ernst said.

—Well, when I am eighteen I'll go all right.

Charley talked with his mother when Ernst was not around, but she did not want her boy to go away to fight and she told him not to think about it but not to mind his father for when he was older he could join the army, but he was still too young.

He asked her could he join the army when he was eighteen and she told him he could, because that would keep him out of the war for at least six months and maybe then it would be over, and

also if she promised him that he wouldn't be so apt to run away
and join up before that time. And when he was eighteen she could
reason with him about it and keep him out for a longer time, maybe.

Ernst sat in his store dejected and unhappy and noticed that
they were not very busy. There were only two customers in the
store and he didn't know either of them. Charles Ross walked into
the office and sat down.

—Well Ernst, by God, it's too bad this war had to be. I know
the way you feel being born in Germany but well, it simply had to
be because the Germans were trying to get this country and they
would have too. All I thought I would do is ask you to see the thing
in the right light and forget that you were born in Germany and be
a real good American.

—Now Charley, please don't ask me to be a damn fool.
I know what I know and how do you think I like it to think of
this country fighting against my relatives over there in Germany?
Would you like it to have your daughter married to somebody in
Germany and have her son fighting against your son or something
like that? Because that's the way I feel about it.

—Now Ernst, you haven't got any close relatives over there
and all your interests are here with this country and your family,
and there is no reason why you shouldn't be a good American. I
just came here to talk to you.

—Well I know what is right and I won't stand up and see
the right thing gone against like it is. Our preacher there is just a
British fool. If Christ was alive do you think he would like the war?
And then the preachers with their British propaganda going out
spouting a lot of lies. And the whole country has just gone plumb
daffy that's all there is to it.

—Well say Ernst, let me reason with you. I know how you feel and I'm related to you and I want everything to be for your good, you know that don't you?

—Well Charley, except for the war no two men could have been better friends, and I always thought you had a lot of sense and good judgment except when it came to the war.

—Well let's forget that now. Now what I want to say is no matter how you feel don't talk, keep your mouth shut and don't talk. You can talk to me all you want to but don't talk. People are watching you and all the Germans in the town, and everybody that is proGerman had better watch out. Now don't do any talking. That's the first thing I wanted to tell you. Oh yes, and don't for God sakes let anybody know you are not all for America. Put a flag out in front. Why haven't you got a flag out in front?

—I won't put one out. This is a business place, not a lecture hall or a recruiting station, and I won't be living a lie the way our preacher does. What can they do to me?

—They can do a lot Ernst. They can make it hot for you and they will. The Vigilance Committee here has been organized and I have been asked to be a member. I can't tell you anything about it because it's secret, but it is part of the American Protective League and they are just out watching for spies and proGermans and they mean business. They mean to protect the country from the inside while the soldiers do it from the outside.

—It's probably that Henry Miles.

—Well yes he is in it, but there are lots of others and they mean business. Now Ernst I'm not supposed to tell you anything about it but they are watching you.

—I don't care.

—You better care Ernst, it isn't fair for Helen and the boy and for yourself for that matter.

—Well what about it Charley?

—If you don't want to be a real true hundred percent American then they won't have anything to do with you.

—I can't be that way and you know it.

—Well you better not go to the business club meetings because they won't want you.

—Do you think I want them any more than they want me? Just a bunch of damn fools that's all they are.

—Ernst please regard me as your friend and don't get mad. I will do all I can for you and I don't like to see my daughter's husband getting into any trouble. Keep your mouth shut or you will get in trouble and if you don't want to act American at least keep still.

—Well I won't go to the business club luncheon then and I can find people who have got some good sound judgment to talk to.

—Don't get in with any of those Germans either or it will just get you in bad. Please Ernst think of Helen and Charley and me. People will look at me bad if they see my son-in-law proGerman.

—Well all right Charley, I won't bother anybody.

———————————

Wagner dropped in the store and looked around and went up to Ernst who was looking sad and downcast.

—We have got to be careful Ernst, they have got a lot of spies watching everything.

—Well we are not doing anything to hurt anybody or throwing bombs are we? They can't do anything to us. We got the right to use our free speech haven't we?

—Well maybe by the Constitution, but I tell you I don't want to take any chances and I wouldn't like to see you get in any mess. Why don't you put a flag out? I did, that's a good thing to do.

—I won't be a damn fool Wagner, not by a long shot. I will be what I am and that is all.

—Well be careful, I got to be going.

Wagner was afraid that he was being watched and he didn't want to get into trouble. He was nervous in Ernst's store talking with Ernst about matters, and he felt relieved to get back to his own store where he would not be afraid of being watched and getting in trouble. He had put a flag out.

Ernst sat doggedly in his store and saw his business growing less and less and two of his clerks left him to go in the army and later two more left and he had only one clerk and that was all he needed, for his business began to get very bad.

The Germans who had been coming in his store began to be afraid to go in there, and not many of them called to see him any more. They were afraid that he might get them in trouble some way because he had always been such a figure in the town of Fairbanks and had always been in with the best people who were all the hundred percent kind of Americans.

Ernst felt deserted and alone. His old friends from the business club were all against him and now the Germans didn't act as friendly as they had been acting. He still had Bartlett to talk to on his way to work and home at night from work.

One day he walked out to old man Schweitzer's green house and saw a flag flying above the door and he hesitated for a minute then went in and spoke to old man Schweitzer.

—Well it's too bad the way things are going.

—Yes it is Ernst, and this country is just a bunch of damn fools, but we have got to be careful.

—You always talking of being careful, hasn't a person got a right to say the things he feels. I'd like to know.

—Well you know the way I feel about it, but I don't like doing any talking.

Frieda walked into the shop and spoke to Ernst and hung back a little because she didn't have much to say and knew that things were going bad with him. Business had been going bad with them for that matter.

Ernst felt disappointed to see the Schweitzers so afraid of the people there in Fairbanks. He had no place to go and no one to talk to.

———————

Helen was getting afraid and anxious and was always thinking that Ernst would get himself in trouble. She did a lot of knitting for the Belgians and went to all the relief teas and parties and tried to act as patriotic as she could and make people think that Ernst was not really proGerman. But they knew the way Ernst felt about it and they thought him dangerous and they treated Helen as if she was an ally of her husband and they were suspicious of her. It made her very unhappy, for even Hazel Johnson began to quit calling her on the phone and coming to see her and she found herself angry at Ernst for getting her in bad with all her friends. But she kept on knitting and going to all the relief parties and teas that she could go to and she tried to talk like a hundred percent American but she could see that she wasn't putting anything over on the canny women in her set in Fairbanks. They suspected her, and behind their nice words there was malice.

She tried to make Ernst act more patriotic and she appealed to him and got real wifely and almost begged him for the sake of his wife and son to be more patriotic.

—Ernst, oh Ernst you make it awful for me. I can tell the way the women act what they are thinking. Why don't you act more patriotic? Please you can feel any way you like but act more patriotic and don't always be talking, that's what you mustn't be doing, talking.

—I have got the right to use free speech and I don't intend to have it infringed on. And if these damn fool women are so foolish what do you care?

—Well Ernst you know very well I am patriotic, why should I be made to suffer for what you do?

—Well Helen I can't help it, it is all the fault of these damn fool people. I can't help it and I am not going to make a damn fool of myself. I tell you that much now.

—It makes it bad for Charley too, he will lose all his friends. You should be thinking a little bit of your family.

—Charley is worse than all the rest, he is right in with a bunch of regular little tigers getting after young fellows like that Wagner boy because their father happened to be born in Germany. Charley needs a good spanking and I said I would give it to him but there isn't much use to spank him. You just encouraged him in all these tricks of his. If you had not been so silly he wouldn't have turned out to be such a young fool about things.

—Oh Ernst please don't talk that way, but do be careful for my sake.

—Well now you know very well that I haven't been doing anything to get us in any trouble. Don't worry.

1 7

Ernst went to the first meeting of the Liederkranz society after the
war had been declared. He was a little afraid to go there and show
himself to be in with the Germans in the town but he had begun
to feel so alone and lonely and that he was being tied and fettered
by his wife and family and by Charles Ross and others of his old
friends in the business club that he wanted to show himself that he
was not afraid of what people might be thinking and he wanted to
find some people to talk to.

At the hall he found only a band of twenty Germans and the
hall looked to him deserted because there had always been between
one hundred and two hundred at the meetings before this time.
These twenty men were mostly men that he knew only slightly.
Most of them were Germans who had not been long in America
and most of them were laboring men. They stood around talking in
groups together and did not hurry to make him welcome. Finally
a leader who had been secretary of the organization called the

meeting to order and a paper was read by him which forbade them to hold meetings and urged the advisability of disbanding.

—I move we disband, said one of the Germans in the hall.

The motion was seconded and carried and the Liederkranz society was disbanded by this handful of members. It was plain to see that the other members had been afraid to attend the meeting, and Ernst, when he walked out, saw why this was. There were ten or twelve policemen standing at the outer door with arms to stop a riot that they had thought these Germans might have in them to start. One of the cops touched his hat to Ernst, he was the cop who had the beat past Weiman's shoe store and he was the son of an old German settler in the town of Fairbanks. Ernst walked home more dejected and downhearted than he had found himself feeling before. As he walked past Bartlett's house he saw a light that seemed to him inviting and he stopped and rang the doorbell and waited for Bartlett to let him in.

—Well Ernst I'm glad to see you, come right in, we'll have a little talk together.

—I went down to the Liederkranz Hall, they have disbanded.

—They disbanded? Well they were fools to do it. They should stick to their guns and to what they believe in. You don't see me getting scared before these people. I say what I want to say and they better not start doing anything to me. I could cause an awful stink in this town if they ever started anything with me. Those German fellows are all afraid. I notice all around the town you see more flags on Germans' stores than on anybody else's. You would think they all wanted to see Germany licked to pieces in the war.

—Yes I guess they are afraid. Old Schweitzer hung a flag out and he doesn't talk at all and acts so funny, and Wagner seems to be getting scared and lots of them are like that. There were only twenty men at the hall tonight and I didn't know more than one or two of them.

—They're all scared Ernst, that's the trouble with them. They had lots of nerve when they weren't afraid of getting into trouble. That fellow Meisel, though, has still got nerve. I noticed that he had a German flag in his window just the other day but they made him take it down. He hasn't lost his nerve though, I can tell you that.

—My wife's father spoke to me and warned me to be careful. He said they were watching and had a Vigilance Committee that was going to watch out for anybody that was not all American.

—Let them try it, they can't do anything at all. They are just a bunch of little kids like highschool boys, and they think they are having lots of fun. Such damn fools I never saw.

They talked a little while longer about the war and America getting in the war and then they began again to talk about Bartlett, and he got to talking about women and about sex, which he was very much interested in even if he didn't care for women and said, phui, phui, when he talked about it. He kept trying to get Ernst to tell him things about his intimate life with Helen. His eyes lit up when Ernst would tell him anything, and he seemed to enjoy it greatly.

—She doesn't seem to care so much for lovemaking. Perhaps you don't know how to make her happy? Do you know?

—Well I guess I ought to know after being married to her all these years.

—That's no way to know. I know a case in my church when I was preaching here in Fairbanks of a woman that had lived for

over thirty years with her husband and had never had a bit of
pleasure out of her lovemaking.

—How could that be Roj? I don't see how that could be
unless the man was sterile or a plain half witted idiot.

—He was one of the biggest men in Fairbanks at that time,
and if I told you his name you would know it right away. She had
always thought that that was all there was to it and didn't know
about it. Here, read in this book what it says about the matter.

Ernst read in a book that Bartlett gave him of a case of a
woman who had three children and who had never really enjoyed
making love to her husband.

—Here, see this Ernst, "Art of Love," they call it. Ought
to be science. All this truck, it isn't worth it, what any man can
see in a woman is more than I can see. Read these books and you
never would want to see a woman. But there's a case just like I told
you. When the fellow saw the doctor and found out what was the
matter then things were all right.

—Well I don't think it is anything like that with Helen and
me because we haven't had anything like that.

Ernst knew that his case was like the case in the book. He
felt it and wondered if Helen could possibly know about it. He felt
ashamed of himself and he felt ignorant and thought that perhaps
he had spoiled their marriage by his ignorance of the things he had
learned in reading just a page or two from the book. He had been
too selfish, if the book was right, and it must be he hadn't made
Helen happy in making love to her.

—No Bartlett, I am sure that isn't the way it is with us
because she isn't that way and I know that with us it is because we
have argued about the war so much.

Bartlett could see that Ernst was thinking deeply and he knew that he had been right in what he said about Ernst and Helen, but he kept still on the subject and let Ernst think he didn't know.

Bartlett felt as if he had been a priest after receiving a confession, and he felt that he had in some way saved Ernst's soul and done him a great service in showing him these things which he had not known before.

—Young men ought to be taught that stuff when they are very young though, instead of having to learn by experience, Ernst said.

—Most boys know it when they're fifteen nowadays, the way they get together and talk. Highschool boys know those things from their classmates. The younger boys are a pretty smart lot when it comes to such things. Times have changed since you were a boy Ernst. You should ask your son some questions. He could probably tell you more about contraception than you know yourself.

—I don't believe it. Things are not as bad as that even in this damned country where everything is about as bad they could make it.

———————

At home Ernst looked at Helen very closely and tried hard to think of her and the things he had been reading, and she only looked sad and angry and spoke to Ernst and told him she hoped he hadn't been doing any silly talking.

—Did you go to that meeting at the Liederkranz Hall Ernst? I heard they raided it and put a stop to things.

—Yes I went there and they didn't raid it and the men just quietly disbanded. There wasn't hardly anybody there though. Most of them were too scared to come.

—It's a good thing they were, it would be good for you to be more scared. Suppose your name gets in the paper. What will people think?

This started a long and bitter argument and Helen went up to her room and left Ernst sitting downstairs feeling irritated and angry that his wife had so little sympathy for him. He tried to read the paper and found his mind straying from the paper to the book he had seen at Bartlett's, and then to the argument with Helen, and then to his whole married life with Helen. He wondered if things would have been different if he had known the things in that book before. He thought he would like to buy that book and read it all. But then he thought of Helen and her anger and her silly attitude toward the war, and he felt he didn't like her. He didn't want to read the book and read about those things. He felt all alone and lonely, for there was only Bartlett left for him to talk to.

The Fairbanks automobile company began to make army trucks and tractors and the stock went up in value and Ernst saw himself becoming more wealthy. The stove works stock was also worth a lot more since the war had started, and the shell casings they were making were yielding big profits for the company. Ernst's fortune was rapidly increasing even though his position among the best people in Fairbanks was not as sound as it had been before the war.

With all of Helen's knitting she could not make the wives of the business men of Fairbanks think that Ernst was anything but a damned proGerman and possibly a spy.

Ernst sat in his shoe store and watched for business which didn't come to him anymore, but which went to Ralph Miller, who was one hundred percent American. His own clerk had very little work to do and spent the day dusting and straightening up the stock and standing around waiting for customers. Ernst sat in his office and looked through his accounts and brooded about the business and the war and Helen.

Harry Johnson, who was out canvassing for liberty bond buyers, walked up to Ernst.

—Well how goes it Ernst? I guess things are looking better for the Allies now that we are in the battle.

Harry wanted to ask Ernst if he still felt proGerman, but he didn't dare ask him straight out.

—I'm on the committee to sell the liberty bonds in our district and I noticed you haven't bought any yet. I thought you ought to buy quite a few because you have got a lot of money.

—I won't buy anything to help the war go on this way Harry, and you know how I feel. I am not acting proGerman. And I am just acting like any decent, self-respecting man ought to act.

—Why Ernst you are completely off your nut and I advise you to be careful. You know very well I am a friend of yours but I can't help you if you don't act patriotic. You ought to buy bonds and show your patriotism. People are all talking about you being proGerman and you are just getting yourself in bad. You will be as bad as that fellow Meisel. They're going to get him. The Vigilance Committee has got their eye out for him.

Johnson began to feel that Ernst was possibly a spy, and he lost his friendly feeling for him and began to threaten him.

—I warn you Ernst, you better be careful. You better buy some bonds.

—I don't want to buy any bonds and I got a right to invest my money the way I want to.

—All the German-Americans in the town are buying bonds and they have got to, that's the way we can tell whether they are spies or not. I'll tell you you better take some. If you don't your name will be put in the paper as not having bought any bonds. We're going to start doing that.

Ernst felt uneasy thinking that his name would be in the paper, and he was afraid that that would completely lose him his position as a figure in the town. It would be a big disgrace, and they had no right to do such things.

—You haven't got any right to do that, that is blackmail.

—We don't care. We're going to win this war and I tell you right now Ernst you better buy some bonds.

—I'm not going to buy any, not a bond to help destroy the world the way the war is doing.

—Well you better. Wait until you see what is going to happen to Meisel tomorrow night. We're going to make an example in the town. I always liked you but if you are going to be a German and anti-American I can't have anything to do with you. You are just hurting yourself by being foolish about the matter. You'll see what may happen to you, I'll tell you that much.

—Go ahead you, that's what you call coercion. I'm a respectable, law abiding citizen and you can't pull tricks like that on me, Harry. I'm surprised that a friend that calls himself a friend would act that way. If you're so damned patriotic why don't you join the army and do some fighting instead of bothering around here making yourself a nuisance.

 —I've got a wife to take care of and I'm exempt from service and you know that. I can do lots of good here at home all right without going to the front. Soldiers are needed at the back of the lines as well as at the front. Don't talk that way Ernst, it won't do you any good. You better watch your step old fellow, you're heading for a big fall, I'll tell you that much. So you won't buy any, that is final is it? Well I warned you, so if anything happens don't lay it to me.

 —No I don't want any. I got good uses for my money.

 Maybe they will do something to me for that, Ernst thought after Johnson left the store. I wonder can they do anything? Will they be apt to get me some way? That Harry Johnson never was a friend of mine to be so damn foolish. What can they do? I got a right to do what I want to. I don't have to buy those bonds. The government don't make you buy them. If they put my name in the paper I'll write a letter to the editor about it. He wouldn't publish it though. They are all together. Just damn fools the whole bunch, gone crazy every one of them.

 Henry Miles had been waiting outside the store when Johnson went in. He was ashamed to go in and see Ernst after having been friendly toward him and then turning against him and saying things about him behind his back. And he felt ashamed because he had bought his last shoes at Miller's.

 —Well Harry, what did Ernst say? Did he take any?

 —No he didn't and we have got to watch him. I wouldn't be surprised if he was just a spy.

—I was afraid of him from the start Harry. I used to tell you fellows he had to be watched. He always did too much talking and then he got in with those Germans and made himself a regular German. We will have to go after him, but I hate to do it. We will have to get some of the boys who don't know him so well to take care of his case. After we fix up Meisel then Ernst may come around to his senses.

—All we got to do is get him to say something in front of somebody against the government the way we got Meisel and we can fix him all right. Only I feel the way you do Henry, I don't want to have anything to do with it knowing him and Helen so long. We were such close friends. I kinda hate to have a hand in it, but there is no question something has got to be done. He isn't safe that's all. Maybe after we tend to Meisel though it will bring him to his senses. I told him we would put his name in the paper.

—That was a good idea. We will have to start doing that to all these fellows who hold out on buying bonds. My boy says his son Charley is one hundred percent and gets it from Ernst for not being proGerman. Can you imagine that fellow going after his son because his son has got the brains to be a real American? If he was half as good an American as his son is he would be all right. You have got to watch such fellows.

18

Ernst told Roger Bartlett about Harry Johnson trying to sell him liberty bonds and threatening to put his name in the paper. Bartlett had also been approached to buy bonds and he was smiling and happy at the way he had taken to refuse them.

    —Richardson came around to see me and I told him where he could go to with his old liberty bonds. Liberty, I'd like to know if they call it liberty. Why they ought to know from the name of them, liberty, that people don't have to buy them if they don't want to. I fixed him good and proper. I just told him he could shove them way up. I haven't got any money to help a lot of damn fools carry on a war against a country that is innocent. That's what I told Richardson and believe me he turned white in the gills and then I told him just what I thought of him and all these childish young fellows who were making such damn fools of themselves. Vigilance Committee, just a bunch of damn fools trying to be smart. I told him all right.

—Well Roj I did the same thing almost. I didn't buy any and Harry Johnson came to see me. We used to be the best friends in the world but I can't stand that fellow anymore. He said he was going to put my name in the paper and all the names of people who don't buy bonds.

—That's what Richardson said, and I told him I hoped he got me in right away because I liked to see my name in print. I told him to telephone it in. I want it in damn it, that's just what I want them to do, the damn fools. Let them try it.

Bartlett was more outspoken than any man in the town with the possible exception of Meisel, but he was known to all the people as just a funny eccentric old fellow, and he couldn't possibly be a spy or really in his heart proGerman because he was almost pure English in his blood.

Richardson had not expected much of Bartlett, but his name was on the list and he had to be called on. Richardson did not think Bartlett was really proGerman, and when he told the members of the committee that were selling liberty bonds in the Fairbanks district about old Bartlett he laughed and called Bartlett a funny old duck and that made the other fellows laugh.

—Yes he is a funny old fellow. Eccentric isn't he? Just a little off his head but he doesn't mean bad by it. That's what his religion did for him I guess.

They didn't put his name in the paper because he was so funny and eccentric.

When Ernst left Bartlett to go to his home he carried the book on love under his arm wrapped in a paper.

—Don't let anybody see it Ernst, Bartlett told him. —It's a pretty strong book, you better be careful with it. Your wife would get after you if she saw you reading such a book. He laughed when Ernst had left him and felt a little excited. He got a great kick out of loaning Ernst this book on sex and talking with Ernst about it.

Helen asked Ernst what he had in the package and he told her it was just a book old Bartlett had loaned him.

—Some German stuff I guess. Oh Ernst you mustn't, mustn't talk to old Bartlett and other people that are proGerman. And you should not read those old German things. I have to hide the magazines you get every day for fear somebody may drop in and see them. It is so hard for me now with everybody thinking you are proGerman and the women act so funny towards me. I wish you wouldn't act proGerman. Act as if you were all for America even if you don't feel that way, but this way it is awful for me.

—Well I don't talk much and you know that Helen. I haven't been talking with anybody. There isn't anyone to talk to except old Bartlett and he is kinda funny. All the German fellows that I know are so scared they never leave their houses. Just a big bunch of cowards. Harry Johnson came in the store and tried to make me, do you hear me, make me buy some liberty bonds. I told him where he could put those bonds.

—Oh Ernst didn't you buy any? People will know you are so proGerman. You should have bought some. What did Harry have to say?

—He threatened me to put my name in the paper if I didn't buy, and I told him I wouldn't stand for any threats like that but if they were decent I might have bought a few. But he was positively insulting the way he talked. I don't know what has gotten into that fellow. I told him where to go though. I wouldn't buy any of them if they did put my name in the paper. People will see that I am honest at least, and that is more than can be said for a lot of these people.

Helen was so worried about the possibility of Ernst's name being in the paper that she hadn't heard the other things he said. She grew nervous and excited and bit her lips and then she spoke to Ernst.

—Oh Ernst if they put your name in the paper what will people think of us? Oh you are horrid. You should have bought some of those bonds, Ernst. I will have to speak to father about it. He can do something. Or you can buy some tomorrow. Or I got some money, I will buy them. I will buy some.

—Now see here Helen, please let me tend to my own affairs.

—Oh but Ernst see what you are doing to me? What will all the ladies say around town? I will buy some.

—No you won't Helen, that is all there is to it. After I have taken care of this thing I won't have you butting in, do you hear me?

—Oh Ernst what will we do? I will see father.

Helen left the house and left Ernst sitting in the front room worrying about what people would be thinking if his name got in the paper.

I guess I ought to buy some. I'll tell Helen that I'll get a few tomorrow. But then Bartlett will just laugh. No by God, I won't get any of the things. I'll hold my own I will. They can't force me to spend my money on these things. Liberty. I guess I got the liberty to spend my money the way I want to.

He went up to his room and got the last copy of the *Fatherland,* now the *American Monthly,* and started to read it, and then he remembered his book downstairs and left the room and the magazine and went downstairs, got the book, and went back to his room and started to read it. He left the door open so he could hear Helen when she got back and started reading the book on sex and love. When he heard her come in the house he hid it and went downstairs and stood there without talking. He couldn't think of anything to say.

—Well did you see your father?

—Yes, and oh Ernst, you have got to use more judgment, he says, and give in to things and act as if you were not proGerman. He says that you will have to buy some bonds, that he can't do anything.

—Well I won't be coerced into buying the things, that is all there is to it.

He felt that he had to hold his ground though he was beginning to feel that it would be easier to buy a few bonds and keep the damn fools in the Vigilance Committee quiet. But he didn't feel that he could be giving in to Helen on the proposition.

—No I won't buy any at all, not one.

—Oh Ernst, maybe, well father said that maybe he could do something with them for a while on it if he fixes it up some way, but it just gets him in bad with the fellows he says. He says he is in bad enough from the way they are talking about you and doesn't like to get in any deeper. Please do something Ernst.

—Well I don't intend to.

—Oh I hate you, you are awful, you are just awful. I never imagined you could be so horrible.

Helen went up to her room in tears and thought about the wreck of her social life in the town of Fairbanks and about how awful Ernst was about the war and how all her hopes were lost and she would like to be dead.

Ernst sat downstairs and thought of Helen and felt sorry
for her and wished that he could give in and buy some bonds and
make everything all right for her. But he couldn't do this after all
that had happened, and he felt bad because he couldn't do it. He
thought about the book he had been reading and thought about
Helen and felt that he loved her and would like to make love to
her. But he couldn't do that after all that had been happening. He
would have to go up to his room and go to bed.

Charley was still out with some highschool boys selling
liberty bonds on the street corners. Ernst didn't know about this
and when Charley came in the house he asked him what he had
been up to this evening.

—Out raising money for the war selling bonds.

—Charley have you been out making a fool of yourself?

—No I been doing what is right and you ought to too. The
fellows all kid the life out of me and it isn't much fun. If they kid
me any more about the way you are a German, I'll join the army.

—Now don't be silly Charley.

—Well I'm not proGerman and neither is mother and
just because you are you needn't think everybody is. You ought
to be careful. They are going to start a lot of doings about the
proGermans in this town. I heard about it and I advise you to be
careful.

—Well I guess when my son begins to give me advice on
how to act it's time to quit. I'll take care of my own things Charley,
and you better quit being such a fool and I don't want to hear
about you joining the army or going out selling bonds and other
truck. You just tend to business do you hear?

Just before closing time at the store Ernst heard paper boys running down the street and yelling,

—Extra! Extra! German spy tarred and feathered! Extra, extra, read all about it!

He called to his clerk Jim, who had heard the boys calling their papers, and he told Jim to get him one. Ernst felt nervous and wondered who the German spy could be, maybe it was somebody he knew. He waited anxiously until his clerk came in the store and said,

—It's that fellow Meisel in the butcher shop.

—Wilhelm Meisel? No, really is it Meisel?

He took the paper and read hurriedly and saw that Meisel had been tarred and feathered because he had desecrated the American flag in front of some men calling on him to sell him liberty bonds. He had poured excrement on the flag, the paper said. This had gotten out and a group of people who were unknown had called him from his store and rushed him into a high powered automobile and rushed him out of the town to the golf links, and just as dusk was falling they tarred and feathered him. It was too early to know details of the case, for Meisel was unwilling to talk and had been rushed to the Catholic hospital. It is thought, the paper said, that some people in their anger at hearing of the deed Meisel had committed had planned the tar and feather bee. No action could be taken by the police because the perpetrators of the deed had been masked and had left the scene before Meisel could ascertain who they were. It is thought, said the paper, that the parties responsible were not citizens of Fairbanks. In the history of the town there is no record of a tar and feather bee ever being held before, though reports from various parts of the country show that summary justice of this nature is being meted out to unpatriotic residents. The police can do nothing to bring perpetrators of the crime to justice.

Ernst was stupefied to think that such a thing had happened right in Fairbanks and right while he had been sitting in his store that evening. And he had seen Meisel only two or three days before and hadn't thought that any people would act so brutal toward a man. He couldn't think that people in 1917 were such beasts as to do a thing of that kind. And he remembered that Harry Johnson had told him something would happen to Meisel and he knew that these fellows in the business club and the Vigilance Committee knew all about it and probably had a hand in it themselves. He was frightened and began to think that he might be next. But Meisel should have known better than to piss on the flag. That was just silliness. Meisel was a little off his head to do such a thing. These fellows must have made him awful mad to do that.

Helen called him on the phone.

—Oh Ernst did you read about poor Meisel? That was awful. Please be careful Ernst and don't do anything to make anybody angry at you.

—They are inhuman Helen, to do such a thing. That is worse than the middle ages. My God what kind of a free country are we living in?

—Do be careful Ernst and come right home.

—I'm going to see Bartlett for a little while.

—Well be awfully careful and don't say anything to him either, Ernst.

After he had hung up the receiver he picked up the paper and read the article again and thought about the reign of terror he was living under. He was so frightened that he decided that he would be more careful and maybe would buy some bonds if it would do any good. And if any of those fellows came in to talk to him he wouldn't say a word and wouldn't let them get anything on him. He thought of the things he had said to Harry Johnson and wondered if they would get him some way for that. He thought of how his old mother had wanted them to go back and live in Germany. It would have been better than staying in this country.

Bartlett was waiting for Ernst when he walked up to the house.

—Come in Ernst, this is a hell of a country and town. What do you think of the age you live in? Meisel wasn't such a bad fellow. They had no right to do that no matter what he did.

—Well I guess he made his water on the flag and that's the reason they did it. He should have known better than that.

—I'd make more than my water on it if they ever asked me. I know who those fellows are too, they are just those fellows in that Vigilance Committee as they call it. Meisel ought to prosecute every one of them that's what he ought to do. I know about it, I heard before. I called the hospital too and let me tell you something. Meisel wasn't in the hospital when that extra came out. He wasn't there. Do you know what that means? Well it means the *Journal* knew all about it before it ever happened. Do you see what that means Ernst? Well I'll tell you, it means that the paper was ready to go to the press before Meisel was even taken from his store. It's a big swindle, that's all it is and if there was any justice in the world those fellows would all get strung up by their necks. They wouldn't dare do anything like that to me and I'll bet with your connections here they wouldn't dare tackle you. They get that poor fellow Meisel and because he is a little runt and in some ways a poor simp they take him out and do that. Cowards, swine, the whole town is rotten, rotten. If the people knew the things I know the world would be a lot better. Such things couldn't happen. Everything would be different if people knew the things I know.

—It isn't safe to leave your house these days with things like that happening Roj. My God what am I going to do? The best way would be to act as if you were patriotic as the devil.

—No never do that. Keep your soul if you lose everything else. Don't give into anybody Ernst. Don't ever.

———————————

Ernst was quiet for the next few days and didn't talk to anybody about the war and went around thinking and feeling afraid and feeling angry at these men whom he had known since he had been a young man in the town of Fairbanks. He learned that Meisel had gone half insane and couldn't talk and was near death in the hospital. And he heard that Henry Miles had been identified by a farmer boy as one of the party in the car. The other men had been masked but the boy had seen Miles with his mask off and had remembered him from hearing him speak to the children in the highschool on higher morality. The boy had finally been assured by the people who had questioned him that he hadn't seen Henry Miles at all because Miles could not have possibly have been there, and the boy, after having a police official call at his house and assure him that it was not Miles, had come to the conclusion that it wasn't really Miles but a double of Miles. Ernst knew very well that it was Miles and he felt sure that Harry Johnson and some other men he knew were in the party.

———————————

A list of names of people who were not buying liberty bonds appeared in the paper and Ernst saw that his name was not listed and neither was the name of Roger Bartlett. The college professor who had stood against the telegram the business club had sent to urge the President to enter the war had his name in the list, and the others were people who had German names and other foreign names that Ernst did not know. Some of them might have been some of the Germans at the last meeting of the Liederkranz society.

19

On his way to work Ernst, feeling alone and suspected, was
unhappy and wanted some kind of consolation, so he stopped in at
old man Kirchner's cigar and newsstand.

—I want a copy of the *Fatherland* … the *American Monthly*.

—We used to keep it, said the son of old man Kirchner, —but
we don't deal in dirty rotten spy magazines no more.

—That's not a bad paper my boy.

—Well you can't get it here.

If old man Kirchner had been still alive his boy would have
gotten a good beating.

My God that kid ought to get it, Ernst thought. His father
never would have stood for that smart aleck business.

But Ernst could not answer back. He was growing docile,
beaten, he couldn't fight back any more. Wife and son and
business, friends and these acquaintances, everything gone to the
devil. He walked down the street past his shoe store two blocks and
turned to his left. Harry Johnson was just going into Ralph Miller's

shoe store. His old friend Harry. Everything was going to the devil and now since Meisel had been handled the way he had been there was no telling what would happen next. Ernst might find himself the next one to be tarred and feathered. He walked on down the street and stopped in Wagner's drug store.

—Hello Wagner. Things are pretty bad just now and getting worse I guess.

—Well Ernst look here, now you know that we are friends. You know that we both feel alike about this thing but we don't dare go doing any talking. Now Ernst you have just got to keep your mouth shut. Meisel never would have got into that mess if he hadn't done so damn much talking. Believe me you don't hear me doing any talking. I can tell you I know enough to keep my mouth shut. They've been after me and I know damn well they're watching you. I got a warning and I tell you I'm going to be damn careful. When you're living around a lot of people like this in wartime then you have got to be damn careful. Here, Ernst, let me show you this I got. It's just a warning to be careful, but I tell you I won't need many. Those damn fools might do anything to a fellow.

Wagner showed Ernst the letter he had received.

In time of great national emergency it is necessary for
right minded citizens to band themselves together in
order to promote the highest interests of the state. Any
actions on the part of residents deemed dangerous
to the state will arouse the action of the united body
of citizens who are trying to maintain law, order and
respect for constitutional government. Your name
has been given to us as being a person suspected of

holding beliefs, opinions, thoughts, or desires which
may in some way be a public danger at this time.
You are warned that any action on your part which
may be interpreted as being against our recognized
government will be promptly dealt with. We trust that
in this great national crisis you will endeavor to do all
in your power toward a speedy victory for right, justice
and democracy.

American Protective League
Fairbanks branch

—That would be for Germany to win the war if you want
democracy. Why that's like the story of the man in Germany who
wanted liberty. Why did he want liberty? Just so he could do his
business on the street. Democracy. God damn it Wagner isn't it
democracy when a man can say what he believes without getting
burned with tar and feathers?!

—Yes maybe Ernst, but Meisel went too far and he was
nothing but a damn fool anyway. And you don't dare go doing
any talking. It ain't safe in Fairbanks. The best way is just pretend
that you are patriotic, go and hear the speeches, buy some liberty
bonds, put them posters in your window. It don't cost nothing
and you win in the end. You know damn well your business
is going all to hell and even if you don't need the money right
away there's no use going in a hole. You can get it all back quick
as nothing. Nothing to it, you do what I tell you. See them
posters in my window? Well, see that Hun, my God, cutting off
a woman's tits? Don't tell me the Germans do that now Ernst
do they? But I got to put it in the window and then I get the

business. And see here just take them liberty bonds and turn them in for goods. You don't lose much money doing that and you can buy more bonds that way and get your name in the paper for buying lots of bonds. Watch in the paper when they print the list next week. I'll be one of the biggest buyers. All my Christmas stuff I'm paying for with bonds. The people will all be saying, my God look at that man Wagner buying liberty bonds! He must have lots of dough and be mighty damn patriotic. I'm going to get more business by it, watch and see.

—I don't think I could ever go putting one of those posters in my windows. That's awful Wagner. That's a plain lie. And damn it everything is just a bunch of lies. You got to live and just go on lying. I don't feel much like buying those liberty bonds but that wouldn't be a bad idea to fool the people that way. Everything is going wrong and there isn't any telling what might happen next. Next, everybody with a German name will be getting hung up by the neck. That's about the way it's coming to, the way they got Meisel. That was terrible. I'll bet that nothing like that could ever happen in Germany, where people are at least a little bit civilized. But I don't think I want to make a fool of myself with bonds and posters, all that rot.

—No use to get excited Ernst and I don't like to have you talking in the store here where people may hear what we're saying.

—Yes maybe you're right. If people hear you breathe a word they would be on our necks, the sneaking dirty damn fools. Say Wagner have you got a *Fatherland?*

—Yes I keep it here underneath the counter for my friends.

—So long Wagner.

—So long Ernst. Remember what I said. Take my advice now damn it.

—I don't think I want to make a damn fool of myself that way. I'm not running a recruiting station.

————————

Back at the store Ernst found that there was a letter like the one Wagner had received and he read it and grew frightened and decided he would keep his mouth shut and not let anybody know how he was feeling. But he wouldn't go putting posters in his windows and flags and buying liberty bonds. They couldn't do anything if he kept his mouth shut, and he didn't intend to go make a damn fool of himself.

That's all a bunch of bunkum, he was thinking. They can't do anything to me and that is just a silly letter like a bunch of highschool boys would write. All they're trying to do is run me out of my business. Those fellows, Miles and Johnson, and those other fellows in the club. American Protective League. What do they want to protect? I'd like to see where I have done anything that needs protecting. They're just a bunch of kids showing off. All my old friends, and now they don't do anything but spy on a fellow. I'd like to show the whole bunch. I'll have to be pretty careful though with all this stuff going on. There's no telling what might happen.

————————

Going home one night from the store after having had a short talk with Roger Bartlett, Ernst thought of Helen and wished that they could some way get closer to each other and not be always arguing and fighting about the war and the position he had been taking. He

could see that Helen was constantly afraid that something bad was
going to happen because he was not acting patriotic, but he could
not find it in himself to act the way Wagner had been acting and
put out flags and posters and buy liberty bonds. He thought that it
would be nice if he and Helen were as close to one another as they
had been when they were first married, but he could not see how
it was in his power to bring this about, and he was quite sure that
Helen would not change her attitude toward him until he became
more patriotic. He would not do that. He would keep quiet and
not do any talking but he would not make a damn fool of himself
with flags and posters and liberty bonds the way Wagner had been
doing.

Ernst walked in his house and, taking off his coat, sat down
in the living room and picked up the evening paper. Helen came
up to him crying and handed him a little note.

> Dear Mother, Richard Miles and I have decided we
> will go in the army. We are going to enlist today in
> another town so don't try looking for us. I didn't want
> to have any argument with you about it so I decided
> to go away and join up with Dick Miles. Don't worry
> about us. Lots of love,
>
> Charley

—Oh Ernst what will we do? I have been almost crazy.
Charley may get killed in the war and he's too young. Oh Ernst I
feel so awful. I don't know what to do.

—Well he should have more sense than that. I wonder where
he went. Maybe we can get him out yet. You were always putting

ideas like that in his head. You were always doing things like that. I knew something like that was going to happen. Go and fight against Germany?! My son?!

He thought, my God there's that little Fransel and my other cousin Wilhelm and my uncle, all of them are fighting in the army and now my own boy goes over there to fight against his own blood that way. I don't know, I guess there isn't anything to do. Helen ought to have known that would happen, the way she was always acting.

—Ernst, he left town with Dick Miles. His mother called me on the phone today this afternoon and she got a note too Ernst, and she is almost frantic and so am I. If anything should happen to Charley I would die, I know I would.

This all comes of having married Helen. If I hadn't got mixed up with Charley Ross I wouldn't have married Helen and I would have married somebody that would not have had my son go away that way. My own boy goes away to fight against his brothers. I don't know. I just don't know. My God. The blood is just the same here as there.

—Oh Ernst please say something and don't sit there without talking that way. What are you thinking, are you thinking? Talk to me Ernst. You think it's my fault, you think I sent him away. I didn't want to see him go away. I can't stand it Ernst, it isn't my fault. I don't want to see Charley go away that way, you know it!

—Well I don't know Helen, I can't think much. He should have known better. Maybe they will put him in the trenches. I got to find out where he is. He's too young. You shouldn't always have been filling his head with ideas.

—Oh Ernst can't you see I never did, I never wanted him to go to war. I just didn't want him to be proGerman. I didn't ever want him to go to war and be killed. Oh something is going to happen that will be awful. Please Ernst it wasn't my fault, can't you see it wasn't my fault? Really?

—That's no son of mine to go over there and fight against his brothers. He is just foolish, that's all there is to it.

—Ernst don't talk that way. What can we do? He didn't ask me. I didn't tell him he could do it.

The doorbell rang and Ernst got up to open it and Helen went out of the room drying her tears with a handkerchief. Henry Miles stood in the doorway. Ernst felt that he did not want to see him. He would like to slam the door in his face and tell him to get out and stay away. But he opened up the door and said,

—Come in Miles.

—Say Ernst, where did those two kids go? We got that note from Dick but his mother is just simply sick about it and we can't find out where they went. Did you find out anything? A nice couple of boys to run away like that.

—I don't know except what the note said.

—Oh well they didn't enlist here in town and I can't find out what depot they left town from. They might have driven in a car. They didn't take your car did they?

—Helen, did Charley run off with the car?

She came into the room and her tears were dried away and her face was ready to receive more tears.

—No it's in the garage. He didn't take it.

—I don't know, Miles, how they got away.

—Well Ernst it's too bad. Dick used to say that your boy Charley had been urging him to run away but we were always firm about it. He's too young, eighteen. He ought to have waited till he was at least twenty-one. My wife is almost crazy and she is sick in bed. You shouldn't have let your boy get those ideas and give them to my boy that way.

—I never gave him any ideas you ought to know that, only I'll tell you this much Henry Miles, when you go talking about patriotism those boys have got more of it than their fathers, how about that? You were always such a strong patriot. I should think you would be glad to see your boy go to help his country.

—Now Ernst you know very well he's too young and there are plenty of men to go to war, and besides with all the work I've been doing here there wasn't any need for my son to go away. You are talking nonsense Ernst.

Helen saw that Ernst was not so sad and unhappy as he had been. He acted almost triumphant. He acted as if he were really glad that little Charley had run away and gone to war. He seemed to be a much bigger, stronger man than the cowardly looking Henry Miles. Miles was white in his face and anxious and worried, and Ernst seemed glad that his son had joined the army.

Helen, seeing Ernst was not so angry and distracted as he had been when she first showed him the note, began to feel less like crying. She dried her tears and said she wished they would hear something from the boys. If they only knew where the boys were it would be easier.

—I have wired to the government and to Detroit and I think we can get Dick out of the army if he is already in. I warned them in Detroit not to accept him. I think they went to Detroit.

—Didn't you tell them not to accept Charley too?

—No we just wired about Dick.

Ernst was thinking lots of things about Henry Miles and the whole lot of the Vigilance Committee, American Protective League fellows in the town. They were just a bunch of coward slackers, he was thinking. He was glad to see Henry Miles suffering a little bit and thought that he ought to get a good dose of it for the crazy way he had been acting.

—I think it will be a good thing for the boys, a little bit of army life, and I like to see that my boy has got that much patriotism.

Helen hearing Ernst say this made her think that he was getting patriotic. Then she thought she knew that he was only talking up to Henry Miles. She could see that Henry Miles wasn't getting sympathy the way he had expected. She could see that Ernst was having a good time talking that way to Henry Miles. She could see that he didn't like Henry Miles and wanted to make him appear to be a slacker and not as patriotic as he had always tried to make people think he was.

—Well Ernst I guess you're not so cut up about it because your boy was always stronger than our boy. It will be bad for Dick, I'm afraid, and he's too young to go to France and fight in the trenches.

—He's older than Charley and we don't like to see Charley go away to fight either. But if everybody felt that way about the war what would become of democracy? We've got to give until it hurts us, that's the way, and giving our sons to save our country, isn't that what they are all talking about?

—Well Ernst I thought you had heard something. My wife thought you might have heard something and she is so cut up she is almost crazy. I don't know what we are going to do about it.

—I don't think there is much to do about it Miles. We have all got to bear the burden of the war.

After Miles left, Ernst fell again to thinking and he felt so bad about Charley going away that the tears began to come to his eyes and Helen saw them coming and she began to cry. She knew why he was crying, and she knew that he had just been doing talking to Henry Miles and hadn't really been meaning what he said at all.

She grew very sad and imagined her son being carried from the muddy trenches wounded and dying and bloody and she cried and she didn't think about Dick Miles at all. Ernst imagined Charley fighting with little Fransel and killing Fransel and then laughing about it and getting himself killed and he felt very very bad about it and began to wish he had told his son to join the Red Cross or go to Washington to work where it was safe. He began to think that he would see the congressman from the state and see if he couldn't get some job for Charley in the army that would keep him from going away to France. But he knew he would have to know where Charley had gone so he could get in touch with him.

He got up from his chair and went to the telephone and telephoned the telegraph office and sent a message to Detroit to stop the boy from enlisting. Henry Miles had never even thought about Charley when he had sent his telegram.

Ernst, seeing Helen so unhappy, forgot to think that she had always been urging Charley to take her part against his father, and he began to feel sorry for Helen and began to wish he could make her so she would not be so unhappy.

They were both so unhappy, each was about as unhappy as the other. Ernst walked over to the davenport where Helen was sitting with her elbow on the arm of the davenport and her forehead in her hand.

—Helen don't be so unhappy, Ernst told her. He put his arm around her and she began to cry aloud now and shake with tears.

—Oh Ernst I was so afraid you wouldn't love me, and with Charley gone I haven't got anybody. Charley was so much to me and I didn't want to have you think that I made him go away because I never wanted him to go away.

—Helen don't feel so bad about it. We will hear from Charley and he may never have to go to France at all. I don't think he will ever have to go to France. Don't cry Helen, I feel unhappy too and I don't like to see him go to war but maybe it will be all right. I think it will be all right with him. Don't cry darling Helen, please don't.

Ernst drew her close to him and put his arm tight around her and she held her handkerchief to her eyes and sobbed a little and sat weak and limp held tight up to Ernst. She felt so much better than she had been feeling since she had seen the note, and now she was feeling almost happy with Ernst's arm around her. She felt a little as she had when she was married to Ernst, and it was good to have herself in his tight arms against him. It had been so long since he had made love to her, and she had always been glad that he had not wanted to be lovemaking and now she was glad that he was making love to her again. She wanted him to make love to her and it made her happy and made her tears flow faster. She was so happy that she cried more than she had been crying.

—Darling don't cry, everything will be all right with Charley, I know it will be and maybe we can fix it up with a congressman so he won't have to go across the water to France and fight in the trenches. We can do something darling. I love you darling. Do you love me? It is so long now. I sometimes think that you don't love me and I am so unhappy.

—Ernst dear, don't say that. I love you. You are so sweet Ernst. It wasn't my fault Charley went away Ernst.

—I know it Helen, but don't worry.

Ernst drew her close to him and kissed her and her face was wet with tears and Ernst had teardrops in his eyes when he kissed her. He felt strongly that he wanted to make love to her and he felt that he would like to make her so she would always be very happy.

He asked her if she had been happy in her lovemaking and he explained to her what he meant by being happy and she said she had felt a little bit that way and he was excited talking to her and wanted to make love to her.

———————

The doorbell rang again and Ernst went to see who was there. He didn't feel like seeing anybody and Helen did not feel like seeing anybody. Charles Ross and his wife were at the door and Ernst was sorry they were there but he told them to come in and Helen wiped her eyes and got ready to do more crying.

Charles Ross and his wife didn't speak because they didn't know what to say to two such unhappy people. They sat down and didn't feel like speaking and starting conversation, and Helen couldn't think of anything to say. She wished they hadn't come and so did Ernst because he was thinking so much about Helen that he didn't like to have anybody come in to stop him from thinking about her.

Finally Charles Ross cleared his throat and said, —Well children it's too bad about little Charley. But there isn't anything to do and I don't think they will send him to the trenches.

Helen sobbed a little.

Mrs. Ross decided she would do some talking.

—You must both feel awful. It's too bad your boy going away the way he did, and so young too. I feel so sorry for you. The war is an awful thing when it comes so close to home. Charles and I have just felt it so much since we heard. I do hope he didn't join the tank corps or the aeroplanes. I think it would be better for him in the navy or the ambulance department. The navy would be the best. I hope he doesn't come to any harm.

Helen sobbed when she thought of Charley coming to harm and dying in France far away where she couldn't see him.

Ernst felt that he must say something.

—He went away with young Miles.

—We heard he did. Isn't that too bad? And that young Miles boy too. Those boys were impetuous.

—Well I don't know, sometimes I think that Charley may find it a good thing for himself. I hate to see him go away, but Helen and I have been talking about it and it may be a good thing for the boy. The influence may be a very good thing for him. It makes me look a little different at the war when I see Charley go away.

Ernst thought he had been saying the right things to be saying at the time. Charles Ross was quick to take him up. He hadn't felt so sure that it would be a bad thing for little Charley to be in the army.

—I think you're right about that Ernst, it may be a darned good think for Charley. I mean it. I don't think there is much chance of him getting overseas and the discipline is very good in the army. And it won't hurt you any here Ernst because you know very well the way the people have been talking about you, and with Charley in the army I don't see how they can say anything.

—I don't care what people have been talking about me, Ernst said. —I don't know what they have been saying, but you know damn well I haven't been acting any differently than anybody else, and you know I have not been acting proGerman. They had no right to send that letter to me.

—Well Ernst that was just a form letter they sent to everybody. I had a deuce of a time keeping your name out of the paper. You ought to buy liberty bonds Ernst. I meant to talk to you about it before but I couldn't get myself to do it. Now with Charley gone you ought to do it, and it would make it easier for you and Helen and you have been foolish about it because you just lost business. But I guess business doesn't amount to much the way that stove works stock has been multiplying. You must be worth a ton of cash in that stock and automobile stuff you've got. But if you want to run a shoe store there isn't any reason to keep it open when you haven't got any business to speak of. You got yourself in bad with the boys talking and that was a bad thing to do. You ought to act more American, then things would be all right. The boys liked you a lot Ernst, and you know it. Don't feel so bad about Charley being gone, but let yourself feel more patriotic about it. Isn't that right Helen?

—Well Ernst has not been acting proGerman and there isn't any reason. You should have heard what he told Henry Miles.

—Was Henry here? What did he have to say about it?

—Ernst told him a few things, and if you had heard him you wouldn't ever say that Ernst was not a good American. He told

Henry Miles what a coward and slacker he is to be whimpering so much because his son goes in the army. Henry Miles says Charley got his boy to go away. That's a lie, it was just the other way because I know the way those boys talk. But we didn't say anything like that did we Ernst? Ernst just told him that he wouldn't feel so bad if he was more patriotic. He told him that we had to make sacrifices for our country, didn't you Ernst?

—Well I'll tell you, Ernst said, —I felt damn sore the way Miles has been talking about me and I know some of the things he has been saying and he buys his shoes in Miller's. And then to come sobbing up to me with this stuff about our boy making his go away to war made me think he was a damn fool. Charley has got more real guts than any fellow in the town and the Lord knows I don't want to see him go to war and you know that because I hate to see him fighting against his relations he's got in Germany, but at the same time I can tell that fellow Miles that he is nothing but a big bag of wind, that's all he is.

—I'm awfully glad to see you taking it the way you are Ernst, Charles Ross said. —You will find things going a damn sight better when you act that way about things.

Ernst wished they would go. He wanted to talk to Helen.

———————

When they went Helen began to cry again, and Ernst went to her side to try and comfort her with his caresses.

They went upstairs and Ernst made Helen feel that she loved him very much and she found herself happy loving him and she no longer felt that she didn't care so much for lovemaking. In her sadness for her son and her fear that Ernst would hate her and blame her because Charley had gone away to the army and in her joy at the tenderness Ernst showed her, she found herself to be more passionate and eager for love than she had ever been before, and she found that Ernst was wonderful and she loved him more than she had ever thought that she could love any man. Ernst made her happy and made love to her until she was happy. And she got the feeling that she had never known before what love was and she knew that she had never before felt all the pleasure that she felt with Ernst that night. She wondered why she had never felt that way before and wondered if she would ever feel that way again. She got to feeling so very happy that she forgot everything about her, and then she knew that she had never known before what love was and she felt weak and happy and drew Ernst to her and kissed him and said that she was going to have another baby because once a long time ago Hazel Johnson had told her how to tell when you were going to have a baby.

—I never believed it, Ernst, when she told me, and I thought then that she was only talking nonsense, but now I know and Ernst dear it is so wonderful and I love you and everything seems as if we had just met for the first time. Oh Ernst I never dreamed that I could feel that way. You darling Ernst.

Ernst was feeling just as happy as Helen felt, and he loved Helen so much knowing that he could make her so happy and he felt as if they had just been married and he felt that he could never leave her and he loved her more than he had ever loved her.

They talked about Charley and most of their uneasiness had left them and they began to think that he would not be bad off in the army and he would not be killed and after all he was very brave and manly and he would be a big man in Fairbanks someday.

20

Ernst walked hurriedly past Bartlett's house and to his store the next morning. He didn't feel much like talking to Roger Bartlett. When he reached the store he asked Jim the clerk to listen to him.

—Jim will you go out and get a service flag, a nice one with a gold braid around it and put it in the window of the door in the front? My boy went in the army and I'm going to show these people here in town just where they stand and where I stand on this matter. I'll show the whole damn town, by God I will.

Ernst was happy because he loved Helen so much and knew that she loved him and he wanted to make everything nice and pleasant for Helen in the town and he was deciding that he would act more patriotic and maybe buy some liberty bonds later, but not right then when everybody was talking about him. And he might make people think in other ways that he was really patriotic. With his son gone to war that ought to be enough to show them.

When Jim got back they hung up the service flag so everybody would know that a member of the family had gone to war.

—Say Jim, now what we want to do is get a flag with four stars for the fellows who were working here and went to war. That will be a good idea. I didn't think of that before. Will you remember tomorrow to get a flag like that?

About ten o'clock in the morning Helen came down to the store with a telegram from little Charley saying he was on his way to Kelly Field in Texas where he was going to be stationed for training in the army. He said that he and Dick Miles had had no trouble getting in the army and were very happy and hoped their folks wouldn't be too cut up about it.

Ernst called Mrs. Miles and learned that they had also received a telegram and were both feeling better knowing where their son was located. They were going to try and get him out, they said.

Ernst was sitting in his desk chair and Helen stood up close to him with her body pressed close against his arm and drew his head over to her breast with her fingers in his hair and she whispered,

—Ernst dear I love you, oh I want you.

She trembled just a little and Ernst felt himself desiring Helen and loving her very very much.

—Don't you think that Charley will be safe Ernst? Do you think we could get him out the way the Mileses want to do with their boy Dick? I don't think Charley would want us to do that but maybe we could try it.

—I think we better let him stay there. I don't think he will get himself killed Helen. I don't even think he will get over there to France at all.

—Oh I hope not Ernst. We must write to him and I will send him some sweaters and some candy and some socks too. I guess I ought to.

—Charley wanted to do that I guess. There was no way to hold him back and I don't think that it will hurt him. Don't they give him all the things like that he needs? He don't need sweaters down in Texas.

—Well maybe not but that's what all the women send their sons.

———————

Richardson walked in the store and talked to Ernst and told him what a noble sacrifice he was making with his son in the army and suggested that it might be a good thing to buy a few liberty bonds, although a man giving his son should be about all that was expected.

—I can understand how you and your wife must feel having your only boy go to war. You are a brave couple and the town will admire you for your example. Doesn't that service flag make you feel just a little bit proud Ernst?

—Well Charley is quite the boy, and when it comes to courage I guess he's got plenty.

When Richardson walked out of the store Ernst fell to thinking that it was easy to make these people think that you were patriotic. And he got to thinking that he wasn't a bit more patriotic than he ever had been before but he was a little proud of Charley for having the guts and courage to run away to war but he did still think that Charley had been foolish and brainless when it came to being reasonable about the war. He was still hoping that Germany might win the victory before his boy had a chance to get across the water and in the war. But he was determined he would let people think that he was patriotic and wanted to see the Allies win the war.

Harry Johnson dropped in a little sheepishly and told Ernst he had heard that Charley had gone in the army.

—Yes, Harry, Charley has got plenty of courage and he isn't afraid to do what he thinks is right. He is a mighty fine boy and I am proud of him.

—I'm glad to see you feel so different when it comes to the war now Ernst. You are getting damn sensible about it. You can make everybody here like you just as much as ever if you only show them how you feel about it. I never felt for a minute that you were really proGerman. I never did and I stuck up for you all the time. You ought to buy some bonds though Ernst and maybe put up a couple of posters and do a little patriotic work for the country. That's the way to do.

—Well I live in America Harry and I'm as much American as anybody. Before the war I felt different and then after we got in, you know the way it is, a fellow can't turn around suddenly against all the things he has been talking and believing. But I am damn proud of my boy, I'll tell you that.

—Say Ernst, you and Helen ought to come around to dinner. I'll have Hazel call you, you haven't been around to see us for a long time.

—Why don't you folks drop over?

When Johnson left, Ernst got to feeling more that he could fool them all and make them think that he was very patriotic and he was glad that little Charley had gone away to war and it did not make him feel so bad to remember that Charley had never showed much sense when it came to the question of war.

But if he ever should kill one of our relations in Germany in the war I don't know what I would do, he was thinking. It's all right as long as he is down in Texas, that was all right. But I don't want that fellow Charley going over there to France.

During the day three or four other old friends of Ernst came in the store and told him what a brave man he was to have his only son go out to fight the enemies of our country. He didn't enjoy talking about it but he acted very patriotic when he talked to these people. Within the next few days business began to pick up a little and Jim found himself being quite busy being the only clerk in the store.

———————

Ernst found himself very happy at home and was always glad to leave the store and go home to Helen. And she was always eagerly waiting for him to come home and they found themselves loving each other more than ever. Charley wrote to them and told them about his army life and told them that he liked it even if it was hard work and he was glad that he had joined.

———————

Henry Miles began to drop into the shoe store and talk with Ernst about their sons and read the letters he had received from his son Dick.

—Well Ernst I guess they're having a good time down there the way these letters sound. We tried to see if we could get him out but we couldn't and I guess it's the best thing not to. My wife doesn't feel so cut up about it now.

—I think those boys have got a lot of courage and are mighty patriotic Miles. Here, I got a letter from Charley. He says something here about Dick cleaning up the cans. That's a pretty good one.

—Well, Dick said the same thing about Charley, only I didn't want to show you the letters. That must be awful for two boys like that.

—That's a good thing for them Miles, a damn good thing. It will do them lots of good.

—Well maybe, but my wife would think that was awful. Well we have all got to make our sacrifices. I guess we have made ours all right with our boys gone in the army. I sometimes think it would have been better if they asked us without running off the way they did.

—We would never have let them go if they did that. They had to show us the way our duty lay.

———————

Henry Miles was talking to Harry Johnson and he told him that Ernst had been a great help to him when his son ran away to join the army.

—You know Harry, the way Ernst took it made me feel sure that these fellows who come over here the way he did make better Americans than a lot of other fellows. He helped me and was a real inspiration to me the way he took it. I thought he would take it hard because I thought he was proGerman, but you know I don't

think that he was very proGerman after his son left. I think he is
probably as good an American as you will find in this town.

—Well maybe Henry, but he used to be proGerman, but I
did a lot of talking to him and I guess maybe he isn't proGerman
anymore. He didn't act that way when I talked to him the other
day.

—Well of course I talked to him too for that matter, but
I was thinking about the way he kept a stiff upper lip and acted
proud and made me feel proud of my boy too. I like Ernst and I
think we should have him back in the club. We never kicked him
out, but you know that he must have known the way the other
fellows felt about it. He has proved himself and we ought to reward
him.

—I think so too Henry, only damn it I hate to go and speak
to him. Let's talk it over with the boys and get a committee to
ask him to come back to the meetings. With his boy in the army,
and he hasn't done any talking, I think he really is patriotic. Only
he ought to buy liberty bonds. But he says he doesn't buy them
because he wants to invest his money in other ways. He just doesn't
understand that that isn't being patriotic. He's got a lot of old ideas
about some things but in his heart he is all right I guess. We'll have
to do something about it with the boys.

———————————

Business at the store improved for Ernst but did not get as good as
it had been before the war, because the majority of customers who
still suspected him of being proGerman and did not care to buy
their shoes from a proGerman.

He sat in his office planning and deciding he would do the thing right and make a big splurge and act real patriotic and show these people of Fairbanks something.

I'll show these fellows something. I'll do like that slick fellow Wagner did and show them. I'll buy bonds and pay my bills with them and I'll put up posters. There's no harm in putting up those posters.

—Come over here Jim, I want to talk to you a minute. Upstairs in the warehouse there is a flag we got in the Spanish war. Go up and get it and if it looks all right we will hang it outside like these other fellows have been doing. It's in one of those drawers on the north side. And I want you to get two more flags for the windows. I got a damn good idea for the windows. Two flags to fit in for a background. Get those things today Jim, and I will take care of the trade myself while you're away. I'll fix those fellows. No I didn't say anything else Jim, I was only talking. I'll pay with liberty bonds. No Jim I didn't say anything else to you. I just said ... well never mind get those flags and I'll tell you the rest of it later.

Ernst sat and planned his campaign. I'll put a picture of Charley in his army suit up there on the front counter. And I'll buy some liberty bonds right away today and pay all my bills with them the way that Wagner fellow has been doing. And I'll do some advertising. *Shoes for the Belgians,* that's a good idea. I can be as big a fool as any of them damn it if I can't.

Jim found the flag and hung it out in the front of the store and went out and bought two flags for the windows.

—We'll wait a while to put those in, Ernst told him. I got an awful good idea planned.

———————————

When the paper published the week's list of biggest Liberty Bond buyers Ernst's name was second, higher up than old man Johnson's, higher up than Charles Ross's. And in the same edition of the paper he ran a half page advertisement.

Weiman's
The American Shoe Store

Military boots, spurs, hiking shoes, puttees. Complete foot equipment for the warrior.

The finest civilian shoes in the state. Best English and American makes.

For every twenty dollars worth of merchandise purchased in our shop we send one pair of shoes to the starving Belgians. Every purchaser of Weiman's shoes automatically assists in putting some poor Belgian on his feet. We will not only give until it hurts, we will give to our limit.

Signed—
Ernst Weiman

PS. Five hundred Belgians will be wearing Weiman's Fairbanks shoes by Christmas if business continues at its present brisk pace.

Wanted—Five clerks. Must be exempt from Government service. No slackers need apply.

21

In half of one of the two windows Ernst had had Jim throw a huge
pile of shoes together and on them place a placard reading:

These shoes for democracy and the Belgians.

The other half of the window was filled with military boots,
spurs, puttees, equipment for the warrior, and Ernst had rustled up
some photographs of soldiers from the best families in Fairbanks,
the families which had formerly been among his customers and
were to be soon again. These photographs he placed here and there
in the window.

The other window had a line of civilian shoes, both men's
and women's, and had a placard reading:

For those brave soldiers who must fight the battles of
their country behind the lines, supplying the man at the
front with his needs, ever ready to do their utmost that

their government of the people, by the people, and for the people, shall not perish from the earth.

Little Charley Weiman was framed and stood proud in ill-fitting khaki on the front counter. Around the walls Ernst had draped flags interspersed by posters. There was not another store in Fairbanks more patriotic looking than the store of Ernst Weiman. There were many that seemed patriotic in appearance but with good German thoroughness Ernst had turned the trick completely. Ernst hired four new helpers making five clerks in all. They were flatfoots and consumptives and men exempt from going to war.

This ought to show them, Ernst thought as he surveyed the scene and thought how easy it was to act patriotic. I can get rid of all my old stock by sending those shoes to the Belgians. I can buy up some bankrupt stuff if I have to or get some factory ends for almost nothing and let the Belgian Relief Commission pay for shipping the junk to Belgium.

––––––––––

When Ernst walked home from work he went around the block that Roger Bartlett lived in. He didn't feel like doing any talking with Roger Bartlett. Bartlett was a funny old fellow and wouldn't understand the things that Ernst was doing. He was a little bit too eccentric and he would be apt to try and do some kidding and try to make Ernst feel uncomfortable and a traitor to his beliefs which they had formerly shared in common. It would be better to just walk around the block and save the trouble of talking to Roger Bartlett.

Helen was pleased with the things that Ernst had been doing and she saw herself being reinstated in the best society of Fairbanks and being just as welcome as she had been before the war started. And she felt now, loving Ernst so much, that what he did was the right thing for a man to be doing. Everything would be so much better from now on. She loved Ernst so much and wanted to be near him always and wanted him to feel how much she loved him. Ernst was a wonderful man and a big man in Fairbanks and the talking all these people had been doing ought to make them ashamed of themselves. All a person had to do was look at Ernst to see what a fine big man he was and how much good he was always doing in the town of Fairbanks.

—Oh Ernst, she said, I am so happy. Hazel Johnson came to see me and she brought her knitting and we had a long talk together and people are all sorry that they didn't understand you. It took Charley's going away for them to understand you. You are a dear boy Ernst, and everybody likes you, and I love you so much Ernst. I never knew how much I loved you, but I have always loved you, since the day I was born. I'm going to give a bridge party to raise some money for the Belgians and the Red Cross and some of the girls have called me up and we are going to have a good time. And Charley may get to be an officer, he says. He is going in training. Won't that be fine to have him be an officer? Such a young fellow, but he is a good soldier and a fine young man now, I know. I hope they never send him over there in the dirty trenches. If he gets to be an officer he won't be so apt to have to go there.

—They better not send Charley over there to be killed in the trenches. I can do all this stuff here in Fairbanks Helen, but I won't have my boy go over there and be killed by the Germans. I do not believe in that at all. If Germany should beat the French before he gets out of that camp down there then everything would be all right. I wish the Germans would get the war over before America gets all her men there, or then it will be too late for her to win. I don't think we had any right to get in this, and I hate to see our country getting all her boys killed for the French and English.

—Ernst please don't talk like that, even if you feel it. Try and act patriotic always, Ernst. I don't care, things are going so well now if anybody heard you say things like that they would think awful things. I don't care how you feel darling, only Germany should not win the war with Charley down in Texas in the army. You don't want Germany to win the war.

—No maybe not, but I do want to see it stop. And I do think it might be better for the world to have Germany win it. What we need most is peace for business and getting all the world back on its feet. That war might go on for years yet if something doesn't happen.

—Yes dear, let's not talk about it. Let's just be happy and remember Charley and everything will be all right.

Ernst still read the *American Monthly*, which had formerly been called the *Fatherland*, and he read the *Nation* now and then. He was anxious for the peace to come. He was anxious that America make any sacrifice to bring about the peace. He could talk to Helen about the things he thought of but she cautioned him not to talk to people, and he knew enough not to do that kind of talking. Helen still kidded him about his views, but she was never very serious for she loved Ernst and found him a source of pleasure to her of a kind she had never known before the time Charley joined the army.

They got along very well together, much better than they had ever gotten on before together, and they never argued because the arguments always found themselves stopped with kisses and endearments. Ernst found it easy to live his life believing the things that he believed in, knowing that Helen wasn't sure what she believed in, for the two were so happy being married and in love with one another that their life together was a happy one for both of them. Ernst knew that Helen didn't understand the way he did and he knew it wasn't necessary for him to try and make her understand, so he never tried to make her believe what he believed. He just went on alone believing in the things that he believed in and he let Helen rule the part of his life that was not him believing the way he did about the war and the peace and the settlement of the international difficulties.

———————

Ernst was in a hurry to get to work in the morning and didn't bother to walk around the block past Roger Bartlett's house but hurried right along the shortest way to his shoe store.

Roj Bartlett came out on his front porch and called to Ernst.

—They got your goat all right. You're a regular scared cat.

Ernst stopped. He wanted to talk to Bartlett after that remark and try to make him understand why he had done the things he had been doing. He wanted Bartlett to have more respect for him and understand that he had been doing only what was right for him to do under the circumstances. He felt that it would be hopeless to talk to Bartlett, but he couldn't stand it being talked to that way and not being thought well of for the things he had been doing.

He stopped and turned around, but Bartlett had his back in the doorway and he turned with half a laugh and slammed the

door. Ernst knew that the slamming of the door was the same
as Roger Bartlett telling him he could go to hell for all he cared.
Ernst couldn't help but feel ashamed a little, and he hurried with a
worried look toward his shoe store.

That fellow Bartlett is a crazy loon, he thought. He's just a
little daffy and a first class fool. He knows damn well they wouldn't
do anything to him. He was a preacher and an Englishman and he
can say what he pleases. Nobody cares about him, they know damn
well he's crazy. I shouldn't have had anything to do with him at all.

Business at the shoe store rapidly grew better. One by one the old
customers came back and bowed almost with apology for having
stayed away for so long. They spoke of little Charley and what a
brave boy he was to fight for his country. And then they said that
Ernst was doing a lot of good for his country.

And then they bought their shoes, and if the bill was not
quite twenty dollars Ernst quietly suggested some comfy slippers.

—Then you'll have your twenty dollars and a pair of shoes
for the Belgians. Would you like to look at some today?

The customer could hardly refuse such a worthy cause.
People liked to buy twenty dollars worth of shoes at Weiman's so
they could say they had donated a pair of shoes to the starving
Belgians.

The old business came back to Ernst, and new business
began to come which he welcomed with delight. He began to feel
a little patriotic thinking of his boy Charley and seeing the way
people came to his shoe store since the change had come about. He
was really changed a little by the changes in his business, and he

found himself having a real good time. It was a good way to get rid of the old dead stock, which went to Belgium, and he knew that he could get more shoes for the Belgians very cheaply from bankrupt sales and factory ends.

There were people in the city who knew that he had been proGerman, and they wondered at the quick change in his outlook. They were suspicious of him, but only a short time was needed to convince almost all of them that he was really quite patriotic and wasn't a bit proGerman.

With all the best people in Fairbanks buying their shoes at Weiman's, it was easy to see that Ernst Weiman was not really proGerman. They liked to go there to show him that they didn't hold it against him that he had a German name and had been for Germany before his country went to war because now they knew that he had become one hundred percent American, and a man's past in America was not a thing to hold against him. They liked it very much that a man who spoke with a German accent was such a good American. And they liked to think that he was very brave to have his only son in the army. And it made them want to patronize his shoe store knowing that he was one of the wealthiest men in the city and was a figure to be respected in Fairbanks. And they knew that he was hand in hand with all the real best people in the town of Fairbanks. They were sorry they had thought that he was proGerman and had avoided him and thought that had been due to the early war hysteria when they had all lost their heads a little.

Ernst Weiman was an example worthy of being followed in the town. It was wonderful for a man brought up as he had been brought up and born in Germany to make himself a big man against all the odds. He was referred to as an example of the finest type of American. But he still read the *American Monthly* and in his heart he wanted a peace that would be favorable to Germany. But these people didn't know the things he really wanted.

————————

Wagner came in the store to talk to Ernst. He walked back to the office.

—Well Ernst you got the right idea. You see what I told you? Well that's what you should have done right off the bat. My jimminy you got the business coming your way all right! Did you read what happened over there? I guess maybe Germany ain't so bad right now. I guess they still do some fighting. This damn foolishness here if this country didn't stick her nose in it never would have gone on the way it has.

Ernst didn't like to have that kind of talk going on in his store. It would be bad for business and might get him in trouble having Wagner come around talking that way. He quietly listened to Wagner for a while but didn't do any of the talking himself. Finally he decided it would be better not to have that kind of talking in his store.

—Wagner I don't like that kind of talking going on here in the store. I don't want you to come here talking that way. I don't like it, not a bit. That's no kind of talk around a place of business and I think you better be careful of what you say.

—Well I wasn't saying anything. You sure have taken a funny way of being with your old friends. I guess I know something about you all right. You needn't get so cocky.

Wagner left the store and was afraid that Ernst might cause him some trouble. There was no telling what Ernst might do. He

was hand and hand with that whole bunch of Vigilance Committee
fellows and he might be spying on the Germans in the town. Maybe
he was always doing that. Wagner got very frightened and began
to think that the reason Ernst had started going to the Liederkranz
Hall for the meetings was to spy on the people there. He became
convinced that Ernst had never been anything but an English
sympathizer. He began to think of the things that he had told Ernst
since the war began and wondered if they would be apt to get
him for treason to America. That fellow was always nothing but a
stuckup fellow from the time he left the German school to go to
public highschool. He made money and got in with all those people
and that's all he's been all the time. Just a dirty sneaking Frenchman
all the time. I'll have to tell the people to be careful. He probably
made them close the hall up. That's the kind of guy he is. By God he
took me in all right with his lying talking. He probably got his son
to beat my boy up. And I bet he had a hand in that Meisel business.
Poor old Meisel. That was a dirty trick for Ernst to do, the dirty spy.

Wagner hurried to tell the German-Americans in Fairbanks
that he had found out that Ernst Weiman was nothing but a British
spy and had been only spying on them when he had been going to
the meetings at the Liederkranz Hall. It was not hard for the German
people in the city to believe this, for they had always felt that he was
not their kind of person, and they had felt it long before Wagner told
them. He had too much money and got in with all those people in
the best society of Fairbanks and that was why he had turned out no
good. His father should have lived to keep him from getting his head
all turned and getting in with those people. They all remembered
that he had always acted funny at the meetings, and they could see
that he had been there just to spy on them.

––––––––––––––––

Ernst had found himself worried when Wagner left his store. He was afraid Wagner might tell people of the way he had always talked and also tell them that he had been acting patriotic only to get their business and keep himself from getting in trouble with the Vigilance Committee. He was really worried when Wagner left the store in such a hurry until old man Schweitzer called in on the phone and talked to him.

—Is this Mr. Weiman? Well I want to tell you that I don't care what you try to do. Wagner told me you were spying on us, but I can tell you you can't do anything at all. I never said a word to you after the war began.

—Why Mr. Schweitzer I don't know what you're talking about.

—Well everybody knows that you were spying on the Liederkranz and I got you down there and I get the blame and I want to tell you now that I never want you to come to my place again and I don't want you to speak to my daughter! I ought to know that you never would be any good and the way you acted when you were a youngster. You and all that bunch that think you are so swell. Your father should have given you some good lickings.

Wagner said I was a spy on them, Ernst began thinking. The damn crazy fool. Can't they see the way I feel about it? All of them are just damn fools, if that's what they all feel like. I'm damn glad I'm not tangled up with any of them. Old Schweitzer sticks his nose in everything. Let them think I was a spy damn them, it won't hurt me any. I can show them damn it. They never did amount to anything.

22

About a week after the change in the shoe store, old man Johnson
went in and looked around at the flags and posters. He walked
back toward the brass barred office and thought of what he was
going to say to Ernst. He had been appointed by the business men's
club to invite Ernst back into the fold.

—Well my boy, you're doing lots of good for dear old
Fairbanks. You have always been one of the hustlers in our
community. I'm mighty glad, my boy, to see you getting on this
way. All we old fellows can do is sit back and see you young men
get ahead of us. There's nothing like good patriotism in the right
direction. Let's walk over to the business club for lunch Ernst. You
haven't been around in a while. We all miss you.

—I've been awful busy. Kinda fixing things up around the
place.

—The boys have all been missing you lately.

At the business men's club luncheon Ernst was made to feel
very welcome. It was Ernst this, and Ernst what have you been

doing, and where you been keeping yourself? Ernst smiled. He was happy to be back there. He couldn't help it. It felt good to be back there and hear them calling him by his first name. They had stopped calling him Dutch, it was too German, but Ernst was good enough for his hearing. He tried to despise these men for treating him the way they had, but he couldn't. They were too glad to see him. Charles Ross was happy to see Ernst back again, and he sat beside him at the table and told him all the boys were glad to have him back. He had done great things at the store. After the luncheon they called on him for a speech.

—Fellow members, it is good to be here to talk to you today. I want to say a few words about our duties to our great free country and our beautiful Fairbanks. You all know that I was born in Germany, the country we are now engaged in war with. Because of this fact I always carried in my heart a little tender spot for that country. Up until the time that America went in the war, my sympathies were with Germany and against France and England. But as you all know I am an American and a citizen of Fairbanks. It is good for me to be here with all of you men who are the doers of the city, the men, I mean, who do the things that are done. All I can say is that we all owe a sacred duty to our country which we can repay only in service. For after all, the main thing is service. There is nothing like it. Each man must battle for his business, home and family and country as if he were fighting at the front with the brave boys. And let me say this much. You are the men who will win the war. It will not be won at the front alone but here behind as well. So as I have said, the heritage is with you. You are the masters of fate. You are the builders of castles. You are the men who will do all for your country and you are all my friends, I am proud to say. And I pledge myself body and soul with you to do all that I can do that the greatest cause may be done and a quick and lasting peace be brought about for us. Thank you.

Ernst was greatly applauded for his speech. He was personally congratulated, slapped on the back, yelled at, hurrahed and bravoed. Each man felt that he had somehow made Ernst into a patriotic American. Each man there felt himself personally responsible for making Ernst into a patriotic American citizen. And then to hear this man speaking broken English speak so forcefully of duty toward the country. They all loved Ernst. No finer character ever was. He was a diamond. Pure gold. If it had been club election day Ernst would have been made President.

And seeing himself admired so highly by the men there, Ernst began to feel a genuine feeling of patriotism. He had never had so much fun being unpatriotic. He almost believed what he had told them.

When the next speaker was speaking Ernst looked around him. The eyes of the men were no longer on him and he looked at them and remembered how they had boycotted him and treated him like an outsider, and he remembered that he had been advised not to go to the business men's club luncheons. His old bitterness came back and he thought now of how he had been fooling them and would continue to fool them. He was happy he had fooled them all, it was revenge for the way they had been treating him.

But after the luncheon he had a group of men around him and things were very much as they had been before the war had started, and he felt like forgetting all the unpleasantness of the war and he felt that he didn't really want a victory for Germany. All he wanted was peace and not the defeat of his old fatherland.

—I got to feeling, he told them, that Germany was wrong and that all war is wrong and maybe we are a little bit wrong too and what we need is peace. We must fight for peace.

—That's right Ernst old boy. Peace, that's the ticket. We are fighting for peace, just as the speaker said. A war for peace to end war. It takes America to do it.

—That's what I say, Ernst said. America is the one country to do it.

The serious conversation did not last very long before jokes were being bandied around and the men began to break up and go back to their businesses.

Charles Ross walked down the street with Ernst.

—That was a damn fine speech Ernst. I'm glad to see you come around that way. Everybody likes you, they always did. Only they all knew that you were proGerman. They will forget that damn quick though with the way things are. I'm glad that for you and Helen things are better.

2 3

Helen found herself having a better and better time of it since the change came about. She found herself going to all the bridge afternoons, receptions, teas and dinners, and she also found a chance to speak of her son Charley and of how many more shoes Ernst was sending than they would ever imagine. So much good work was being done considering all the knitting, and Helen felt the world was getting much better.

Ernst found himself enjoying the position of a big man in the town of Fairbanks. His auto stock and stove works stock and bank stock were worth much more than they had been worth before. And business at the shoe store was better than it had ever been. He was on terms of good friendship with all the big men in Fairbanks and life was very good to him. Only the thought of Charley in the army and the thought of the war's destruction bothered him. Peace at any price he wanted.

—Oh Ernst, Helen said, I am now so very happy. And we got a letter from Charley and everything is all right. Oh, but you shouldn't read those crazy magazines downstairs here. You might forget and leave them and somebody might see them. I don't care how much you read them upstairs, only don't leave them down here where people might see them. And Ernst did you really get a letter from those men, that Vigilance Committee? I heard somebody talking but I shut them up all right.

—Well yes I got a letter a long time ago but that had nothing to do with those changes.

—Well that doesn't matter Ernst, those men were awful silly but I won't have people say you got a letter. They better shut up when you think of all the things we've done and Charley in the army. It was Minnie Hackett, but she is always talking.

—Well I guess I got along all right Helen. I kinda fooled them. I got more business now than I can handle. And I sent some money to the German prison relief commission the other day, that's the least I could do.

—Now Ernst you shouldn't do that, really. Don't ever let anybody know a word about it. You must be awful careful with your son in the army. People are awful sneaky and they might hold that against you. And Ernst, I meant to tell you about that letter Charley wrote and they had made him an instructor down there and he won't have to go across. He was madder than a hatter, but I'm glad it happened and I hope he doesn't ever have to go across.

—That's good. I'm glad to hear that. Old man Johnson took it up with the Senator for me and he said he would get it fixed up someway because he is our only boy. Johnson bought out most of the Senator's holdings in the auto factory. If they ever sent Charley over there Helen I don't know what I would do, but I would do something I'll tell you that. I don't think we had any right to stick our noses in this war. It wasn't our business. I'd show those fellows, Helen.

Then Ernst wiped off his reading glasses and settled in his arm chair with a feeling of satisfaction to read the *American Monthly* which had formerly been called the *Fatherland*.

Charley Weiman

From Contact *(October 1932).*

Charley Weiman liked it very much being in the army. He was in every way a good soldier and was always anxious to get across and do some fighting. He and Miles both got to officers' training school. Charlie determined to get ahead in the army and he began studying hard in order to get a commission and be an officer.

Young Miles was not such an ardent soldier. He didn't like the drudgery of life in the camp and he began to wish he hadn't joined the army. Feeling the way he did about it he began to make new friends among fellows who didn't care much for army life, and who were sorry they had ever joined the army. Charley Weiman made friends with fellows who, like himself, were anxious to get ahead and he began to grow away from Dick Miles and they finally got to the point where they seldom were around together.

The letters the two boys wrote to their friends and to their families in Fairbanks were very different. Ernst Weiman liked it seeing the way things were turning out and the way Miles was complaining about the army. Old man Miles didn't like it and felt sorry for his son but it was too late to do anything about it. When Charley finally got his commission as a second lieutenant Ernst put a new picture in the shoestore, with a gold frame and Charley in a slick looking officer's uniform. Ernst was really feeling proud of Charley and wanting peace at any price but not talking too much about it.

A short time after Charley got his commission he was sent to a camp in Georgia where he was to be an instructor. He didn't like the idea of being an instructor and was a little discontented about it. But he liked the army and the uniform and it seemed good to him to be an officer. He said good bye to Dick Miles.

—Well Dick we joined up together but I suppose I had more luck than you did. Anyway Dick, for God sake work and you can get a commission soon enough. You try, you ought to get it easy. Then I'll see you when we get over and we ought to have some swell times in Paris when we get there. God, you know that would be great if we could be there and have leave and go around and see Paris.

—Jesus, Charley, the way you talk makes me sick. I was a darn fool to join the army, now I know it.

—Don't go talking that way Dick for God sakes, you'll get yourself in trouble talking like that.

—I don't give a damn and I don't care if they send me over now and get me shot up to hell, I don't care. You can talk all you want to, what the devil good is it I want to ask you that.

—Well Dick I guess there's no use us talking. We don't seem to see the thing the same way any more. You used to be crazy about it. You have got funnier ideas than my old man ever had. There isn't any use us talking Dick. So long and get over that kinda stuff you got in your bean now.

—So long Charley I hope you have a good time, you are God damn welcome to it.

That was the last time Charley and Dick, who had joined up together, spoke to one another. Charley went to a camp in Georgia and Dick stayed on for quite a while there at Kelly Field.

In the letters he wrote home, Charley Weiman was saying how much he wanted to get across, but he seemed to be stuck in the camp in Georgia. Ernst always wrote and told him that he was probably doing more real service for the country just staying on this side than he could do over there and that somebody had to take care of the army business on this side and get the men ready to go across and do the actual fighting. Charley Weiman always said that he wanted to be doing some of the actual fighting himself and was getting tired of it sticking in camp and watching other fellows who had come in long since he had, getting orders and going overseas to the front. He said he felt that some one was trying to hold him back from getting any real honors out of the war. He said he was afraid it would be over before he ever got across and then he would feel like the devil about it.

Ernst and Helen Weiman were glad that Charley didn't get across and they both wrote letters to him telling him that it was his real duty to stay on this side and that he shouldn't fret and get up in the air about it but should decide that was doing the best for the country that was in him. Charley didn't see their point of view in the matter.

Another second lieutenant who was a friend of Charley's who was from Detroit showed Charley a picture of his girl and told him how they had gotten married just before he left for camp. He said they just got married and then he took the train, that was all there was to it.

—Didn't you even sleep with her do you mean, Charley asked him.

Donald Phelps, who was the friend of Charley spoke up.

—No, that's what I was telling you. You see the way it is if I should get killed or something like that then you see it wouldn't be consummated and then you see it would be just as if we hadn't. That was the reason. But you see when I get back then everything will be that way and we're married. She thought it up, the idea. She writes to me every day and has got a flag for me. We just did it that way.

—Jesus Don I don't think I would have done that. I mean getting on the train. I would have wanted to be with her once anyway.

—Yes, but you see the point don't you. It wouldn't hardly be fair to the girl taking chances in the war. I think it was noble. That's what her mother said. She said it was noble of us.

—I suppose it was, Charley said. Only gee whizz. Well come right down to it, it was noble Don. Only you might as well have just been engaged.

—It isn't the same Charley, you don't feel so close to her that way. Here let me show you another picture. This one here with her, that's her sister, she's eighteen, her sister is I mean and damn good looking. Her name's Clarice and my wife's is Mabel. Clarice Howard, I don't like it so well for a name but she is a knockout. Snapshots don't show it up so well but she is, she's a knockout Charley.

—She looks damn good to me, said Charley.

Donald Phelps hemmed and hawed around a little and then cleared his throat and started speaking without looking straight at Charley.

—What it was Charley, I wanted to ask you if maybe you would like to write letters to her. I mean Mabel wrote to me and she told me Clarice would like to write letters, you know, and Mabel told me to ask some good chap, somebody you know who I liked and I thought of you Charley. It may sound funny, but girls like that like to write and Jesus, nobody doesn't like getting letters. So I thought I'd ask you, that was all it was.

—Christ yes I'd like to write her, give me her address and give me that picture so I can look at it and I'll write her. Say it would be funny wouldn't it, I mean if we could get leave and go back there. Of course then you could stay with your wife.

Donald Phelps looked at Charley and he seemed to be sad and thoughtful.

—No we don't start that till after the war is over, that was the way we arranged it. If you and I go back there we would be on the same footing. I mean if you and Clarice hit it off all right we would.

—I'm damned if I don't write to her right today Don. It would be funny if maybe something happened about her. Both of us in the same camp and brother officers and them sisters.

—Jesus Charley if you would that would make it nice for me because I practically told Mabel I would fix it up and that'll help me with her if you and Clarice should make a go of it. I hated like hell to say anything about it.

—For Christ sake don't think that, don't you think I get a kick out of it too. Why I'm glad you didn't ask anybody else. I don't give a damn about any girls in Fairbanks.

This started Charley Weiman writing letters to Clarice Howard and exchanging snapshots and photographs with her. It didn't take long before their letters were love letters and they were planning on getting married.

Clarice thought it would be nice to get married the way her sister and Donald Phelps had been married and to wait until the war was over to consummate the wedding. Charley Weiman almost gave in to the lure of this idea but he hadn't really decided that he was deeply enough in love with her for that. Clarice wrote and said that she was sure she was more than enough in love with him and she told him how proud she would be to have her husband in the army and an officer and such a fine looking one as Charley.

Charley decided he would like to see her first so he kept right on writing love letters and talking about the future and telling her how much he wanted to see her. But he always wrote a little with his tongue in his cheek. He also did a lot of talking with Donald Phelps and he began slowly to think that Mabel wasn't being absolutely fair with Donald, he thought to himself that she should not have insisted upon a wedding without going through with the thing. But Donald Phelps, although he went around looking sad and thoughtful, was really satisfied with the arrangement and was getting more and more anxious for the war to be over.

Donald Phelps didn't say anything about this to Charley but he had been thinking since his wedding and even a little before the wedding that it might be a good idea not to consummate it. He knew that Mabel, once she had him, would find it very difficult to wait for him to come back from the army. He figured to himself that it would be cruel to let her taste the joys of matrimony and then to suddenly deprive her of them. And he couldn't help but feel that when he got back from the army, in case the wedding had not been consummated, he would know for sure that she had been faithful and true to him while he was away fighting the battles of his country. He got a lot of satisfaction out of thinking that he could now tell whether she had been always true to him. And besides the whole idea was very noble, just as Mabel Howard's mother had said. Donald thought it was just as well not to tell Charley all the things he had been thinking.

Charley Weiman considered the thing as noble but at the same time as a sort of damn fool thing to do. He wished he could get leave to go back to Fairbanks and on the way stop off in Detroit and see Clarice and decide what to do about marrying her. He thought it over and decided to write to his mother and tell her all about it. He told her just how his acquaintance with the girl had come about and said that he was really in love with her and expected after the war was over to marry her. He said he had thought a little about marrying her while he was still in the army but that he was not sure what he wanted to do and would have to think it over carefully.

Mrs. Weiman and Ernst were alarmed about their boy. They held a long consultation and decided to write to Charley and try to get the idea of marriage out of his head. They decided he was much too young to get married, and he had no way to support a wife. They decided it was just plain foolishness for Charley to think of a wife and marriage and besides to have been making such arrangements through correspondence was ridiculous.

—That's what the war and the army does for fellows, Ernst said.

—Well we won't worry about it, Mrs. Weiman said. We'll put a stop to this foolishness right away. Who ever heard of such a thing. And he's never even seen the girl. I wonder who those Howards in Detroit are anyway. I never heard of them.

—Well Helen that doesn't matter so much, they are probably good enough people but I don't like this, I don't like this way of doing things. He better not think of getting married when he hasn't even seen the girl.

—I wonder who those people are. Probably they are just some scheming people trying to get any young soldier they can, and Charley an officer. That girl probably just wants to get his insurance money if anything should happen.

—Well he said he was thinking about waiting until the war was over to marry her didn't he.

—Now Ernst you don't read between the lines. He said he was thinking a little about marrying her while he was still in the army, you ought to know what that means. That's just as clear as anything could be. You ought to know Charley well enough to see that.

—Well maybe, Ernst said.

Mrs. Helen Weiman went to Detroit to visit friends that lived there and she spent a lot of time trying to find out just who the Howards were. Her friends did not know them but she found out that Mrs. Howard was a widow with two daughters and that they had some money but not very much and that the girls had gone to Liggett school, which made them somebody. Helen Weiman decided she would call on them and meet the mother and the daughters and she was very sure that she wouldn't like Clarice Howard. She didn't like the name in the first place and in the second, the idea of a girl carrying on like that through the mails and with her own son Charley. Helen Weiman thought it would be best to see these people and plan a way to stop the affair before it could get serious.

She telephoned the Howard house and told Mrs. Howard that it was Mrs. Weiman speaking and that she was in Detroit and would awfully like to meet them. Mrs. Howard said she didn't recognize who it was speaking and then Helen Weiman said that she was the mother of Charles Weiman who was a close friend of Clarice Howard.

—Oh, said Mrs. Howard.

—I thought I would like to meet Clarice, Helen Weiman said.

—Oh we would be delighted to have you come and see us. Won't you come this afternoon and have tea with us.

—I would like to very much Mrs. Howard, Helen Weiman said.

—At four then.

—Good at four then, I shall be awfully glad to see you.

Helen Weiman hated to do it but she thought it was her duty toward her son and it would be a good thing for the girl too. It would be dreadful for the girl to get her expectations all aroused and then have something come along and break her heart. Mrs. Weiman felt that it was her duty to put a stop to the young people's silliness.

Mrs. Howard met Helen at the door.

—Oh Mrs. Weiman I'm so glad to see you. Just put your coat here won't you. It's so warm, and your hat, won't you take your hat off.

—Oh thank you, I'll take it off, yes, thank you.

Then Mrs. Howard led Helen into the living room and introduced her to her two daughters. Clarice hung back a little at first and then went up and took Helen Weiman by the hand and spoke to her.

—Oh Mrs. Weiman, I'm so glad to see you. I care so for Charley. It was nice of you to come and see us. I wish Charley could get a furlough.

—Then you are Clarice, Mrs. Weiman said. Charles has written so much about you to us. Mr. Weiman and I wanted to see you. He couldn't come but I had to come down to see some friends of ours and I thought it would be nice if I could meet you.

—It was awfully nice of you to come, said Mrs. Howard.

—Yes, said Mabel.

—I think it was lovely, Clarice said.

—I get to Detroit so seldom, Mrs. Weiman said.

—But Fairbanks isn't really far from here.

—I know but I am kept so busy there with relief work and one thing and another, I just never seem to be able to get away.

—Isn't that too bad, said Mrs. Howard.

The conversation began to drag a little so Mrs. Howard went out and brought in the tea service. While she was out of the room nobody did any talking. Helen Weiman noticed that they had no maid and decided the three women were just scheming to marry money or get the war risk insurance. It looked perfectly obvious to her but she kept on smiling and when tea was served they talked about the weather and the war and the theater. Charley was not even mentioned.

When Helen Weiman left they all three told her how much they had enjoyed meeting her and she said she had enjoyed it very much herself and hoped she would see them again soon. After she was gone the two girls and their mother talked it over and decided they didn't like Mrs. Weiman.

—But Charley isn't like that, I can tell from his letters, Clarice said.

—They have got a lot of money, Mabel said. Don wrote and told me.

—She looks as if they had money and good family, Mrs. Howard said. But she is too stuckup I think. I don't know about the boy but if he's like his mother you'll have a life if you marry him Clarice.

—He is a fine man, I can tell from his letters and pictures and I love him mother.

—Don said he was a fine fellow and everybody likes him, Mabel said.

—Well I don't exactly like all this business of arranging weddings and love affairs all through the mail. You can't tell by letter the way you can some other ways, Mrs. Howard said.

—I think you can too mother, Clarice said.

—Well I'll just bet his mother doesn't like this idea, I could tell the way she acted.

—I don't care a bit about his mother, Clarice said.

Helen Weiman told Ernst that it was plain to her that the three women were just scheming together to get Charley into marriage and either get him to support the whole outfit after he got out of the army or in case anything happened to him to get the life insurance. She said that they would have to put a stop to the thing right away.

—Did they say anything about the getting married part of it, Ernst asked her.

—We didn't talk about that, Helen said.

—Well what makes you think then that this girl is trying to get Charley. Maybe she's in love with him Helen.

—You can't fool me about such things Ernst Weiman, I know what I know about such things and they are just scheming to get our boy and I won't have it.

—Well I don't like the idea of Charley getting married like this before he starts out in business myself.

—I won't have it, Helen said.

—I think maybe we ought to do something about it, Ernst said.

—If I have to I'll go down there and see Charley and put him in his senses.

—We better just write him first and get him to hold off until after the war is over and then we can do something about it.

—All right then Ernst, you just write him. That girl is just a little foolish thing and the mother acted just as silly.

Ernst sat down and laboriously wrote a letter telling Charley not to do anything rash and to wait until the war was over. He said that his wife had met the girl and they thought it would be best for Charley to see her and know her a lot better before marrying her or getting himself tied up in any way.

Mrs. Weiman wrote and said, My dear boy, you will make an awful big mistake if you do anything rash. I really think if you see the girl you will not feel so strongly toward her. She is really quite a common little thing though she is quite charming. There are so many nice girls here in Fairbanks it is a shame you have to pick one out through the mails. Your father and I are very upset about this. Your father thinks that it is possible that this girl is just scheming to get you into marriage for the money that will someday be yours if you remain always the good son to us that you are. You know you have responsibilities and your father is not a poor man and there are a great many girls in the world who would do anything for money. I am not saying you will have a fortune but you will have enough. And of course it would be absurd for you to marry before the war is over and you are again a civilian and settled down into business and that will be a long time, for you have college still ahead of you and you simply cannot marry before you are out of college. It is such a shame that you will be behind all of your classmates. Oh Charley please don't string that little girl along any longer. Do this for your mother Charley. I want such big and wonderful things for my boy and have hoped for so much. Please darling if you love me don't go on with this silliness.

Charley Weiman at first took offense at the letters his parents sent him and he answered them in anything but a good spirit. Finally reading over the letters they had sent him and at the same time reading a letter from Clarice in which the girl said something Charley took to be slighting of his mother, he changed his mind about Clarice and doubted more than ever that he loved her. From then on he began to find things about her that he did not like and before long he wrote to his mother telling her the whole thing was off and that she should not worry. She wrote and told him that she and his father were both relieved and were glad Charles was sensible about it.

He didn't stop writing to Clarice with this new decision but he was careful when he wrote her and made it quite plain that he wouldn't marry until the war was over. Clarice wrote and told him she was glad because she thought Mabel had been silly to tie herself

down to a man by marriage when an engagement was just as good
as marriage. She said that she had had a few dates with men in
Detroit but that she never even kissed them and didn't want to kiss
anybody but Charley. That started Charley thinking and he went to
Donald Phelps and told him he could see how it was a good idea to
get married the way he had.

—What do you mean, Phelps asked.

—I mean you'll know when you get back that Mabel has
been true to you.

—Yes, that's true too, I never thought about that though, I
was thinking more about it from her point of view, don't you see
Charley, for her sake I mean, I never thought of that. But it's true
isn't it, I never thought of it.

—Well I just thought of it and wondered if you thought of
it, said Charley.

—No, that's funny I didn't. I wish this damn war was over.

—I wish we could get across.

—I don't know, but I think sometimes we do as much good
here as across. And I got a wife to think of.

—I would like to get across.

When the war was almost over Charley Weiman was given a
two weeks furlough after which he was to be sent overseas. He was
very glad that at last he had a chance to do some actual fighting
and he was tired of it, being an instructor in an army camp for such
a long time without seeing actual service at the front. He started
back to Fairbanks very happy and lighthearted.

He wired to his parents that he had ten days leave so that
he would have three days to spend with Clarice. He thought he
might decide that he loved her and he was curious to see her and he

knew that he would at least get a little good necking from her. So
he stopped off in Detroit and called her on the telephone and she
asked him to stay at their house as long as he could, they had an
extra bed and everybody would be glad to have him stay there.

Charley walked boldly into the house and Clarice walked up
to him and they kissed each other and held each other in their arms
for a while and then he met Mabel and Mrs. Howard. The whole
family treated him so cordially that he felt very much at ease and
happy and he liked Clarice more than ever.

—I only got ten days leave, he told her. So I got to go home
in just a couple days and see the folks and then we go overseas.

That made it out that he was giving Clarice a bigger portion
of his leave than he was really giving her. She pouted a little and
told him he should stay longer with them. He said he couldn't
because he had some business things to take care of in Fairbanks
as well as seeing his folks. That settled it because it was all right to
have business to take care of.

Clarice and Charley went out to teas and dances and made
love. Mrs. Howard and Mabel always knew when to leave them
alone for lovemaking. Neither Clarice nor Charley were bashful
about kissing but they both knew the limit they could go in
lovemaking and neither of them tried to go beyond the point that
they considered proper.

The streets of Detroit were lively with soldiers and sailors and
now and then band music, and flags were flying all over the city. It
all made the lovemaking very exciting and the thought that Charley
was going overseas and would be in danger and might never come
back had something with it. But they never went beyond the point
they considered proper.

—Charley you love me don't you, Clarice asked him.

—Sure I do and you love me too don't you.

—I wish we could be married.

—We will be when I get back, Charley said.

—It may be so long and if something should happen or you should fall in love with some French girl Charley. I don't know what I would do.

—Don't worry about me Clarice. You're a wonder you are. I wouldn't forget you very soon, don't worry about me.

Charley got to thinking that it wouldn't be bad to fall in love with some French girl, but he didn't say anything about it.

They sat up late each night and made love and talked about the future. The day before Charley was going back to Fairbanks he began to get tired of the lovemaking and talk and promises and he began to get a little tired of Clarice. He was glad when he left and kissed her good bye and said good bye to Mabel and her mother. He felt guilty about having spent the three days with the Howards instead of with his parents and he hoped nobody would find out and tell his folks what he had done. When he got off the train in Fairbanks he was wise enough to complain of the long dull trip from Georgia and to say that he was very tired from it. He really was tired from the late hours with Clarice in Detroit.

Helen Weiman and Ernst were feeling bad to think that Charley was going overseas but they both tried to make a brave front of it and appear to be only happy to have him with them for the few days of his furlough.

Ernst Weiman had slowly come around to a way of blaming the German Kaiser for the war and he still had a great deal of sympathy with the German people. He no longer felt so bitter about it and was not so upset at Charley fighting against his relatives as at the idea of Charley running to any kind of danger. But he felt that as a lieutenant, Charley would run into less danger than he would have as a private and this eased his mind a little. Helen Weiman was very frightened and tried not to show it.

The time in Fairbanks passed by slowly and Charley was red with it and was anxious to get overseas. He had planned on a happy time in Fairbanks but he was only bored and anxious to get away once he got there. His parents asked him questions and talked so much and gave him so much advice about taking care of himself that he got tired of it.

Ernst took him aside for a private talk and warned him about the French girls and told him there were no women in the world more immoral and more diseased than the French women. He said that there was one thing Charley should promise for his sake and for his mother's and that was to lead a good clean straight life in the army.

—Don't worry about me father, Charley said. I've always been able to take care of myself and I know about all those things. I'll be careful, don't you go worrying about me now.

—Well you can't be too careful Charley, I just thought I'd tell you.

Mrs. Weiman took Charley aside once and told him almost the same things and Charley was a little embarrassed talking with his mother about these things. He told her not to worry about him. She said that a mother could not help worrying about her boy. She said that she was glad he had come to his senses about that little girl in Detroit.

—Well that wasn't anything after all mother, Charley said.

—But you mustn't go getting yourself into any mixups.

—I won't, Charley said.

There was crying and more advice when Charley left Fairbanks and after he had gone Ernst was the man of the moment at the business men's luncheon and everybody spoke his praises. Ernst felt a little as though he himself were on his way abroad to fight for democracy and to preserve America. He was beginning to be really patriotic and was less interested in the American Monthly and the Nation.

Charles Weiman was made a first lieutenant. He was very happy about it and hoped to make a very good record for himself in the war. But he was only in France two weeks and then the armistice was signed and his chances were all shot to pieces. He was really unhappy about it. He couldn't understand it seeing everybody else so happy that the war was over.

He found his duties in France more monotonous than they had been in camp in Georgia and he couldn't make himself enjoy the life in France. It was too different and to be suddenly thrown into France was not much fun for Charley. He thought the women were homely and men there were unpleasant. All around him he thought he heard the Americans being laughed at. He never imagined they would be treated in that way. He heard people say America had waited until it was certain the Allies would win and then had gone into the war. Charley took it as a personal insult.

He wrote love letters back and forth with Clarice and she was glad the war was over and hoped he would be back soon. He hoped he would be back soon too. His parents were very glad the war was over and they were so relieved they no longer cared if Charley

couldn't get right back again. Now there was no more real danger
for him.

Charley sometimes wondered why he kept on writing love
letters to Clarice but every time he got a letter from her he sat
down and answered it. He began to think that he didn't want to
marry her and he wondered if it would be hard to get out of the
agreement they had made about getting married. But he kept right
on writing love letters to her.

Charley saw the Americans leaving France and found himself
in some troops that were going to Coblenz in Germany in the army
of occupation. He thought there might be some excitement in
Germany and was glad to be going there. The Germans might start
the war up again in some way, he thought. There might still be a
chance for him to win some glory.

Before he left for Coblenz two other officers and himself got
leave and went to Paris. The other officers wanted to see the sights
and Charley wanted to. They didn't have a very good time but they
went to the House of a Thousand Mirrors one night and Charley
was drunk enough on champagne and *fines* to go with one of the
girls and she showed him the kind of time he had heard the boys
talk about. He didn't enjoy it very much and was glad to get back to
the hotel. Next day he went to a doctor and the doctor told him not
to worry because the girls in the House of a Thousand Mirrors were
all safe and there was nothing to worry about. Charley thought he
better have a prophylactic just the same. It was all right with the
doctor and Charley felt much better when he left the doctor's office.
He was sure he didn't really want to marry Clarice Howard.

Walking along the streets in Coblenz, German men raised
their hats to Charley with a pleasant, guten Morgen, and girls

smiled and even little children looked with pride at Charley. The Americans were liked by the people of Coblenz and these people hated the French soldiers and they feared them. Charley began to like it very much being in Coblenz and thought it was much better than being in France. He began to think that it might not have been the Germans' fault about the war as much as it had been the German Kaiser's fault. He liked being called Herr Leutnant and being looked up to and his chest stuck out with pride and he was having a good time there in Coblenz.

One day some hungry German people raided the bakery of Herr August Wohlleben which was one of a chain of bakeries scattered all over Germany. The Americans stopped the raid and no loss was reported. Herr Wohlleben was in Garmisch-Partenkirchen in the Bavarian Alps with his daughter when the raid occurred. He and his daughter came to Coblenz and they gave a dinner in the Rathskeller for some of the American officers and for some of the big guns of Coblenz. It was a very good dinner and the Rhine wines were good. Charley Weiman had a long talk in English with Herr Wohlleben and his daughter and they invited him to come and see them in their Munich home. Charley said he would like to if he ever could get down to Munich.

—Oh you can certainly come some time to Munich, Herr Leutnant, said Frieda Wohlleben.

—I would like to, Charley said.

Then they talked to several other officers and gave out several other invitations. Charley Weiman thought Frieda Wohlleben was a swell looking girl and better than anything he had seen in France. He wished he could get down to Munich. She smiled at him very sweetly after the dinner was over and the guests were leaving the

Rathskeller. Herr Wohlleben had been very profuse in his thanks to the brave Americans and had told them that the citizens of Coblenz were very happy that Americans had been stationed there instead of Frenchmen. The American officers were all very much flattered.

Clarice wrote to Charley Weiman and told him her sister Mabel had fallen in love with some University of Michigan student and had decided that she didn't love Donald Phelps anymore. She went to a judge in Detroit and had her marriage annulled on the grounds that it had not been consummated and that she had married Phelps because of the war hysteria and that she had not loved him. She had no trouble getting an annulment and was going to marry the Michigan student. Donald Phelps was all cut up about it and was going around threatening to commit suicide.

God, he was a damn fool not to sleep with her, Charley thought. She just wanted to have a husband in the army that was all. Now the war's over a soldier isn't any good to her. That darn fool Phelps. I wonder what he's doing.

Clarice wrote that she hoped Charley would be back soon. She said she didn't like it waiting so long for him. Charley felt good about that. But he was beginning to be more interested in Frieda Wohlleben than in Clarice Howard. He began to think Frieda would make a better wife for him than Clarice. He wished he could see her and make her love him. He wrote to Clarice and told her that he didn't think it was fair of him to keep her tied down so long and he said he didn't have the remotest idea when he would be coming back to the states. He told her that if she was interested in anybody it wouldn't be fair for him to try to hold her.

Clarice Howard was nobody's damn fool and saw plainly enough that Charley didn't care for her anymore. She had really

seen that a long time from his letters. She thought she had
better end the engagement with Charley herself and she began
running around with a fraternity brother of her sister Mabel's new
sweetheart. She became engaged to the fraternity brother and wrote
and told Charley about it and said that she could see he didn't love
her and she really loved her new boy friend better than she had ever
loved Charley. She said Charley's uniform had carried her off her
feet and she wasn't any longer the impressionable girl she had been
and she thought it was better to end things.

When the letter came Charley felt bad even though it was
what he had been wanting. He thought he ought to try and win
back her love but he didn't make any efforts in that direction. He
just slowly let the matter drop from his mind and smiled at the
German girls in Coblenz, who seemed so pretty to him. He was
beginning to like the Germans and he felt sorry for them in their
poverty and with the mark collapsing and making paupers of the
comfortable class Germans. The rich got richer and the poor got
poorer, not only children, Charley said.

—That's a good one, another officer said.

—Those people are better than the frogs, Charley said.

—You're God damn tooting, the officer said.

Charley was invited to the homes of some of the better
people in Coblenz and he began to learn the German language.
He wished he had learned it in school. He made a lot of friends in
Coblenz, partly because his name was so obviously German and
besides he told them his father was born in Germany and in the
Rhineland. This made a bond between Charley and the Germans
and they liked him. They told him his name was really Karl, so he

let them call him Karl and really liked it. They were very nice to
him these people, and he liked them.

Ernst Weiman sent Charley the addresses of some of his
relations and Charley got leave and went to visit them. They liked
him and some of them remembered his father from the time he
was a boy before he had gone to America with his parents. They all
complained about their poverty and because it wasn't safe to save
their money which was losing value day by day. Charley gave them
all some American dollars which made them feel like millionaires
and they were very fond of him. They told him more and more
troubles but he didn't have too many dollars with him. After he left
his relatives and went back to Coblenz he thought a lot about the
awful time the people were having making a go of living. He wrote
to his father and advised him to help their relatives with money,
and to send him some to use to help out the poor people. He
grew sentimental about the people and wanted to help them and
he began to be sure the Allies were more to blame than Germany
for the war. He laughed at Wilson and the fourteen points, along
with the Germans. And he agreed with them that Wall Street had
made America enter the war and that if it hadn't been for America
Germany would have won and should have. If Wilson had stuck
to his fourteen points things would have been different. He was
against the occupation of Ruhr by the French troops. He had many
very good and close friends among the people of Coblenz.

Old Charles Ross, back in Fairbanks, died and left half of
his money to Charley Weiman and the other half to his widow.
Ernst wrote and told his son about it and Helen Weiman helped
Ernst write the letter. They advised Charley to come back as soon

as he could and said they would try to use some influence to get his discharge from the army. They said they thought he should be back in Fairbanks and should go to college and then should settle down into the automobile company or do some good work in the community. He was a rich man, that was true, but he should settle down and keep on doing things for his good and for the good of the community. They said they thought he would get his discharge if he applied for it and they hoped he would make every effort. You must realize that now you're a man of responsibility and must be an example to the community.

Charley Weiman thought it over very careful. He felt bad to hear about the death of his grandfather but he felt very good to hear about the money. His father hadn't told him how much it was but Charley knew it was a small fortune and he began to swell a little and think about the things he could do with the money. He thought about Frieda Wohlleben. He didn't like the idea of going back to college when he thought how all of his old highschool classmates would be already out of college. He would feel like an old man among little kids. He didn't want to go to college. But he knew he would have to have a college education if he wanted to be anybody in America. There were lots of them didn't have a college education, he thought, but now, in this modern civilization you have to have it. He had heard a speaker somewhere say that and it sounded reasonable.

Suddenly he decided that he would go to Munich and to the university there and get a doctor's degree and then go back. A doctor's degree was better than an A.B. degree any day. And it could be done in three or four years if he worked hard. He wrote and told his parents what his plans were and he explained that he just didn't feel like going to college in America and that it was broadening to be educated abroad the way he intended to be.

Helen Weiman thought it would be nice to have a degree from a foreign university and none of the Fairbanks boys had gone to school abroad. Ernst thought it would be a very good thing for Charley to learn German and he had always understood that discipline was stringent in the German schools and he thought it would make a man of Charley to study there in Germany. They wrote to Charley and suggested Heidelberg because they had never heard of the University in Munich. He wrote and explained that the climate in Munich was healthier than at Heidelberg and the Bavarian institution was better than Heidelberg. He told them Heidelberg was terribly run down since the war.

Ernst Weiman told him he could have all the money he wanted because it was his own, but he advised him to be careful how he used it and not to get himself into any trouble.

Charley got his discharge from the army shortly before the American troops left Coblenz. His friends were sorry to see him go and they feared to have the Americans leave the city. They hated even the thought of French soldiers being quartered in the city.

Charley said good bye and when he left he had a lot of little presents from the people he had known and liked so well in Coblenz. He grew very sentimental and tears formed in his eyes and he waved his handkerchief out of the window of the first class carriage long after the platform was out of sight. He knew his German friends would still be waving handkerchiefs because they always did that even after they had lost sight of the person they were saying good bye to. Charley was going to Munich and he was thinking about Frieda Wohlleben.

The mark had been falling steadily and Charley rode all the way from Coblenz to Munich in a first class carriage for about fifty cents in American money, which was several thousand marks at that time. Knowing that he was rich in America he felt as if he owned the whole of Germany, but he was interested in Frieda Wohlleben and did more thinking about her than about his financial status.

He rented a suite of rooms in the Hotel Vierjahreszeiten and got a small outfit from the best tailor in Munich. He found out that Frieda Wohlleben and her father were in the Bavarian Alps, so he idly roamed around Munich staying away from the University, where he intended to pursue his studies. He went to the American Church and Library and met some young American artists who had come to Munich because it was so cheap to live there with American dollars. There were a lot of Americans living in Munich for almost nothing and they all acted as if they were broke and having as hard time of it as the Germans.

The first Saturday night in Munich he went with about twenty of the wilder members of the American colony to the Pavillon Gruss where there was much drinking and dancing and indiscriminate lovemaking. When the Gruss closed the whole party went to Walter Goldberg's studio and took the cabaret orchestra with them. There there was more drinking and dancing and kissing.

Charley Weiman had a good time and was glad he was out of the army. Now and then he thought about the poor German people and he wished Frieda Wohlleben would come back from the mountains. He got to thinking so much of Frieda and the party kept on getting wilder so he called a taxi and went back to the Hotel Vierjahreszeiten.

When he got back he began to think it was wrong for these Americans to come to Munich and live for almost nothing with their American dollars, but next day Jules Rawleigh and his wife stopped in the hotel to see Charley and the three people went out to tea and met a little American named Dora Dancer, who was in Munich studying to be a painter. They had imitation absinthe for tea and went to the Rawleighs' apartment where they had more to drink and where Charley got in a little necking with Dora. At dinner they met some more Americans and there was more drinking and that night Charley invited them all over to the Vierjahreszeiten and there was more drinking in his suite of rooms in the hotel. The party grew so wild that the hotel manager asked them to make a little bit less noise. The party stayed wild for a couple hours more and Charley had a good time and forgot the German people and Frieda Wohlleben.

Then for two weeks Charley Weiman kept it up, drinking and going to parties and buying champagne and he found that he was spending very little real money with the mark falling so rapidly. The drinking and late hours tired him out and he felt guilty because he hadn't been around to see about getting into the university.

A German merchant, who owned an art goods shop in Munich, had been running around with the wilder members of the American colony and he helped Charley arrange to get into the university. It was difficult because Charley didn't have the proper credentials and his knowledge of German was not yet very great. However the German managed things for Charley and he was enrolled in the university.

Charley rented a very high class apartment in one of the best sections of Munich for about fifteen dollars a month and furnished it with furniture he bought for almost nothing. He wrote home and told his parents all about the university life in Munich. He went to a few lectures in the university and found them dull and very difficult to understand.

Finally Frieda Wohlleben and her father came back to Munich and Charley went to call on them.

—Oh Herr Leutnant, we are so glad to see you, said Frieda.

—Yes, and now I suppose you speak good German, said her father.

—Not very good yet, but I'm going to the university here to learn it, Charley said.

—Oh that will be so nice and you can come and see us often, won't that be nice papa, Frieda said.

Charley liked the talk with Frieda and her father and he was very fond of Frieda. In her home she seemed more formal and not so easy to get at as she had seemed in Coblenz.

The next day Charley sent her flowers. He called again and both Frieda and her father knew something was going to happen. Frieda was all excited having an American officer a man with lots of American dollars coming to call on and sending her flowers. The Wohllebens had plenty of money from the bakeries and August Wohlleben knew how to turn the money he got into foreign currency, into dollars, Swiss francs and Swedish Kronen. He was a rich man and the fall of the mark wasn't going to hurt him any. But he complained constantly about it and said that he would be bankrupt if things didn't soon take a change for better. Nothing could have been better for him than just the way things were going because he sold bread and changed his money into good hard dollars.

Charley told them that he knew some of the American colony and they said the people in Munich were not very fond of the Americans there, although they themselves thought it was a silly prejudice. They said that it was the French that the Bavarians hated mainly. They talked about American dollars a great deal and they found out that Charley was a rich young man.

—You ought to go to some country where things are better, Herr Wohlleben told Charley. Everybody would rather be in America than here, if they could be there. I wish I had gone to America before the war myself. It is too uncertain here the way things are going and they only get worse all the time.

—Yes but the university here papa, that is something, people come here from all over the world for the university, said Frieda.

—Yes everybody knows about the university here, Charley said. And Munich is such a wonderful city. For an American there is nothing like studying a while abroad. Just like for a German travel is a good thing.

—Travel is a good thing, we always used to go to Italy in the spring, but now it is difficult to get the passports, said August Wohlleben.

Charley invited Frieda and her father to the opera and took them out to dinner and they enjoyed it having a friend in the young American dollarprince. He didn't seem to be able to find a way to be alone with Frieda. And he was in love with her. He thought she was in love with him too and she was, although she never thought of telling him or showing him in any way but in her smiles and in the warmth of her handclasp.

Finally Charley wrote to his parents and told them he was in love with Frieda and told them that her father was very wealthy and very highly respected and that Frieda herself was beautiful and a wonderful woman. He said that he wanted to marry her if he could win her.

He went to the lectures in the university but he wasn't learning anything from them. He studied the language though and read a few books in German and finally found himself becoming quite proficient in the language. He began to talk German with the Wohllebens when he could speak it as well as they could speak English. It was his beginning to speak German that made Frieda fall really in love with him. She liked to hear the broken German from the big tall American dollarprince and it made her feel like a mother talking to a great big baby. Her heart was soft and she was sentimental. When she heard Charley talking broken German she wanted to run her hands through his hair and kiss him and talk baby talk to him. She began to really love him.

Herr Wohlleben thought it might be a good thing for his daughter to be married to the rich American. There were very few eligible Germans and Frieda couldn't be expected to marry into some fallen family.

—You and Frieda are quite fond of each other, he told Charley one day.

—Herr Wohlleben, I love Frieda and would like to marry her, said Charley.

He thought he might just as well come right out with it. August Wohlleben smiled and said he thought they ought to speak to Frieda about it. He smiled and said he thought it ought to be all right.

Charley cabled the good news of his engagement to his parents. The cable reached them just after they had received his letter. Ernst Weiman thought it was all right but Helen didn't like it.

—I don't want him marrying any little German girl. They are all just housemaids. There are so many nice American girls.

—Now Helen they are not, there are lots of just as good German girls as American and didn't Charley tell us what a good family the Wohllebens are. They have got a good name and I'll bet it would be a better thing for the boy to get a good German girl than one of these young flappers. He should settle down and now he has got that money he ought to settle down. There is no use of that college.

Helen Weiman and Ernst argued about it and decided to take a trip to Germany and see Charley and his fiancée. They thought they ought to make a trip to Europe and Ernst wanted to see Germany. Helen thought she would get some clothes in Paris. And they really thought they must see the girl before they gave their consent to a marriage.

Frieda and Charley were engaged and that meant they were practically the same as married. Charley didn't know all of the customs in Germany but Frieda taught him things he ought to know and when there was a question between the usage in Germany and the American usage she was always with him in choosing the American. She was proud to think that she would soon be an American lady.

—We will be so happy Karl, and I love to go to America she told Charley.

Charley Weiman was careful not to introduce Frieda to any of his American friends and he drifted away from them and every day spent some time at the home of Wohllebens. Frieda began industriously to study English. She was anxious not to have an accent when she reached America.

August Wohlleben always acted as though he were going to be brokenhearted when his daughter left him but he began calling on the widow of the former Bavarian court painter, who was a charming English lady with very little money and a grown up son to care for. Wohlleben had to find somebody to replace his daughter in his affections.

Frieda dragged Charley to tea in the better restaurants and hotels in Munich and seemed to enjoy being seen there. Charley liked it better alone in the house with Frieda but she was as good looking as any girl he had seen in Germany and he was proud to notice people staring at her. He also got angry sometimes when Germans would stare so hard they seemed to be taking her clothes off. But Frieda didn't mind it, she was having a good time. And she was very anxious to get to America.

—You will have to stop the University, she told Charley.

—I don't care, I want to.

Charley thought it would be great to take Frieda back to Fairbanks and show her off to the people. She would knock their eyes out, he thought.

Ernst and Helen Weiman got to Paris and didn't like it. Helen Weiman bought some expensive clothes and then they started towards the Rhineland to visit Ernst's relations. The mark was falling faster and faster and there was more misery among the German people. Everywhere they went they saw and it got on their nerves and before Ernst saw his relatives he was ready to leave Germany. Everything was different. He was disappointed and almost sorry he had come back to Germany.

His relatives were all poor and they acted like begging servants. Helen didn't like them and Ernst began to think they were just trying to milk him of his money.

—America is the only country, he said.

—Well I'm glad to see you coming around to your senses. You were just foolish about Germany, Helen told him.

Ernst gave all of his relatives checks for American dollars and they thought of him as having unlimited money and he began to think they considered him stingy for not giving them more money. It got on his nerves.

—That's what the war did. Made them all beggars. Just low down beggars, Helen. Their morale is all gone now. I never saw anything like it. We ought to get out of here. They haven't got any principles at all.

Ernst and Helen Weiman went on to Munich and felt better when they were settled in Charley's very good apartment. Ernst began telling Charley that Germany was no place to be anymore.

—Before the war it was different. But it's no good now. You ought to get out of here. You'll get just like these people. Beggars. In the hotels they try to rob you.

Ernst had never paid more than two dollars for a room with bath but that was Auslander price and Ernst didn't like to think that he was paying more than the Germans were paying.

—It is bad for you, you come back with us Charley. You don't need college. You can go into the automobile factory. I am giving up the shoestore. I'm president of the new Building and Loan Association and I'm not going to keep on with the shoestore. I have got a buyer for it. But you come back Charley.

—Yes you must come back, this is frightful here, Helen said.

—Well I'll be taking Frieda back with me. You better get ready to go around and meet her.

Helen Weiman had decided not to say anything until after she had met Frieda, but the temptation was too great for her.

—Charley are you sure you are doing a wise thing. Everything all upset the way it is you may be just carried off your feet.

—Now mother, this is all settled and there isn't any use talking.

—We better wait and meet the girl first Helen, Ernst said.

—Well all right but I'm afraid. And that's no way to talk to your mother Charley. You have grown into a very inconsiderate sort of boy.

They went around to meet the Wohllebens. Both of them were impressed by the splendid home and the servants and the oil paintings and the beautiful old furniture. Helen Weiman was not very much against the marriage, after she had looked around the house a little.

Frieda and her father were very pleasant and liked the Weimans and there was much talk in German and in English. Helen Weiman tried to be very cool and she couldn't help liking Frieda and Herr Wohlleben was such an impressive looking gentleman in his cutaway. Ernst thought this was something like it. He had never seen such a fine German household and he liked Frieda and thought that Charley ought to have a good time of marriage.

Frieda and Charley were very happy and planned to go to America with Ernst and Helen Weiman. Wohlleben said he would be very unhappy, especially the way things were in Germany. Ernst spoke up and said that it was terrible and it would be a good thing for Frieda to get to America when things were so bad in Germany and there was no telling what might happen.

Wohlleben said there was talk of revolution and he said he was afraid he might lose everything he had made. This led to an arrangement to take the money Wohlleben had hoarded to America and invest it safely. Wohlleben said he would get it to Switzerland for them to take to America. All this was against the laws of Germany but that didn't matter. The money had to be cared for some way.

When the four people were leaving Germany Ernst had some trouble with his passport not being properly visaed and had to go back to Munich from the border to get the matter fixed up. Helen and Charley and Frieda waited for him. This was the last straw for Ernst. The way he was treated in the passport office and the trouble he had and the imagined discourtesy of the railroad officials and the beggars made Ernst hate Germany and want to get back to America.

Crossing Lake Constance Ernst told them how he felt about it.

—I am glad I'm an American. My father was the wisest man in the world to come to America when he did. Your father made a big mistake in staying there in Germany Frieda. America is God's own country and you don't have any bother there with passports or any of this darn stupid business. I am going to tell the boys at the club just how I feel about it when I get back. And Charley we got you out of there just in time. A regular nest of thieves and no morals or anything.

Frieda didn't get it all because Ernst talked fast and was very much excited thinking about the fine speech he would make to the members of the business men's club. If she had heard it all distinctly she would have felt bad about it.

—It's too bad you had to go back for that visa, Frieda said.

About the Author

John Herrmann was born November 9, 1900, in Lansing, Michigan. He grew up in Lansing and later attended George Washington University, the University of Michigan, and the University of Munich. After spending a brief period of time in Paris as part of the expatriate literary circle of the 1920s, Herrmann returned to the United States, where he married fellow writer Josephine Herbst in 1926. Herrmann wrote three novels and over two dozen other publications (novellas, short stories, and essays) over the next two decades, and when he was not writing he often worked as a traveling salesman to supplement his income. His moment of highest literary acclaim occurred in 1932, when he tied with Thomas Wolfe for the *Scribner's Magazine* prize for short fiction. During the 1930s, he became increasingly involved in political issues and workers' rights struggles. Herrmann and Herbst divorced in 1940, and he married Ruth Tate that same year. He served in the U.S. Coast Guard during World War II, and by the late 1940s, honorably discharged, Herrmann fled to Mexico after discovering that the FBI was investigating his earlier political activities. He died April 9, 1959, in Guadalajara, Mexico.